The Distant Steps

To Kitty,

Thanks!

Deb

To Nithy,
Thanks!
DXB

The Distant Steps

A Novel

Ann Webster

The Distant Steps is a work of fiction. Names, characters and incidents are products of the author's imagination. Any resemblance to actual events or persons living or dead is entirely coincidental.

Copyright © 2019 Ann Webster
All rights reserved.
Chaleur Bay Creative

ISBN-13: 9871793184832

For Sadie

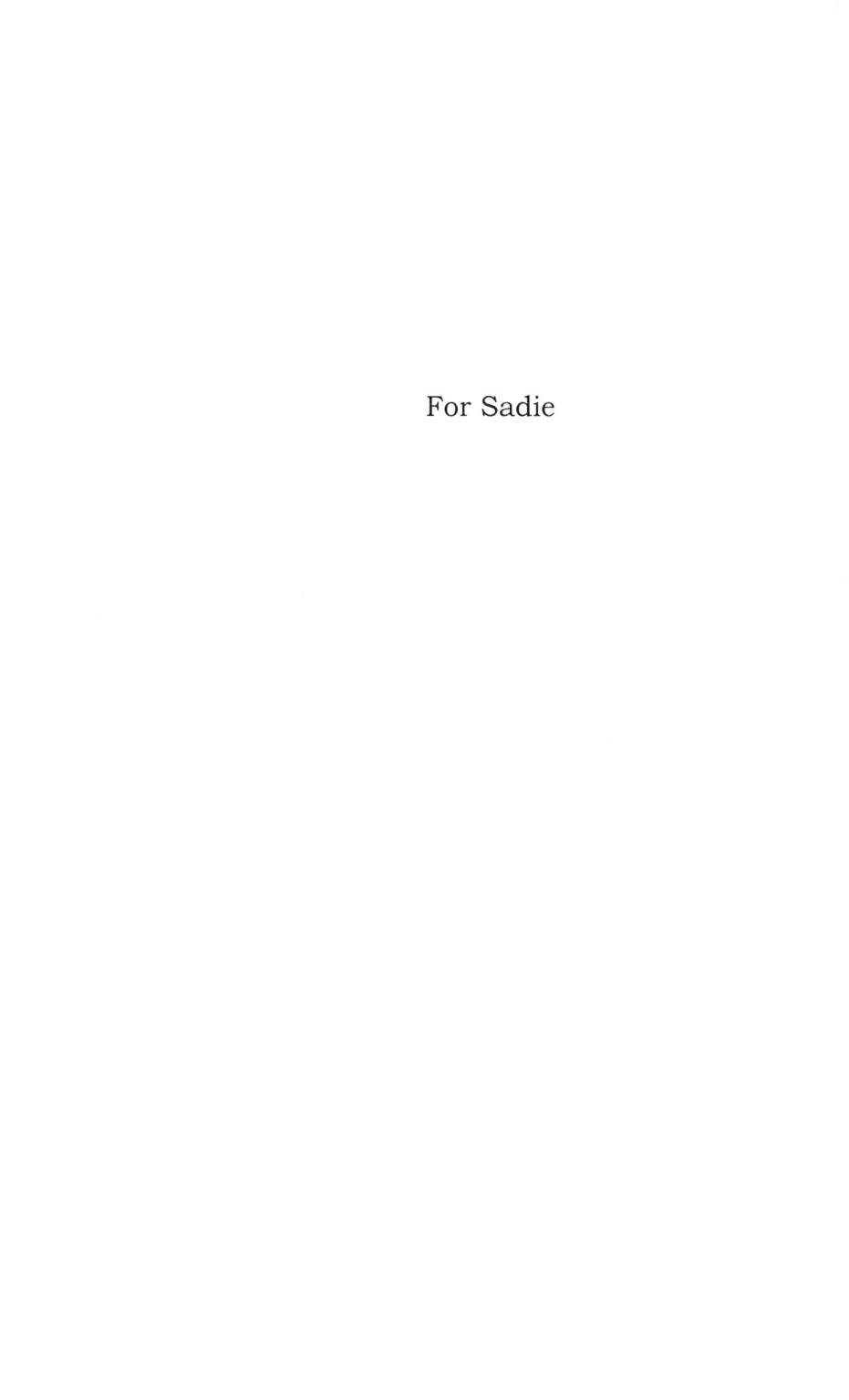

1

Isle of Arran, Scotland

1834

Whisper voices. That's what Margaret called them. The voices so soft she couldn't hear the words inside them. What could it be this time, she wondered, allowing fear to overcome her thoughts. Whisper voices seemed to appear when bad things were about to happen. A hollow feeling was building inside her as she climbed the sloping field towards the farm.

It had only been two years since the last whisper voices filled her small dark home. Duncan, the youngest child, had become ill and Mama didn't know what to do. Those whispers hung like clouds in the air, wrapping his weak body until he died. And they refused to leave when he was placed in the small grave. The whispers lingered for months. Mama and Papa had difficulty finding their regular voices. It made sense, it was too painful to talk. He was their baby and they couldn't save him.

But now whisper voices were back and growing louder every day. Had the fever returned? It couldn't. It wouldn't. She replayed those difficult days in her mind. Each day a repeat of the previous one. Every hour filled with worry and fear. Mama and Papa were like strangers. Ignoring her when Duncan was sick. How could it happen again?

Was there anything different about these whispers, she wondered. They murmured in the fields, and in the school yard when the pupils arrived, but they never went inside the house. Why would they stop at the door? All the voices inside weren't whispers. Even Mama used her regular voice. What was everyone whispering about? What was the big secret?

Margaret was baffled and no one was coming forward with an explanation. Even as the whispers grew louder, nothing was said. Complete silence. No questions were asked, not even from her sister, Janet who liked to challenge everything. Her oldest sister Liza, would never ask questions, but Janet? It was strange for Janet to remain silent. John, the oldest and only brother, also remained quiet. He was the center of the family. The one Papa and the three girls counted on. The tension increased in her body as she wondered if the whispers were directed at her.

Margaret headed toward the house, looking for signs of sickness or something out of place as she walked up the path. Had she missed something before? A warning sign? Something, anything to whisper about? Nothing seemed different. She watched the smoke from the cooking fire rise above the roof. Everything looks the same, she thought, increasing her glance to include the fields. Her eyes were drawn to her two sisters digging at something, then John up in the meadow tending to the animals.

She couldn't help but stare at Liza. In an hour, Liza would be standing beside Mama cooking the evening meal. Maybe tonight Liza would ask about the whisper voices. Margaret let out a sigh, knowing it wouldn't happen. Liza would never ask. She would wait for someone, anyone to tell her. Someone to provide the daily direction.

Margaret wondered why Liza always let others make decisions for her or agreed with everything Mama said. It was foolish to wait for an explanation or be told what to do. She shook her head as her decision became clear. To get an answer, she must be the one to ask the questions.

Margaret decided to approach her mother first. Mama wasn't good at keeping secrets, so a few innocent questions could reveal the answers Margaret needed. Mama wouldn't hide her feelings. If her voice didn't share the answers, her body would carelessly give them away. It was late afternoon, so Mama must be alone in the house. Margaret turned toward the front door. In a few minutes, she would know the truth. At least something, she thought.

Mama was standing over the fire, when Margaret burst into the house. Unable to hold back her curiosity with the tension of not knowing, her voice filled the kitchen.

"What are the whispers about this time?" Margaret asked, not letting her mother to look up.

Mama stood still, stiffening her back, while barely changing her posture as the words from the question left her daughter's mouth. She winced knowing any answer would fall short of Margaret's expectations. Her young daughter would want a quick response, nothing short of the truth. Not knowing what to say, or how to answer, Mama let the large pot of fish stew became her focus. The sound of the wooden spoon scraping the sides of the black pot in a rhythm of worry was the only response she had.

It was as though her mouth froze, unable to assemble words in a response to Margaret. Where was her husband James, when she needed him, she thought, raising her eyes to glance toward the door? He should answer. It's his dream the family was preparing to follow.

An immediate sense of fear fell over Margaret. As she looked at her mother, she knew something must be terribly wrong. Her mother wasn't speaking, causing the silence in the room to grow louder than any of the whispers. After a few deep breaths, Margaret stepped closer to the fire and tried to make eye contact with her mother.

"Mama, the whispers," she said attempting to force an answer from her mother's mouth.

Mama removed the large spoon from the pot and looked directly into her young daughter's eyes.

"Corriecravie is changing," she said, pointing the spoon in Margaret's direction. "We can't farm here anymore."

Mama inched toward the bench propped against the back wall of the kitchen and sat down, the spoon never leaving her tight grip. Margaret stood completely still and watched a woman she didn't recognize. A woman filled with tension and fear. She waited for more words but couldn't imagine what else would escape her mother's mouth. After a long silence, Mama looked up at Margaret.

"We must leave," she said, turning up the corners of her mouth.

Mama felt a sense of contentment for freeing the trapped words. But the feeling wasn't shared by her daughter. Margaret hadn't prepared for this type of answer. Whisper voices for leaving? Leaving Corriecravie? Whisper voices were meant for sickness, for fever. This didn't make any sense, she thought.

"What do you mean leave?" she asked. "This is our home. Why would we leave?"

Margaret burst into tears, afraid of the change that was about to happen and headed toward the inner room. In their tiny house there was no escape and Mama quickly followed. She wrapped her arms around her daughter, trying to calm her fears.

"We'll talk about this when everyone's in the house," Mama said. Margaret kept her head down and her body tense. She couldn't accept her mother's embrace.

"Yes, Corriecravie and Arran have been our home," Mama said. "But Arran is changing and changing in ways a young girl may not understand. We need to leave," Mama declared, not waiting for a rebuttal.

She knew Margaret had difficulty accepting change after Duncan's death. It had been a trying time for everyone but finally, after several months, they had settled into a routine. The calmness and predictability of that routine would be broken when the family left Arran. Mama was confident they would find the path forward, but it would take time.

Margaret was filled with questions. Too many questions to ask and Mama's voice was too firm. Worst yet, she wasn't cooperating with the type of answers Margaret wanted to hear. She had heard enough. It was more than she bargained for.

Where would the family go, she thought, silently questioning her mother's answer. Other places? What other places? It sounded too late to talk about it. Mama's answers were absolute. Margaret immediately felt very small. Too small to have a voice in her own family.

She nodded to Mama, managing to keep her questions locked inside. As Mama released her embrace, Margaret pretended to accept her answers, smiling and nodding while quietly making her way toward the door. She would find John, she thought and ask him the same questions. Just like Mama, Margaret knew exactly where to find John. In the late afternoon he would be in the upper pasture so off she went, climbing the rings of farmland toward the open field at the top of the hill. Maybe that's what she liked about Arran. Things were simple. People were always where you expected them to be. Life was easy. As she ran across the strips of land, the grass and plants tickled her legs, reminding her of the bouquet she had picked last week. She ignored the urge to stop and make another. Today she had to talk to John.

Her mind raced with Mama's words. Words about change and leaving Arran. She thought about all the changes she had experienced with the loss of Duncan. For months Mama couldn't talk about him. And now Mama wanted to leave Arran. Why? What could be so horrible to make the family leave? Margaret wanted her old life. The way things were before all the whisper voices.

She looked up the hill for John, trying to place him against the low green plants and brown rocks. Margaret depended on John. She knew he would explain everything, especially the reason the family needed to leave. And he wouldn't make Margaret feel like a child when he spoke to her. John always treated Margaret as an equal to her sisters, Liza and Janet. Being equal in age was important, but not equal in ability. Margaret thought she could outwit her sisters any day. She found ways to disrupt the status quo, poking and prodding when things were settled. She never wavered from sharing an opinion, an ability that brought plenty of criticism and trouble for Margaret.

She was almost out of breath when she finally caught a glimpse of John. Immediately her arms went up, waving for his attention. Disappointed in not catching his eye, she stopped to collect her energy and to shout his name. He would certainly hear a shout, she thought.

"John, John," she yelled, her pitch rising with each name.

John turned and smiled, not expecting to see Margaret and her fiery red hair in the field so late in the afternoon. Knowing his sister, John wasn't sure what to expect. His smile disappeared as she approached and John noticed the tense lines in her face.

"What is it?" he asked. "Is anyone hurt?"

Margaret ignored John's questions. "Why must we leave?" she asked, not waiting to answer. "Papa is --."

"Wait, wait," John insisted. "Look around you. Before you complain about change and decisions by Papa, you should understand what's happening."

Margaret flinched as her questions were halted in midair. John ignored his sister's reaction and started to sweep his arm across the horizon. As the words about Arran spilled out of his mouth, Margaret grabbed his arm to halt its movement, insisting John must listen to her first.

"I should have a say, a voice in what happens to me," Margaret declared, her hands settling on her hips to show her displeasure in John's lesson on Arran.

"No, you don't have a voice or a say," John replied, holding back his anger toward his youngest sister. "You're thirteen and Papa will decide for you and for the rest of us. You barely contribute to the farm, so how do you think you can decide for yourself?"

Margaret was shocked. Almost too shocked to speak. The words stung. She bit her lower lip to keep from crying but her eyes welled up anyway. John never spoke to her this way. His words continued to flow and John insisted Margaret must listen.

"This might be where you want to live, but I can't," John continued. "There isn't any land for me to farm."

John knew Margaret was too young to understand the farming changes on Arran but she wasn't too young to listen.

"Archibald McKinnon left Arran over a year ago and found beautiful farmland with trees as tall as sailing masts in British North America's New Brunswick," he said.

He stopped to see if she was listening. He wanted to be clear.

"I want to go there and so does Papa," John finished.

Once again, Margaret found herself pretending to listen but this time the sound of John's lecturing voice forced her to ignore his words. She stared at John without blinking. This day was getting worse, she thought.

In spite of her wanting to be an equal in age, Margaret covered her ears and ran back toward the house. Acting out like a thirteen year old, John thought as he watched her run away. The truth was she didn't want to hear anymore. The words were the same from everyone she spoke to. Her family had plans to leave Arran.

First Mama and then John giving her a lecture on life. Why would they want to leave Arran, she thought? It was beautiful too. Yes, the trees weren't as tall as masts but the ocean, the fields. Everything was home! And now her brother had become someone she didn't know.

She entered the house and found Mama cooking over the fire. Liza and Janet were sitting next to each other and sharing the meal chores with Mama. Janet immediately reacted upon seeing Margaret.

"Here she is," Janet said. "Why don't you stop fretting and help us?"

Janet and Margaret lived together, always on the edge of tension. Two sisters attempting to outshine each other for Mama's attention. They knew Papa would have none of their harsh words, but Mama let it play out on most days. Tonight, she decided to intervene.

"Girls! Enough of your arguments," Mama said. "I will not tolerate your squabbles."

Both girls looked at Mama, barely believing their mother's directness. But Mama knew the pending discussion would add stress to the family. These girls would need to behave tonight.

Papa entered the kitchen straight from the field and immediately sensed the evening would be difficult. The house was too quiet. Not a single voice. There was none of the normal chatter of three girls and their mother around the fire. The only noise he could hear was the sound of John bringing the animals into the far end of the house. Papa decided to remain silent until John entered the kitchen. No point in starting a discussion without him, he thought. Papa walked over to the fire, looked into the large black pot and waited patiently for his son to join them.

John was filled with excitement and didn't notice the dark silence as he entered the room. He glanced at Margaret to see if she was ready to listen because he was more than ready to finish their conversation. As he opened his mouth to describe New Brunswick, Papa decided to speak before the words came out.

"I need everyone to sit and listen," he said, without smiling. "We have a challenge and a problem with the farm," he continued.

Papa was matter of fact, his voice low as he stared at the kitchen floor.

"The owner of Arran has decided to reduce the number of farms and increase taxes," he said. "We cannot pay the taxes and will be forced off the farm. There isn't a future here."

A silence filled the room as the children tried to make sense of their father's words. The owner of Arran, Margaret thought. She hadn't given any thought to who owned the farm.

Papa didn't wait for any questions. He continued speaking in a voice that Margaret strained to hear.

"No farm, no food," he said while wiping his hands against each other.

It was as simple as that. Margaret watched as her father spoke to the family like a teacher. None of this makes sense, she thought. How could the family be forced to leave? What were taxes?

Papa knew his younger children would have difficulty understanding, so he kept talking.

"Many farms in the north of the island have become sheep farms or leased to mainlanders," he said. "We can't stay and take our chances on what happens to Corriecravie. There's barely enough food for all of us today and too many problems, so we must leave."

As Papa explained the changes on Arran to his family, Mama was wringing her hands and looking at him. It was clear they had worried about this discussion for some time. They both looked tired and worn down. The future unclear, except for the many difficult days ahead.

The children's questions were immediate but not from Margaret. She didn't know what to ask. But the words flowed freely from the others. Janet wanted to know when and how. Liza wanted to know what they could bring and John wanted to know more about where they were going.

"Tell us about Archibald's new land," John asked almost giddy with anticipation. "Tell us so we know what it looks like."

John was sitting on the edge of the bench ready to take it all in as Papa described the land, the ocean, and the forests. He even described the winter. The kind of winter everyone should respect.

"Snow and cold beyond what Arran sees," Papa said.

John kept smiling, ignoring the description of the winter.

"Snow doesn't matter," he said. "We'll have our own farm."

Papa raised his eyebrows and looked at John.

"Yes, it'll be our farm," he said. "But we need to get there first."

Papa stopped short of describing the voyage across the Atlantic. He heard about the difficulties. The rough waters. Now wasn't the time to bring it up. Stay positive, he thought.

"The trip is an adventure," he said. "An adventure across the ocean."

He knew there was a regular schedule of ships that sailed between Arran and New Brunswick. According to the locals, there were several ships leaving from

Lamlash Harbor each month. The gossip spread quickly about each pending arrival and the willingness for the ship Captains to take emigrants to British North America. Lamlash was awash in gossip of the ships, the voyages and the opportunity for farmland. Papa wanted his children to hear some of that gossip.

"If you go into Lamlash village you can see the ships, the ones that sail to British North America," he said, not certain if any ships would be in the harbor. "You can ask about the schedule for the next several sailings and find out what families take with them on the voyage."

The children should be more than passengers in the biggest change to their lives, he thought. They must understand why leaving Arran was the family's only option. He knew the risks of staying. How the farmland couldn't support Arran's growing population and now it was time for John and his sisters to know more. In time, they would appreciate their new home.

Before he stopped talking, the father of four children started to smile as he described their future, relaxing his words and taking a seat on the bench.

"We'll have our own farm on Bay Chaleur," he said. "One hundred acres for every man over the age of 20 is offered by the Crown. That's more land than we work here and it would be ours, not the Duke of Hamilton's property. The land would be ours, registered to James Murchie."

Margaret heard the optimism in his voice. It was intoxicating. Moments earlier, when Papa was discussing the changes on Arran, he spoke like a broken man. A man who couldn't support his own family. A man who knew more than he wanted to share. But now she was listening to a different man. The Papa she knew and loved. She wanted to follow this man to New Brunswick. To Bay Chaleur, but something didn't feel right. It was too much. Too soon. The family had barely recovered from Duncan.

Margaret decided to remain silent while her brother and sisters barraged their father with questions about Bay Chaleur. She watched as the excitement built with each answer. There was nothing to add she thought. No one seemed to notice how quiet Margaret was.

A week passed before they all jumped in the dory for a quick trip to Lamlash. The small boat's carrying capacity was outsized by the curiosity and excitement of three of its four passengers. John was filled with a sense of helping his family. It was more than checking on schedules. He sat straight as he rowed, each oar getting lighter as they approached the Lamlash dock. Margaret and Janet sat at opposite ends and kept quiet. Always wise to keep them apart but on this day, Janet's optimistic smile was countered by Margaret's sulking. He knew something was wrong with Margaret. She had been too quiet over the past few days.

"Look at this, I've never seen so many people," Janet said, as Lamlash harbor came into view. "All the people, the ships. There are four large ships in the harbor."

Lamlash was exploding with activity, forcing the children to stare at the people on the dock. This wasn't the sleepy harbor they typically saw. Families were gathering and forming queues at the dock's edge to board the tenders that ferried them to the ship waiting out in the harbor. Children were clinging to a hand, a piece of clothing, anything that would connect them to their mother or father as they stepped off Arran for the last time. Tears were streaming down faces as families said goodbyes and headed toward the ship. Some wore smiles behind the tears but many children had a bewildered look. As Margaret watched the children, she couldn't help but feel helpless.

"Papa's right," John said. "Arran is changing and it'll never be the same with so many families leaving the island."

The Murchie children tried to take it all in, barely moving as the events of the harbor occupied their imagination.

"Where are you going?" Janet asked the first crew member she saw. "Greenock," he replied. "Then off to Bay Chaleur."

"That's where we want to go," she said.

"Did you ask what we can bring?" Liza whispered to Janet, trying to hear the conversation.

"No, it's your question to ask," Janet replied, shaking her head at Liza.

Liza wanted to listen and hadn't planned to ask any questions. She would let Janet inquire. But at that moment, something changed and Liza rushed to ask the remaining families what they were bringing onboard the ship.

Margaret was trying to make sense of the dock and the harbor activity in front of her. And now she watched as her sisters acted like complete strangers. They never behaved this way. She was always the excited one. The one who asked questions. Always wondering what was next and trying to understand. Now, in Lamlash, Janet was asking about the voyage in a voice that shared her level of excitement. There were so many questions Margaret wanted to ask, but she couldn't find the words or the voice to deliver them.

Margaret watched as Liza ran over to the dock's edge to talk to one of the families. Normally, Liza walked in Mama's long shadow, never acting as her own person. Everything she did was Mama's way of doing things. Seeking permission and approval. On the dock in Lamlash, this was a different Liza. She was engaging in conversation.

And Janet, well she could be counted on for at least one major adventure or mishap, but today she was thoughtful and organized. Margaret thought of Janet as a risk taker, willing to act before thinking. But something was different and Margaret couldn't believe her eyes. What was happening to them? First John treating her like a child and now Liza and Janet acting like adults. Margaret was always the outsider but today she felt completely outside. Different.

Margaret tried to fight her feeling of helplessness. No one was listening to her and she needed to find a way out of her sinking mood. She must ignore what her sisters were doing and take control, she thought. Ignore them. Scanning the dock area, Margaret looked for familiar faces. Families the Murchies knew, maybe friends from school.

"Do you recognize anyone?" she asked John, waiting for an answer filled with the names of the many families he saw. Today, John was staring at the ships in the harbor, almost in a trance and didn't answer. Margaret decided to look for herself, continuing to wonder about her family. She scanned everyone, trying to identify familiar faces, but the chaotic scene took over her view. The ship, the boats, the passengers. Dock workers telling people what to do, babies crying and parents raising their voices so their children could hear them.

She locked her gaze on one family. It looked like the Kerr family, a neighbor in Corriecravie. Margaret squinted to see their faces. Anna, their youngest was clinging to her mother's dress as they left the dock. Her eyes were so wide, Margaret could see the fear in them. Margaret felt scared for her. Anna kept looking up to her mother and crying and Margaret desperately wanted to cry with her. She saw herself in Anna. So afraid of everything going on around her. At that point she knew, it was fear holding her back on Arran.

As she watched the Kerr family leave, a member of the crew nearly knocked her over.

"If you aren't on this ship child, you best get out of the way," he said motioning with his arms to clear the area.

Margaret jumped to the side, letting the men move the barrels and containers with the ship's provisions. She nervously looked for John and her sisters and saw they had moved toward the buildings at the far end of the dock. Without hesitation, she rushed over to join them.

The buildings were surrounded by containers and large barrels labeled with "WOOL" in large black letters. Margaret thought she better ask more questions before John wondered what was wrong and gave her another lecture.

"Are these wool barrels going to New Brunswick too?" She asked.

"I don't think so," John replied. "They appear to be waiting on another ship."

Margaret decide to continue with questions on the provisions.

"What's inside those barrels?" Margaret said, pointing to the barrels the dock workers were loading on boats.

"Biscuits and water would be my guess," he said. "Why don't you ask? You haven't been asking many questions. We came here to get answers. Go ahead and ask one of the men loading the barrels."

John wondered about this quiet version of Margaret. Was it possible she was still angry with him? Not Margaret. Why was she asking questions about the provisions, he wondered? John shrugged it off and focused on his excitement and future plans.

To Margaret's surprise, the dock worker didn't mind the questions she raised.

"Water, mostly child," he said. "Some oats, potatoes and biscuits. Enough for all the passengers."

John nodded, almost pleased with his sister as she came back with answers.

"We must tell Mama to bring extra oats for us," Margaret said. "I don't think they'll have enough in those barrels for everyone."

That should be enough to keep John quiet, she thought. Margaret didn't need him meddling inside her thoughts. She was scared and the visit to the dock wasn't helping.

"Single file, hurry up, the ship's leaving in one hour," the dock worker yelled.

The Murchie children watched as the final group of families made their way to the large ship waiting to set sail. Loud voices could be heard shouting orders to anyone ready to listen.

Finally, the noise level started to ease as the last family boarded the tender. The hum of emigration stopped and now it was up to the ship to take the families away.

"We should be on that ship," John said, wishing the next few weeks would pass quickly.

He was convinced more than ever he needed to go.

"In several weeks, those families will be walking on new land, land with a great future," he added.

Liza and Janet nodded in agreement. Margaret gave a half nod, not capable of releasing her fear. She knew deep down inside, she didn't want to leave. Arran was her home.

They made their way back to the dory for the trip home and settled into the seats for the ride. The conversation was overflowing with excitement and ideas about the voyage. After a few short minutes, John stopped realizing they didn't get any information on the schedule. Too much excitement, he thought.

"We need to go back," he said. "We forgot to ask about the schedule."

They turned around and headed back to the dock.

"I'll go ask," Janet offered and jumped out before John could stop her.

She returned with a huge smile, revealing good news to share.

"There's a ship leaving next month, the middle of the month," she said. "It's going to Bay Chaleur, where Archibald has his new farm."

"That's the best news," John said.

He put his arms around his sisters and they hugged.

"Wait until Papa hears the next ship is sailing three weeks from now," he said.

A minute of silence fell over the children that ended with a yell of excitement from both Liza and Janet. John was grinning from ear to ear as he watched his sisters.

John maneuvered the flat oars around the coastline with ease, stopping only when the dory was next to the Corriecravie dock. Their little boat felt lighter when they pulled it out of the water and beached it.

The four children ran up the hill and burst into the house. Their noise level reached Mama and Papa well before they arrived at the door. Papa smiled when they rushed into the house.

"What'd you see," Papa asked. "Mama and I want to hear about Lamlash Harbor."

They were out of breath, barely pronouncing the words, as they recounted the harbor, the dock activity and finally stopped at announcing the next ship. Papa nodded when they told him about the May sailing.

"You already knew?" John asked.

"I knew they were monthly at this time so I'm not surprised," Papa said. "You didn't think I'd send you to Lamlash without knowing a few things. Did you?"

John smiled at his father.

"Of course not," he lied.

Truthfully, John hadn't thought about it. He was so wrapped up in thinking about his future. His own farm weighed heavy on his thoughts. At sixteen, he knew one hundred acres could be his in four years.

Margaret watched in horror as the whole family shared stories about the upcoming journey. They had no idea about British North America, she thought. And no idea about New Brunswick or Bay Chaleur for that matter. A few letters from Archibald and everyone wants to leave. Arran was home. She didn't know what she would do. She was afraid to leave her Arran. Afraid to get on the ship and sail across the ocean for a month or two.

As Margaret climbed into the sleeping area for the night, she knew it would be impossible to fall asleep. Her mind racing from a fear of the unknown to a fear of the next three weeks. With the three girls sharing the bed, Margaret tried to remain still and not awaken them with her worries. It was difficult. When she closed her eyes, she was back on the dock, staring into Anna's eyes. It was the scene she played over and over in her mind, until she fell asleep. Anna's fear became hers. The next morning everyone was eating their breakfast meal when she finally crawled down the ladder.

"Someone had a good sleep," Mama announced when she saw her youngest daughter.

It was Mama's way of saying good morning.

"Yes, good sleep Mama," she said.

Margaret didn't dare to tell her it wasn't a good sleep. Better to stay quiet. No one would understand her anyway.

"Great news," Papa announced as he walked into the kitchen after an early morning trip to Lamlash. "The Duke of Hamilton will pay half of the sailing fee to New Brunswick, so we'll be joining other Arran families on Bay Chaleur soon. Very soon.

2

Lamlash

The next several weeks were a blur in the Murchie house. There were animals to sell and debts to settle. More importantly, it was a time of endless visits to friends and family to say goodbyes and farewells. Many of the friends promised to see them in the future, requesting letters with descriptions of their new home on Bay Chaleur. They each had their own dreams to emigrate and wanted to learn more.

The family visits challenged Papa's optimism. Margaret's grandparents and elder aunts and uncles refused to leave. Arran was home and they were at peace with their life on the small island. They shrugged their shoulders as Papa described the upcoming changes to Arran, ignoring him completely when he claimed the number of farms would be reduced. These changes could force everyone off the land, Papa insisted. The response was always the same. Arran was their life and they would find a way to adjust. Margaret nodded along with them. They were telling Papa what she wanted to say.

Land grants were not enough to make them leave. It was the idea of a long voyage across the Atlantic to a new home that scared them. Few had traveled across the Clyde to the mainland, making the trip across the Atlantic an impossible journey. Margaret found these conversations soothing. She agreed and wanted to stay on Arran too. But Papa had made the decision and the calendar would not stop for her.

Between the tears and farewells, Mama made cleaning the house a top priority. It was a small island and she didn't want any gossip about Elizabeth Murchie's housekeeping after they departed. Bay Chaleur was far away but Mama feared the gossip words could carry over the ocean.

"Sweep the floors as best you can and scrub down the walls in the kitchen," she said pointing to the dark layers of soot lining each wall.

Margaret called it impossible work. Years of smoke had filled every rock crevice on the walls and the dirt floor couldn't be cleaned. Yet Mama would not relent. Instead of arguing, Margaret chose the laundry chores. Janet and Liza could take Mama's orders and tend to the walls and floors, she thought. The laundry could be done outside and done alone. Away from her mother's watchful eye. It would give her time to make a plan. Her plan to stay on Arran.

The weeks of visits and chores turned into days. Nothing could dampen the excitement. Not even the impossible cleaning. The anticipation was building inside the Murchie house with each passing day. Soon their ship would be arriving in Lamlash harbor.

Papa decided the family would spend their last evening on Arran at his sister, Isabella's house in Bennan.

"Bennan is closer to Lamlash," Papa said. "Our home is no longer ours and we'll need a place to sleep. Isabella and Neil will have us for one night."

His words sounded complete, yet the family wasn't quite ready to leave. John was the exception. He kept pushing everyone to load up the trap Uncle Neil had brought over. His sights focused on Bay Chaleur, and the prospect of his own farm. John wanted to leave Arran behind and start a new life. He imagined the new world would be an improvement over this one. Far away from the controls and stifling rules of the land owners. On Bay Chaleur, he could be his own landowner.

Mama's pace slowed as she placed the final chair into the trap. She looked around the house. One last glance, she thought. A few final moments inside her home. The emotion of leaving everything she knew weighed heavy on Mama. The small memories grew in size and importance as Mama walked the earthen floors one last time. This was it. There would be no going back to their life on Arran.

Uncle Neil's trap could barely hold the additional six people and everything the family needed to start their dream on Bay Chaleur. It didn't matter, the mood was too somber and no one dared complain. As melancholy continued to take over the excitement of a new life, Papa tried to intervene. He knew the future was off the island and worried the past was reaching for his family.

"Let's not dwell," he said, hoping his words would break the stillness of the silence.

Papa looked at Mama and watched her eyes well up. She must be rebuilding the past in her mind, he thought. Best to let the moment pass quickly.

"Yes, these footsteps are our last in Corriecravie," he said. "But better ones lie ahead."

Margaret stared at the house, incapable of sharing her feelings of sadness with anyone. It didn't seem real and she had few words to explain it. As they rode down the narrow lane to the main travel road, John refused to look back. The small house and farm were no more.

Mama kept a gaze on the old buildings until they were completely out of view. So many memories, she thought. Duncan. Poor little Duncan. He would forever be their link back to this farm. She sighed, trying to think about the future on Bay Chaleur. There would be new memories waiting for her with the Arran families already settled.

The pony and trap made its way along the road surrounded in silence from the farm and worries of what lie ahead. As they crossed the Sliddery Water, Papa forced his thoughts from the farm in Corriecravie to the Atlantic crossing and the days ahead

"Our ride to Lamlash from Bennan will be quick in the morning," he said, hoping his family would change their mood.

"Ah, yes," Neil replied before any of the Murchie children could respond.

He wanted to be on the ship with them, but family obligations forced Neil and Isabella to stay on Arran.

"Yes, you'll be closer to the ship," he said. "Soon enough, it'll be our turn."

Neil smiled knowing those obligations would change in the next several years. His father was too ill to make the journey, forcing Neil and Isabella to stay back, and care for him. It would be difficult with many unknowns but the family depended on Neil and he accepted his responsibility.

Similar to the Murchie family, Neil and Isabella MacNair were tenant farmers and subject to the whims of Arran's owners. Neil's family had worked the same piece of land for as long as anyone could remember and he hoped that would be an advantage. It was good land, producing a small crop, but anything could happen with the reduction in farms. The future was dimming with each day.

Isabella tried to hide the jealousy she held for her brother's future. The freedom to leave and start a new life. She wanted to believe Neil and his promise of their own voyage across the Atlantic. Only time could make it real.

The evening at the McNair home was filled with laughter and tears as storytelling took the spotlight. For a short time, everyone forgot the tension of the day and joined in the many stories about the Murchie family. The stories of Papa were special for the children and Isabella didn't hold back. Margaret watched as her father sat on the edge of the chair when Isabella shared a few embarrassing moments.

As the pause between the stories grew longer, Neil announced it was time for bed. Reluctant to stop the warm conversation and the mood of his family, Papa eventually agreed and everyone headed to their sleeping areas.

Sleep would not come easy. John imagined what the land on Bay Chaleur looked like. His new farm, covered in tall trees, ready to be tilled and planted. The next day was the beginning. As the images of land, trees and freedom floated in his mind, sleep remained elusive.

Margaret also found it impossible to sleep. With only a few hours before they boarded the ship, she continued to believe she could stay on Arran. But she needed a plan. A plan to convince Mama. She was confident Mama wanted to stay. She felt it during the last few hours at the farm. Her mind raced with options, hoping it wasn't too late. Would Mama listen to her now? What could she do?

She finally fell asleep only to awake an hour later from the loud voices and noise in the house. The sun hadn't risen, yet the house was filled with the energy of a mid-day. Everyone was awake and talking over each other.

"When are we leaving? Will we be too early?

Mama could sense the anticipation and anxiety buried beneath the questions. She immediately took control.

"Children, it's time to thank Aunt Isabella and Uncle Neil. Where are your manners? Let's be orderly or we'll forget something."

The voices settled and the questions stopped. Within a short time, the family was leaving Bennan for Lamlash and Margaret found herself sitting in the trap between her two sisters. A strange feeling washed over her body, sweeping her up with the excitement. Unable to fight it, she struggled to consider her Arran plan.

Papa's voice broke her concentration and Margaret strained to hear his words.

"It'll be chaotic and disorganized when we arrive at the dock," Papa warned.

He was worried. The children were too excited to realize what was going on around them.

"Hold onto each other and listen to the officers for instructions," he said.

The early morning fog wrapped the island in a soft blanket as the trap meandered down the narrow road towards Lamlash. Papa's instructions hung inside the fog, too muffled in the damp air to reach his children's ears. Hours later John would try to replay those instructions, but for now he was filled with the anticipation of boarding a ship to Bay Chaleur.

Margaret remained in a trance as they approached the dock. Part fog and fear, she sat quiet, deep in her own thoughts.

"There she is," John shouted, pointing to the ship between Lamlash and Holy Isle. "I'm sure those masts came from Bay Chaleur."

Papa stared at the ship. It looked small from the road with her masts resolute to the fog. It was a good sign, he thought. The ship would need strong masts to carry the sails on the open ocean. He smiled, relaxing his gaze and thinking about his family. This small barque would transport the Murchie family from an old life on Arran into a brand new world.

Isabella sensed it was time for her last goodbye.

"Safe journey to you," she said, trying to hold back her emotions.

"I'll write," Papa replied. "And soon, you'll join us."

Isabella couldn't keep her tears inside. She gave her brother a final embrace and turned to Neil. It was his clue to head home. James Murchie and his family were on their own.

They walked toward the end of the dock, all eyes fixated on the ship. It would be their home for the next several weeks. As they made their way, the chaos and confusion of the early morning took over. The dock was filled with noises, voices, and people milling about. Mama was immediately overwhelmed and tightened her grip on Papa's hand. She had never seen so many people in one place. This wasn't her Arran she was leaving behind. This was another place. A place she didn't recognize. She closed her eyes trying to feel and smell the Arran air one last time. Perhaps it was good they were leaving.

The dock officer started yelling at the families, pointing to the tenders ready to take the passengers.

"A few families at a time," he said. "Keep moving."

As one tender filled, another was ready to take on passengers. There was order inside the chaos. Finally, the Murchie family reached the front of the queue. It was their turn. Papa stepped on the plank, leading his family into the boat. They all held hands, with Mama and Margaret at the end of the line. This is it, Margaret thought. How did this happen?

She played out the earlier visit to the dock in her head. This time, she was Anna, clinging to her mother's side. But this time had to be different, she thought. She couldn't be Anna.

Margaret waited until everyone ahead of Mama was in the tender. As Mama steadied her foot to step inside, Margaret let go of her mother and raced back across the plank. She continued to run as fast as her little legs could carry her, stopping only when she was well out of view of the ship. She looked back and saw that no one had followed her.

Completely out of breath and filled with panic Margaret found a few "WOOL" barrels standing next to a building. They must be waiting for the next ship, she thought. Without hesitation, she nuzzled between them, dropping down as close to the ground as possible so no one could see her. Covering her head with the bag she had been carrying to the ship, she felt hidden from passersby.

She thought someone would find her. The loudness of her heartbeat must be enough to signal her location. No one came after her. No one. After a few hours, the fatigue of not sleeping the previous night forced her to doze off. When Margaret finally awoke it was almost dark, the sun casting its final light on Lamlash.

A full day had passed for Margaret. The sun was beginning to rise when they arrived at the dock and now it had dropped below the Arran hills. Afraid to get up, she peeked around the outer barrel and gradually stood on her feet.

Margaret edged out from behind the barrels and walked toward the end of the dock. The ship was gone and with it all the chaos of the people. A sense of fear and the excitement of being alone raced through her. Before she could decide what emotion, she preferred, someone grabbed her arm and pulled her toward them. As Margaret let out a scream a hand covered her mouth before she could make a sound.

"Where'd you go?" John asked. "What were you thinking? Do you know how dumb you are?"

A flurry of questions came out of John's mouth, not hiding the anger he felt for his sister. Margaret started to cry. Frustration and fear collapsing in on her.

"I want to stay on Arran," she said between her tears and sobs.

"Well you've turned this into a complete mess and now I must stay on Arran because of you," John said. "I needed to go to New Brunswick and now I'm stuck here with you. You ruined everything!"

"Me?" Margaret asked, not realizing her selfish behavior. "That's nonsense. Where's Papa and Mama?"

John couldn't believe how things turned out for him. His whole future was in the hands of his youngest sister.

"They're heading for our new home," he said. "I'm stuck with you until we can get on the next ship."

"I didn't think--"

"That's right," John interrupted. "You didn't think and now I'm paying the price for it."

Margaret remembered the day in the field and started to cry louder. She felt awful. Awful that John had found her and awful that he would take her off Arran. How did this go so badly? John let go of her arm and hugged her. There was anger but more forgiveness than he realized.

Margaret was convinced she could have lived alone. Nothing had changed about leaving Arran. Her last minute decision only made it worse.

"Let's go back to the house, John said, trying to take control of the situation. "At least we can discuss the next few days, weeks or months. All I know is we need to be on the next ship."

John started walking toward the road, then abruptly stopped in his footsteps. He realized the house in Corriecravie wasn't theirs. A new tenant could be in it. They couldn't go there.

Unsure of how John would react, Margaret kept quiet instead of offering any suggestions.

"Let's go back to Isabella and Neil," John blurted after thinking through their options. "They're family and will understand. It's our only option."

John found a dory next to the dock and asked one of the remaining workmen if he could borrow it.

"Don't know if she works," he said. "Take it and bring her back whence you can."

It was a dark and quiet ride back to Bennan that night. There was a small leak in the dory so Margaret kept bailing the water as John rowed to the MacNair home. The leak was enough of a distraction for the two of them but not enough to sink the boat. John thought the leak was like Margaret. Not enough to sink his hopes of leaving and starting a new life. He'll make it to New Brunswick.

Margaret stared into the dark water as the oars glided to the rhythm of her water removal. Soon they would be back in Bennan, still on the island. She had somehow managed to stay on Arran, but would it last? Had she gone too far? Was her fear of leaving Arran justified? The questions rolled over in her head as she thought about Mama. Could she live without Mama and Papa?

3

County Cork, Ireland

Four hundred miles from Arran, a cloud of whisper voices were asking a similar set of questions. But it wasn't just distance that separated the whispers. On Arran the whispers were filled with changes to the farms and farmland, a reduction in land available to the tenant farmer. In County Cork, Ireland the whispers surrounded concerns of rebellion.

Religious conflict was at the center of those concerns. The tension between the Catholic majority and a small privileged group of Protestants had continued since the 1798 rebellion. Most of the time resentment remained hidden beneath the surface, with both groups accepting the events of the past. But on occasion, the anger would erupt in a conversation or during a story about a lost relative. Robert Blacknell saw the conflict as a cycle of simmer and burn. A cycle that appeared to be heading out of the simmer phase.

Robert's ancestors had immigrated to Ireland over two hundred years earlier. They left England for the Munster Plantation, a planned settlement for loyal English farmers in southwest Ireland. After years inside the Bandon town walls, the family eventually settled in Timoleague, in the townlands of Ardgehane. The Blacknell family enjoyed the rich farmland and rolling hills of Timoleague. Close to the River Bandon and the seaport of Kinsale, Timoleague gave the Blacknells more than they had in England.

The Munster Plantation was the English Government's response to a series of Irish rebellions and uprisings in the late 1500s. They had grown weary of the incursions and demanded loyal subjects must populate Munster Province. In response, large swaths of land, an expanse of thousands of acres were confiscated from the Irish and sold to gentlemen undertakers. These men were tasked with filling the land with Protestant tenants based on an English model.

And now, two centuries later, Robert was deciding whether to stay in Ireland or leave for New Brunswick, in British North America. It was a repeat of the Blacknell family history and a major decision for Robert to make on his own. His father wasn't alive to share in the making of this milestone for the family. He had died a year earlier leaving Robert to care for his mother and three siblings. The days leading up to his death were painful. A man not yet fifty, shouldn't die, Mother would repeat to anyone who would listen. Pneumonia doesn't select its victims by age, Robert thought as he watched the grief overflow. His mother would eventually come to terms with Father's death, but it did little to lighten her grief.

If only Father was here to decide with me, or for us, Robert thought. What would he do? How would he convince Mother? He knew it was pointless to wait for answers. They wouldn't come and a decision had to be made. Times were changing in Ireland and West Cork was no exception.

The local economy was still in turmoil from the end of the Napoleonic wars. At the height of the war, the Bandon textile mills were in high demand, exporting to England and America. With the war between Britain and its former colony over, the Irish textile market collapsed taking the livelihood of many in Bandon with it. Unrest always followed economic troubles and this time wasn't any different.

Families were already struggling when the Government imposed additional taxes and tithes in support of the Church of Ireland. The anger increased as the situation went from bad to intolerable. Everywhere Robert went, emigration from Ireland was in the whispers.

Irish families made plans to leave for British North America or to New South Wales in the Pacific. In less than two months, a family could cross the Atlantic and start a new beginning in New Brunswick

All the whispers peaked Robert's thoughts about leaving Ireland. The latest skirmish in Bandon only added to his interest. It was another small one, but the frequency of the attacks was changing. Every week he heard a new story about a business in the town repairing window damage.

Several cousins had left Ireland a decade prior and insisted Robert should join them in New Brunswick. Their new home on Bay Chaleur sounded inviting with its bounty of forests, fish and land. Robert read and re-read each letter from cousin Matthew. He imagined the life Matthew described in detail. An opportunity with less friction. He only needed courage and hard work to fulfill a lifetime of possibilities, according to Matthew.

Robert struggled to balance the farmland he had in Timoleague with Matthew's description of Bay Chaleur. The labor required to build a farm didn't scare him, but at the same time, the uprisings in West Cork certainly did. The more he thought about the options, the more he wished his father was still alive. He would know what to do.

As the merchants continued to shutter their shops in Bandon, Robert grew concerned that time was not on his side. But there was more to leaving than sailing on the next ship out of Bantry Bay. He would need to convince his mother to leave too. She loved Timoleague. Her family history was tied to the farmland and she would be difficult. Robert was facing a repeat of the Blacknell family history. The British Government once again was offering land grants as an incentive to emigrate. This time the destination was New Brunswick and not the Munster Plantation. It would be a new chapter for the Blacknells.

Robert was shouldering the burden of acting as both son and the eldest with the ease of an older man.

He knew his father's shoes were too large to fill but each morning after the burial, Robert stood a little taller with the added responsibility. At nineteen, his business and farming skills had been fine tuned while his father was still alive. Negotiating with his mother however, was still a challenge. A challenge his father did not prepare him for.

Robert knew his mother would reject the prospect of emigration if he brought it up in conversation. His words would be brushed aside as soon as they left his mouth. Ireland was her home with deep memories in County Cork. She loved the farm, the nearby townspeople and her monthly trips to Bandon for the little extras. He would have to convince her.

Lacking the finesse that life experience brings, he chose to gather information and evidence to make his case. Early one Thursday morning, Robert made his way to Cork City's emigration office. It would be the starting point for collecting the information he needed.

Once in Cork, Robert made his way to the Customs House to inquire about New Brunswick. After standing in queue for the better part of an hour, the official barely looked up when Robert reached his desk and asked about the emigration opportunities. The officer pointed to the wall behind Robert.

"All your questions can be answered on that wall," he declared. "Nothing more for me to add."

Robert thought the officer was rude, but turned around to find a wall filled with notices about sailings, passages, British North American ports, ships, and various offers for new settlers. He could hardly believe it. The officer didn't need to speak. It was all in black and white for anyone to read.

Robert focused on the New Brunswick notices. Generous grants of 100 and 200 acres could be obtained. The grants came with a set of expectations. Clearing, building a home and land improvements through farming. Robert liked what he saw. The pace of land clearing seemed reasonable. It would be hard work. Much harder than farming in Timoleague. This was exactly as Matthew had described.

The Customs official continued to keep his head down to avoid questions but Robert still had a few unknowns and didn't want to stand in the queue again. He decided to ask the older man standing next to him.

"I'm sorry to bother you with my questions, but do you know where the voyage schedules are posted?" he asked. "I'm thinking about taking my family and need to know when the ships sail."

The man shrugged his shoulders forcing Robert to return to the queue. After a shorter wait, he finally reached the officer's desk again and immediately blurted his question.

"Can you point me in the direction of the sailing schedules to New Brunswick?" he asked without waiting for the officer.

Without changing the expression on his face, the officer pointed to the door.

"Outside on the dock's notice boards," he said, keeping his eyes focused on the papers in front of him. Robert was amazed at this man's behavior and left the building for the dock area. Again, he was presented with the exact information he needed. The ships were leaving from Cobh Harbour, just down the road, on a regular schedule. The schedule included arrivals and departures for the next three months.

Robert searched for arrival ports in New Brunswick, looking for Bathurst or Miramichi. These ports were close to Matthew's home in Gloucester County, so they were Robert's first choice. Matthew advised Robert to sail on a reputable ship with an experienced captain. A good captain will bring you safely across the Atlantic so be wary and ask questions Matthew had written. Robert already saw the difficulty in asking questions but he took a chance and walked over to the officer working on the dock.

"Can you tell me more about the ship schedules and passage to New Brunswick?" Robert enquired.

When the officer smiled and started talking, the tension in Robert immediately faded.

"Yes of course," he said. "The sailings are weekly now with the timber trade as busy as it is. New Brunswick has so much timber arriving in Cobh for shipbuilding, the captains try to fill the hold with paying passengers for the return voyage. Most ships are adjusted for these passengers but you must be careful. There had been several issues with ships not caring for the people."

This was exactly what Matthew had described. Shipbuilding was a strong business in New Brunswick and the ship's owners did not want to sail back empty.

"Anything to make a profit," he declared.

The officer wouldn't stop talking and Robert didn't interrupt.

"The days of horrible treatment are over," he said. "Governments have placed new rules for the safety of the passage. The north Atlantic is not forgiving. I must tell you having the right captain is essential. A captain that knows the Atlantic and all she can dish out."

Robert couldn't believe his good luck and the honesty. He started to feel better, hoping this officer would tell him everything he needed to know including finding the right Captain.

"Tell me sir, is there a method to selecting the right Captain?" he asked.

The officer just shook his head and told Robert to look at the upcoming schedule and ask questions.

"The Captains are expected to keep good records of the voyage, the sick and dying," he said. "They must also track the provisions. Upon arrival the documents are handed to the customs agent in New Brunswick."

He went on to describe how the laws were getting stricter and forcing bad Captains from carrying people across the Atlantic.

"Go over to the schedule on the board and tell me the Captain's name for the sailing you want," he said. "I'll nod if he's known as a good one."

Robert eyes scanned the sailing schedule for the remainder of spring. He thought he could finish his farm business quickly and sail with an upcoming ship.

"What do you know about Beegan?" he asked.

The officer shook his head forcing Robert to continue down the list. The next several names had the same response, raising Robert's concerns of finding the right Captain. When Robert said the name Power, the officer immediately nodded. Robert could feel the weight of the world leave his shoulders.

"The ship, Eden?" Robert asked almost afraid his good luck would run out.

"Captain Power would only set sail aboard a good ship," he said.

Robert started to smile knowing he had the information he needed to persuade his mother to leave. Everything was falling into place. He thanked the officer for sharing his knowledge, but remained puzzled by the behavior of the first officer.

"Not everyone is as helpful as you have been," he said. Without hesitation it became clear.

"A hundred people show up each week to learn about passage across the Atlantic," he said. "I don't mind answering the same questions but some officers grow tired."

It made sense to Robert. With the recent challenges and a growing economy in New Brunswick many Irish were seeking opportunities. It was clear from the day's events, he wasn't alone in the search for answers.

Back to Timoleague he went as the setting sun started its descent. Alone in the cart, he practiced his upcoming conversation with his mother in the cool Irish air. There would be several obstacles and she would want him to stay in Ireland. Who would work the farm? Take care of her? He knew all the standard questions she would ask and he would have to stay strong. She would have to join him. It was as simple as that. No other answer could be given. The entire Blacknell family must be on the Eden.

Once he arrived at the farm, Robert put the horse and carriage away while the final conversation played in his head. He was ready. At least he thought so.

Robert took off his hat as he entered the house. He would have to abide by all the important courtesies his mother expected. Mother was sitting in the rocking chair next to the fire. She was holding her usual knitting needles with the yarn quickly moving through her fingers. Robert pulled up a chair and sat across from her.

Never one to avoid a good debate, Robert wasted no time in getting the conversation started.

"I've been thinking of sailing to British North America to join Matthew," he announced.

It didn't make sense to attempt any small talk. Mother hated conversations that didn't hit the main point.

"British North America say ye," she said, not looking up. "Is there not enough for ye here?"

Mother dropped the needles into her lap and straightened her back. Folding her arms across her chest, she immediately put Robert on the defensive.

Robert knew he should stay seated out of respect, but decided to stand and take charge of the conversation. She could be stubborn and Robert was concerned she would dig in for a long argument. He tried an emotional approach first.

"Mother, I fear for our safety," he said. "Our long term property—." Mother would not listen.

"Everything's fine here," she said. "We've enough to eat. Our neighbors treat us well. Even that small uprising last week was about the Barry farm. This land has been with the family longer than the Barry's."

He knew she was ignoring the warning signs.

"Yes Mother, but times are changing," he said. Robert moved toward the stove taking his eyes off Mother. No need to provoke her by staring he thought.

"First the Barry's farm then others, even ones from centuries ago are under attack," he said. "I'm sure you heard about the Wexford barn burning."

Mother stood up immediately dropping the knitting onto the floor. She walked toward the door to leave the room. He had pushed too hard.

"I don't believe ye," she said, walking away. "And that barn burning is made up to scare people. It's County Wexford, not Cork. I've heard enough."

She made her way out of the room but Robert fell in pursuit. He knew he had hit a nerve discussing the barn burning but she needed to hear it. Her ancestors had lost their farm many decades ago after an uprising and it was his final shot at getting her to think about leaving.

"If you're up to it, let's go into Bandon on Saturday and I'll show you the changes," Robert offered.

"It's a pack of foolishness!" Mother grumbled under her breath.

Robert could hear her talking to herself as she closed the door to her bedroom. There wasn't any sense in trying to talk about it after Mother shut the door.

Robert walked back to the fire and took her seat. He looked around at the room in front of him. They had a grand house in addition to several barns on the property. Rich farmland and nearly one hundred acres were known as the Blacknell farm. He understood why she would be reluctant to leave. His heart was heavy but he knew things were different now. He was scared.

The noise level was increasing. Many of the farmers had to sell their cattle to pay taxes. It was just a matter of time before the Catholic families would insist on more than taxes paid by their Protestants neighbors. Robert knew the Plantation families lived on land taken from the Irish a few centuries ago. Seemingly far removed from those ancient times, concerns remained. With the added responsibility of caring for his family, Robert watched and listened, trying to extract meaning from the whispers of the day.

Taxes were a hot issue and the crime rate against the Protestants was increasing. Ireland had seen many of these battles in the name of religion. This was not the time to be complacent.

With Ireland in transition and the potential for history to repeat itself, Robert knew the family could be in danger. The Blacknell family had to change or leave. He would need to provide more evidence. Without asking, on Saturday morning he pulled the horse out of the barn and hitched the cart.

"A quick ride into Bandon town is all," Robert pleaded. "If you see what has happened since your last trip, perhaps it'll help. The family's safety is at hand."

Mother sat down to take in the seriousness in his voice.

"But this is all I know," she said. "We've everything here."

"We do but we don't have our long term safety," Robert replied.

"If your father was alive, he wouldn't listen to this. He would find a way to keep us safe," she said.

For a moment, Robert bristled with hearing what his father would do, then he moved on.

"I can't argue about what father would be able to do. I only know this. There's a ship leaving in a month and another one leaving in two. We need to be on one of them."

Robert knew better than to argue about how his father would have acted in this situation. His father wasn't alive and he couldn't ask him. Mother was reaching.

"What about the farm?" Mother asked.

Robert felt a shift in her questions. They were about the future not the past.

"Cousin William can take care of the farm," he said. "William would like the option to purchase our farm after several months," Robert carefully added.

His land was next to the property and William had no desire to leave. By suggesting the purchase in the future, Mother could leave knowing she had property to return to if necessary. Robert had thought of every argument.

Robert had discussed British North America and New Brunswick with William on several occasions. He shared Matthew's letters and the conversations always ended with William's desire to stay. William understood the risks yet he saw no future in leaving. He would take his chances in Timoleague. Robert felt differently, but he offered William the option of joining them in the future, if things worsened.

Robert had prepared for this day. He took his responsibility for his mother and siblings seriously, adjusting his future for them. He wasn't thinking about marriage or courting any of the women as mother suggested. The farm and his family were the top priority.

Getting the grant in New Brunswick upon arrival would take time but the process had been started by

Matthew. In two weeks, he would know if the family qualified. British North America was giving preference to Protestants. He felt confident.

Robert helped his mother into the cart for the ride to Bandon. As they turned onto the road, she filled the air with questions. A few, Robert attempted to ignore but he was quickly called out.

"How much can I take with me?" she asked. "What's it like in British North America? Why aren't you answering me? I'm an old woman. This won't be easy."

Robert tried to hide his smile. He was convinced his mother would make the trip. As the horse made its way over the bridge and onto Main Street South, Robert felt a sense of relief as Mother saw the vandalism in the form of broken windows and damaged buildings. It wasn't a significant amount of damage but enough to indicate trouble. One of the large windows of the dry goods store where Mother purchased her cloth was boarded up. His points were evident.

"Please stop the carriage," Mother asked. "I want to visit with Mrs. Hanson and see how she is. I want to see how is she's handling the damage to the store."

Mother stepped into the store and quickly returned.

"Mrs. Hanson is at home," she said, trying to hold back her tears. "She's unable to come to the store because of an injury. She was in the store at the time of the vandalism and a piece of glass cut into her arm."

Robert helped his mother back into the seat as she held his hand tightly. Several minutes passed before she collected her emotions and Robert felt the carriage could move. He slapped the reins to the horses and they headed home. As the carriage rounded the corner toward the bridge, Mother made up her mind. She could leave. She had seen enough and knew the history. This was not the first bit of trouble Ireland had seen. And it wouldn't be the last. Robert had shown her the evidence.

Over the next several days, Robert prepared his brother and sisters with the news of their upcoming voyage. He approached the two girls, Rebecca and Sarah with caution. They were reluctant to try new things, preferring the safety of the predictable. He knew it would be easier with Thomas, a twelve year old with the carefree spirit of the youngest child. He was ready to try anything new.

Robert explained where they were going, leading with the excitement of traveling to a British colony. Crossing the Atlantic Ocean would be the first challenge, he told them. It was a vast open water and it would be dangerous. Robert saved the hardest part for the last. They would leave Timoleague behind. A home they all loved.

"We know all about your plans," Sarah claimed. "We've been listening to your conversations with Mother."

Robert was pleased that he didn't have to describe every detail, but there was a different tone in her voice. He would use caution in his explanation.

"I know this is a big adventure and a complete change to our lives," he said. "We must go for our family's safety and I'll need your help. As the oldest daughter, Mother will rely on you during our voyage. She will also need you when we set up our new home."

Sarah appreciated Robert's reliance on her as the oldest daughter. It made her feel important to the family. But leaving Timoleague would be a burden on her too. Sarah had friends in Bandon, especially Samuel Dixon. She hoped to marry Samuel in the near future and now this voyage to the other side of the world would change all that.

Robert waited for his sister to share her concerns. He was certain the Dixon family was staying in Ireland, so he avoided the topic altogether. It would be best to keep the conversation strictly about their own family.

The Blacknells were tight knit and rarely did things without a discussion. Father's death forced all of them to grow up and evaluate every decision. He had left Mother everything according to the will and had asked Robert to take care of the family in the event of an early death. The younger children were asked to abide by family decisions. It made an impact on everyone. Even in death, Father was leading the family.

Rebecca and Thomas were less concerned than Sarah. The ship's voyage sounded like an adventure. They had seen the ships in Kinsale harbor but never dreamt of taking a long voyage across the Atlantic on one. Their older brother could worry about the risks. They simply didn't see any.

Sarah was different. At sixteen, she was old enough to stay behind if she decided but a promise to Father weighed heavy on her. She asked Robert for his advice on staying behind or going.

"I'm old enough to stay in Timoleague," Sarah pointed out, attempting to gauge Robert's reaction.

Robert knew she would agree to travel but he allowed her the time to ask questions and make the decision.

"Yes, you certainly are old enough," he said. "But what are your plans? How will Mother stay in touch with you? Can you manage the farm for William?" Sarah shook her head and dropped her shoulders.

"I hadn't thought about all of that," she said. "I will travel. I want to be with all of you. I've already asked Samuel about his plans to travel to New Brunswick."

Robert tried to keep a straight face as Sarah made her decision in front of him. He doubted Samuel would make the trip, but was surprised Sarah had asked him. It didn't matter. The Dixon family would never let him go alone, Robert thought. He remained silent, not commenting. There was little advantage in deflating her dreams.

"Wonderful news," he said. "You won't regret creating our new home in New Brunswick."

It was settled. The Blacknell family would be on the next ship to Bathurst, New Brunswick. The only question remaining was whether Samuel would join them on the ship.

4

Bennan, Isle of Arran

The oars moved swiftly through the dark water on the ride to Bennan, the dory thrusting forward with each stroke. John's grip was methodical and crisp, his frustration flowing with each pull of the oars. Margaret didn't speak. There wasn't anything she could say.

John thought about his situation. A few hours ago, he was in a boat heading toward a new life and now he was back in this old one. He would hold Margaret responsible. There wasn't any other option. He would tell the story of what happened on the dock. It was time for others to know how she behaved. Her impulsiveness created the mess he was stuck in.

After beaching the dory, they ran up the hill to the MacNair home. It took a few loud knocks before Isabella opened the door and let out a loud gasp at the sight of the two children standing in front of her.

"What happened?" Isabella asked with excitement and worry wrapped in her voice. "Where's James?"

John didn't wait for Margaret to answer.

"Papa is off to New Brunswick," John answered. "Everyone boarded the ship, but Margaret decided to stay on Arran. She ran and hid so we couldn't find her. Papa sent me after her."

The words fell out of John's mouth with ease. His anger and frustration visible to his aunt.

"How is this possible?" she said, barely believing what she just heard. Isabella motioned for the two children to step into the kitchen. Neil heard the commotion and joined everyone standing near the door.

"Come in, come in," he said. "Sit by the fire. Tell us what happened."

John repeated what he had shared earlier with Isabella. He gazed at Margaret as he described his father's instructions to find her.

"So here we are," John said. "We're hoping we can stay with you until the next ship sails. And Miss Margaret, you'll be on that ship."

John continued to stare at his sister, not expecting a response. Margaret kept her head down during the conversation. She didn't like John speaking for her, but she had few options. Besides, no one would listen to her now. She knew her voice was silenced. Everything had gone so terribly wrong.

"You can stay here," Neil said. "But I'll need you to help with the chores like the rest of the children. It can't be a visit."

"Thank you," John said. "Papa and Mama will thank you too." John was relieved and grateful. At least they had a place to sleep. He could manage chores. That would be easy. Keeping his sister in line and getting her on the next ship would be more difficult.

The next morning, Neil had plans for the two children as soon as they finished breakfast.

"I could use your help in the fields," Neil said pointing to John as the last spoonful of porridge left the dish. "Margaret can work in the house."

John stood up and followed Neil out of the house, almost relieved to be away from Margaret. He glanced at her over his shoulder as he stepped outside. She'll be safe here, he thought. Isabella will watch her.

A few minutes after they left, Margaret felt safe enough to talk.

"John's upset with me," she said looking into the bowl in front of her.

"He should be," Isabella replied, not feeling sorry for the predicament her young niece found herself in. "You took a terrible risk and put your family's future in jeopardy."

"I didn't think about it that way," Margaret said revealing her youth.

Aunt Isabella heard the innocence in Margaret's voice. She moved closer and put her arm around her.

"There'll be times in your life when you question your mother and father," she said. "This wasn't one of them. What you did was wrong."

The words hung in the air with the smoke from the fire, but only the smoke escaped. Margaret put her hands on her face and started to cry. They were tears built up from the past few weeks and Isabella didn't try to console her.

"Time to start on the laundry," she said.

Isabella had made her points and now there was work to be done. Margaret rubbed her eyes with her sleeve and finished eating. There wasn't time for tears with Aunt Isabella, she thought, as her hands gathered the bowls from the table for washing.

Margaret knew her place. She would be expected to clean and wash and mind the children. John was different. He could escape to the outdoors, away from Neil's watchful eye. Inside it was different. Margaret felt Isabella's eyes were always upon her.

The routine of daily tasks was established and the two Murchie children set about to keep their end of the bargain. Soon enough, they would be sailing off to New Brunswick, John thought, but first they needed to know the ship schedule. After his chores were finished on Thursday, John made his way to Lamlash harbor. He scanned all the signs and posters for sailings for Bay Chaleur. There were a few but none were direct like the ship Papa had taken. He sat down at the end of the dock trying to evaluate his options. A voyage with multiple ports and ships would give Margaret more opportunity to run and hide. He also knew if they boarded the wrong ship, they might never see their parents again.

The situation started to wash over him. Staying behind with Margaret, farming for the MacNairs and now a complicated sailing schedule. The temperature was rising in his body. Everything seemed impossible. His whole life was a mess. Several days ago, his future was clear and now he was searching for a new sailing schedule. They would be lucky to leave Arran this year, he thought. And luckier to be on a ship sailing to Bay Chaleur. Overwhelmed, John yelled at the first dock worker he saw.

"How do I get to New Brunswick?" he asked. "Would the ship honor the paid passage from a previous sailing? When could they leave?" The rapid set of questions fell on deaf ears.

"I just work here," the man yelled in response. "I don't run the place. Go ask the man in that office," he said, while pointing to the small building near the entrance.

John realized he wasn't thinking clearly. He knew all the information was at the Harbor Office, but somehow the situation had clouded his thinking. He walked toward the small building and opened the door to find an old man with grey hair and glasses behind the desk. The old man immediately looked up at him.

"Can I help?" he asked.

John described his situation without stopping to take a breath. The old man winced and shook his head as John filled the small building with questions.

"You just need to be ready for the next ship," he said. "Don't know if you can get on it, but I do know there is one leaving for New Brunswick from Port Glasgow on the mainland in three weeks."

John immediately perked up.

"Three weeks from now?" he asked.

The old man nodded his head again and tried to explain the schedule.

"You will need to board here, sail to Port Glasgow and change ships in the harbor," the old man explained. "You best be here early and ready to board."

It was too good to be true. Three weeks. John hesitated for a minute and asked about the payment.

"Your passage was covered on the Lady Campbell who sailed last week, so no payment is due."

An hour ago, it was overwhelming, but now John had hope. He tried not to think about the farm waiting for him in New Brunswick. Slowly, he thought. One day at a time. John thanked the old man and hurried back to the MacNair home. He had no doubt, Margaret would be ready to board that ship to Port Glasgow.

The following day, John sent a letter to Archibald with their potential arrival date. Six weeks from the Port Glasgow departure, he assumed. There was no way of knowing whether Archibald would receive the letter in time, but John had to tell Papa they were heading across the Atlantic. Another worry, but it was the best he could do.

The weeks before the departure passed slowly. Each day was filled with the anticipation and excitement of leaving. The concern of finding his family in New Brunswick weighed on John causing nights of fitful sleep as he went over and over the voyage in his head. All the port stops, the voyage from Lamlash to Port Glasgow, Port Glasgow to where? Maybe he should have told Archibald eight weeks. Once in the Atlantic, the ship could make port in many places in New Brunswick. Bathurst was his preferred port, but he needed to be ready for anything. He had seen a map of New Brunswick and knew it was a larger than Arran.

There was no choice but to take the next ship and work through each challenge.

And there was Margaret. With each port call, she could jump, increasing the size of his mess. Without her cooperation, his plans were doomed. Could she be trusted with the schedule, he wondered.

With one week left before their departure, John decided to share the details of the voyage with Margaret. She needs to know about the number of ship changes, he thought. Surprising her on the day of departure could create bigger issues.

"It's difficult to find ships sailing directly to Bathurst," John said, one evening after the supper meal.

"Does that mean we must stay on Arran longer?" Margaret asked while trying to hold back a smile. This time she was torn between her love of Arran and her mother's warm embrace. There was an emptiness on Arran without Mama.

"Oh no, it just means we'd take a ship to Port Glasgow and then, another to New Brunswick," he replied. "We could also arrive at a different port than Papa did, making our voyage more difficult."

John wanted to remind Margaret about the mess she created but held back staring at her instead. Margaret saw his eyes and decided to keep quiet. No point in challenging him, she thought. It was clear his anger had not gone away.

When the day finally arrived, the house was alive before dawn. Another day of departure filled with the anticipation of a long journey. Isabella had developed a fondness for the children and secretly wished they would stay. It wasn't possible, she thought. As much as she wanted them, her brother was waiting for John and Margaret to join the family across the Atlantic. Perhaps she would see them in New Brunswick, in only a few years. Neil had made that promise and it was one she expected him to keep.

After a few tearful goodbyes and long hugs, John and Margaret headed for Lamlash in the dory they had borrowed a month earlier. John had repaired the leak so there was pride in bringing the small boat back in better condition than when he borrowed it. This was it. John was confident, but Margaret was nervous. She was afraid of travelling so far away from Arran. This time however, she had no choice but to leave.

They placed the dory above the tide line where they had found it and headed to the dock. The scene was all too familiar at Lamlash harbor. A rising sun and a growing crowd of people filled with excitement and anxiety. Everyone appeared ready. Ready to board the ship to Port Glasgow and to ports unknown. The Murchie children had New Brunswick as their destination, but many of the other families were leaving the island for England or America. Most would never return to Arran.

Families started to assemble near the planks to load into the tenders. It was a smaller crowd than the day Papa left, but the noise level of excitement and anxiety, was similar.

"You must hold my hand," John declared, staring into Margaret's eyes. "I know you think you're old enough to walk on your own but you've already tricked us. I can't let you go, I promised Papa I'd bring you to Bay Chaleur."

John kept a watchful eye and hold on his sister. He rushed to the ship's boarding officer to ensure their passage, pulling Margaret behind him while squeezing her small hand in his fist. He knew the risks of letting go. Besides he yearned for New Brunswick more than his young sister could imagine. Margaret didn't fight him that morning, but kept pace with his rapid steps and winched under his tight grip.

The officer gave them the nod and pointed to the plank with the shorter queue. They navigated around each of the families and found themselves standing behind a mother with three children. Margaret tried to imagine the next several weeks. She was scared, but she had John. Suddenly, his grip didn't seem so bad. It felt reassuring. Comforting. She closed her eyes and imagined their arrival on Bay Chaleur. Mama would meet them, she was certain. Oh, how she missed her.

At the signal, Margaret crossed the plank ahead of John, keeping her head down while John's grip pushed her along. After she placed her foot inside the tender, John let out a long sigh. Step one, he thought. There were so many transition points ahead of them, and he wanted to celebrate this one but knew better than to drop his guard or relax.

"We made it," he announced loud enough for everyone in the tender to hear.

"Yes, we'll see Mama soon," Margaret replied, deep in thought about her mother. She wanted to be alone with those thoughts, imagining Mama's arms wrapped around her.

John's voice continued to interrupt her thoughts. He was annoying. He insisted on talking. Filling the air with sentences and pointless words.

"We're on our way to Bay Chaleur," he said. "Look at that ship. It's a steamer. We've never been on a ship, much less a steamer. It's the largest ship I've ever seen."

Margaret smiled expecting John to stop talking. Finally, she reacted as he tightened his grip.

"You're hurting me," she said.

"I'm sorry," John replied, without relaxing his hand.

He was excited, yet apprehensive and a bit scared. He was closer to his dream and couldn't stop the words flowing out of his mouth. Margaret closed her eyes and tried to ignore the pain and John. She could do this. She could leave Arran, surrounded by strangers.

John didn't notice Margaret's legs shaking as she stepped onto the second plank. His eyes were fixed on the ship, his grip tightening with each step. Another transition, he thought as Margaret placed her left foot onto the deck. Step two. They were on the steamer. John briefly closed his eyes and smiled, acknowledging their progress. Closer, they were getting closer. The crew instructed the Murchie children to take a seat and remain seated until the ship set sail.

As the steamer left the harbor, they knew they would never see their island home again. Surprisingly, Margaret wasn't alone in feeling melancholy. John took several deep breaths, trying to take in the island's air for one last time. Arran had been their entire world, their home, but in the future, it would be the tiny island they came from.

Within a short time, the buildings on Arran became smaller and smaller until they looked like dots on a green field. Holy Island stood majestic giving Margaret a focal point to stare at. It had always been a landmark. A compass. A navigation point for Lamlash Harbor. Now it was just another rock in the Firth of Clyde.

Despite the cold east wind cutting across the steamer's deck, Margaret and John didn't go below for warmth. They had never stepped foot off their island home and now the Scottish mainland was closing in. Papa had shared many stories and tales about this Scotland, but it was all foreign to them. They stared intently as Port Glasgow harbor came into focus. Arran had not prepared them for the scenes unfolding in front of their innocent eyes.

The bustle in Lamlash harbor seemed calm by comparison. Port Glasgow was exploding with activity. Buildings, people and ships. More than they had ever seen in one place. John counted the ships in the harbor and stopped at twenty. It didn't matter. What mattered was keeping Margaret beside him. Another transition was upon them. The biggest step toward New Brunswick.

They gathered their belongings and followed all the passengers toward the plank. John was unsure of where to go next. So many ships, but which one would take them to New Brunswick? He couldn't let Margaret know he was lost, so he kept his head high and tightened his grip.

Margaret led the way off the ship and onto the dock. Just a few hours and they would be on the next one. But where was it and how would they find it? John searched for the first dock official and tried to appear calm as he approached him.

"Can you point me toward the Harbor Office?" John asked, sounding breathless.

"Off to your right about 300 yards," the worker said.

John thanked him and pulled Margaret toward the office. He couldn't lose her now. Not here. She would be gone forever. There were so many people collected on the dock. No one would miss the two children from Arran if they never boarded the ship. John felt the sweat bead up on his forehead as he made his way. He was scared.

Margaret was deep in her own fear. She was adjusting to the sounds and odors of the city. It wasn't anything like Lamlash. There were people everywhere. And the smells made her stomach flip. She covered her nose with her free hand while keeping her arm over her small bag. It was difficult. She kept bumping into strangers. She wanted to find the ship as much as John did.

After a quick conversation in the office, John and Margaret followed the directions to the ship at the end of the dock. It was a few minutes away and scheduled to leave within a few hours. John's heart raced as he carved a path through the crowd. There weren't any complaints from Margaret as she struggled to keep up.

Their ship, the Eden was surrounded by crew and passengers when they reached her. John was out of breath as he handed their papers over to the ship's officer.

"Take your place over there," the man said while pointing to the queue near the stern.

John took back the papers and followed the directions. He could relax. The ship was in front of them and shortly they would be boarding her. He wanted to let down his guard but they were so close. It was the Eden, then Bay Chaleur. Almost giddy with his luck, he looked around not believing how close he was to his dream.

"What do you think of Port Glasgow?" he asked Margaret.

"I'm too scared to think about it," she replied.

It was true. The dock at Port Glasgow made Margaret feel small, insignificant, and almost invisible. John's tight and painful grip was surprisingly reassuring.

Before long they were heading up the plank to the Eden. Another transition. John sighed, dropping his shoulders from the exhaustion of the day. Soon we will be out in the Atlantic and I won't need to hold her hand, he thought. He touched the side of the ship with the palm of his hand as he stepped on the deck.

"Touch the ship," he told Margaret.

"Why, why would I do that?" she asked, confused.

"This ship has been across the Atlantic," he said. "It's carried many families to British North America. It --"

"Alright," she said interrupting John. She didn't know what to think. John was acting strange, but she reached over and touched the ship anyway.

Within a few minutes, the crew instructed the passengers to go below deck to their assigned areas and John followed Margaret into the opening. After a few steps, Margaret was overcome by the odor of damp wood and the smoke from burning oil rising toward her. She quickly covered her nose and continued down the ladder. The thought of living with this smell during the voyage brought her to tears and John reacted immediately.

"What's wrong with you?" he said.

He couldn't relax his guard until the ship set sail so he found himself always overreacting.

"The smell is making me feel bad," she said.

John's mind started to race. Would she jump off the ship? He was tired of tending to his sister and worrying about her sudden moves. Besides, they weren't near Arran and she was afraid of Port Glasgow. It was time to calm down.

The ship's atmosphere started to change as more families boarded and headed below deck. It reminded John of the church gatherings in Kilmory Parish. Loud voices, familiar songs and conversation filled the air. Soon the ship was flowing with the laughter of excitement and anticipation. This should help, John thought, as it changed both their moods. They were among strangers but somehow everyone appeared to be friends. Margaret wiped her tears with her sleeve and covered her nose on her way toward the stern.

Once their small bags were placed below the table in the center aisle, John stared at the bunk he would share with Margaret for the next six weeks. It wasn't anything he expected. Steerage was worse than a stable, he thought. Two rows of slatted wood about five feet high made up the bunks on both sides of the ship. He smiled at Margaret, trying to disguise his thoughts. She didn't return his smile as she moved to their assigned bunk. Margaret dropped their only blanket onto the bed. Privacy would be impossible across the Atlantic.

At the same time, the Taylor and MacMillan families were setting up next to the Murchie children. It was clear both families were excited about the new beginnings in British North America. Their conversation reminded them of Papa and the bright future he described in New Brunswick. Margaret followed the Taylor girls as they headed up the ladder. She wanted to get away from the musty odor and John's tight grip. He was smothering her. She understood why but didn't like it.

How she missed the days of playing with friends and the freedom of living on Arran. Those days were gone. She tried to imagine the next several weeks on this ship. It was an impossible place. As she reached the top of the ladder, she turned to see John following her topside. He would stop at nothing to reach his dream on Bay Chaleur.

5

The Firth of Clyde, Scotland

The Eden left the dock at Port Glasgow with the outgoing tide, drifting slowly down the River Clyde as the crew unfurled the mainsail for the short trip to the open water. They seemed to communicate without words, an exhibition of seamanship John had never witnessed before. He was torn between watching the ship preparations and enjoying the familiar landmarks of Arran and Ailsa Craig as they sailed into the Firth. He chose to observe the crew. Enough time had been spent on saying goodbye.

Margaret kept her eyes on Arran. The island would remain visible for the first part of the voyage, on the starboard aft, a reminder of what she left behind. John glanced at the coastline in between watching the skilled crew climb the rigging. He looked at his sister and saw the tears rolling down her cheeks. He couldn't understand why Margaret was making such a fuss.

"Why is this so difficult?" he asked realizing the question could never be answered.

"I don't know," she said. "I could've stayed behind. I think Aunt Isabella would've kept me."

She wanted to believe it. Instead of staying on Arran, she was heading to a new world and trying to imprint the old world of Arran in her memory forever. John shook his head. She was an impossible dreamer.

Margaret's sadness was interrupted by a crew member shouting directions and orders to the passengers.

"Everyone to the stern of the ship," he said. "You'll be given instructions for the voyage."

Still in the trance of crying, Margaret moved along the deck as directed. This ship was different than the steamer. So high above the water's surface. It made her nervous slowing her steps with the other passengers. As she settled in to listen, John put his arm around her.

"We'll see Mama soon," he said, trying to make his sister think about the future.

The resentment they felt toward each other would have to wait for another time. A time in the future, after they get off this ship, John thought. Today, at this moment, the Murchie children had to focus on the voyage ahead, inside the ship destined for New Brunswick.

He knew his little sister was scared and unhappy with leaving Arran. It didn't make any sense to him.

He only saw opportunity while she resisted change. His emotions were exactly opposite hers. Was it possible she couldn't see the benefits of leaving? He brushed the thought aside. The immediate focus was bringing Margaret to Bay Chaleur. John had a promise to fulfill.

The crew informed the passengers the ship had one more port to call on before sailing into the Atlantic. John braced. Another port meant more time to watch his sister. Margaret was unpredictable and that worried him, although she seemed to have settled and accepted the voyage. But anything could happen. Thankfully, her mood told him what she was thinking. Strange how a thirteen year old girl had so much influence over his life. He shook his head as he thought about her foolish actions before the first voyage. It was pure luck they were on the Eden and John didn't want his luck to run out.

"The next port is Cobh in County Cork, Ireland," the sailor announced. "We'll stop and collect passengers for our voyage across the Atlantic."

There was an immediate burst of conversation on the deck, mostly inquisitive about seeing Ireland up close. From Corriecravie, Ireland was the land across the water, a place where the Gaels lived. Soon John would see the details of the land that appeared as a small spit in the distance. He tried to take it all in. In two short days, John had seen more new places than he had seen in his previous sixteen years.

It didn't stop with the ports. There was much to learn about the Eden and how the passengers would live over the next several weeks. Below deck, the crew had instructed the families where to sleep and how to stay out of the ship's operations. On deck, the instructions continued. John watched as the Captain joined the crew and called everyone to gather. The Captain waved his arms and motioned silence as he prepared to speak.

"My name is Captain William Power," he said, loud enough for everyone to hear. "I've been traveling the Atlantic for many years now. He paused to allow everyone understand his experience.

"The Atlantic is not friendly and we'll be out on the open ocean for many weeks," he continued. "If the wind cooperates the voyage will last five weeks and if the wind isn't with us, well, the voyage could be more than six."

Once again, he paused and looked around to make sure everyone was listening.

"My crew is first rate but they are here for the ship and not for you." he said. "Please stay out of their way. You must always stay out of the ship's operations."

John looked around and noticed everyone was nodding with the Captain's words.

"I expect everyone up by 7:00 A.M. and below deck, in bed by 10:00 P.M.," he said, moving his head side to side to ensure he had the passenger's attention.

The passengers remained quiet, listening to each word the Captain spoke. His eyes turned toward the man in a black coat.

"Many of the passengers will become sick," he said, while nodding at the same man. "Sick with illness or sick from the rocking ocean. Our fine Doctor Nichol, will do his best to tend to the ill so he'll need to know if anyone is feeling more than sick from the ocean."

A low hush fell over the ship. Everyone seemed to share what they knew about ship sickness. The Captain cleared his throat to gather their attention.

"For those of you who paid for your meals, they will be provided daily," he said. Breakfast of porridge at 8 o'clock. Dinner at noon. Supper at 6:00. The crew will distribute the food. Take only what you are given. Do not take more."

The words hung over the entire ship as the Captain turned toward his quarters. Captain Power's stern voice commanded everyone to listen intently. Everyone except Margaret. She was too busy trying to make sense of the families on the ship. She counted the number of people including children at sixty. There were babies in their mother's arms and plenty of little ones holding tightly to their mother's skirts. Several men that reminded her of Papa were also on board. John elbowed Margaret.

"Listen to Captain Power," he said.

She turned quickly and glared at John. The level of frustration was climbing in both of them. John grabbed her arm for emphasis.

"I'm not your father," he scolded. "And Papa wouldn't put up with you like this."

Margaret lowered her head and attempted to listen but Captain Power had left.

"How can I listen when he isn't talking?" she asked.

Margaret knew her words would frustrate John but didn't care. It was time for John to leave her alone. For the next few hours, John and Margaret remained on the deck but didn't speak. There would be many days and nights ahead to work through their differences. It was time for quiet before the 10 o'clock curfew.

Margaret tried to listen to the conversations around her. Her ears were drawn to a few young men standing near the ship's rail. They seemed to be bragging about their future. It wasn't difficult to hear them, their voices carried across the ship. The tallest of the four was the loudest.

"We'll make our fortune in Pictou," he said. "There's coal there and we know how to mine it. Nova Scotia needs us."

Nova Scotia? Margaret's head almost came out of her body as she turned to John for his reaction.

"Nova Scotia," she whispered in his ear. "Did you hear Nova Scotia? Where's Nova Scotia and are we on the right ship?"

Margaret's questions were filled with panic. John stayed calm and kept one eye on Margaret while he walked toward one of the men to ask about their destination.

"I overheard you talking about heading to Nova Scotia," John said.

He was careful in his questions because they were so loud and he didn't want to show any vulnerability. One of the younger men jumped at the opportunity to talk.

"Yes, we're off to Nova Scotia," he said. "New mines and our fortune," he claimed.

The stories grew in number as each of the men shared their plans with John. They were experts in mining coal and Pictou, Nova Scotia needed them.

"Would you be familiar with mining?" the youngest man asked, not caring about John's answer.

John tried to balance his interest in the conversation and his need to get answers.

"I'm not a miner," John said. 'I don't know anything about mining.

"It doesn't matter, the young man said. "Pictou needs men."

Finally, John was brave enough to ask the question he needed answered.

"Will this ship take us to Nova Scotia?" John asked.

A grin came over the young miner's face as he anxiously shared how much he knew.

"Nay, this ship was only going to Cobh, where we'll board another ship to Pictou," he said. "But you should come with us. You're a capable young man with a bright future in the mines. You can make a fortune with us. And bring that lovely young lass with you. She would be treated well by us miners."

John thanked him for the offer and explained they were joining family in New Brunswick. He felt his stomach settle and his legs grow in strength knowing the ship wasn't going to Nova Scotia.

He returned to a pale Margaret and quickly calmed her down. Suddenly something changed in John. It was immediate. One minute he worried about her jumping ship and the next he didn't care. John had enough of the mess Margaret created for him. Despite the promise he made to Papa, he was done with her. Jump, stay, go to Pictou, Nova Scotia. It didn't matter.

If Margaret wanted to be alone, let her try, John thought. He was tired of solving her problems, especially the ones she created for the two of them. Only three years separated them, yet John was shouldering the responsibility of a man, a man much older than John's sixteen years.

79

Without a word, he headed below deck to their small bunk. It wasn't much more than a bed or a place to lay on. Margaret knew he was angry and followed him. Just when he wanted to be alone, she chose to be with him. Traveling with his sister was a challenge and the ship was only in the Firth of Clyde. He feared for the open ocean, his patience depleted by Margaret's unbelievable whims.

As the ship sailed toward Cobh, Margaret felt her stomach turn so she headed top side as fast as her legs could carry her. On the deck several passengers were hanging over the side of the ship. They were vomiting while trying to avoid what the wind delivered from the passenger next to them. If Margaret's stomach was better, she would have worried about passengers falling into the water, but not now. She couldn't worry about anyone else, her own stomach was her top priority.

She walked to a quiet place at the stern where a few passengers were sitting and sharing stories. As she made her way, her eyes caught the Scottish mainland as it faded from view. A surprise goodbye she thought, adding a little sadness to the day. Arran was gone, and now Scotland. Margaret limped her final steps to a small place near the stove and sat down. She closed her eyes expecting sleep to settle her upset stomach. Nothing could take care of her sorrow. The rocking ship lulled her tired body to sleep.

Margaret awoke to the voices of families gathering around the stove. It seemed as though everyone was on deck ready to eat. She scanned for John but couldn't find him. Alone, she thought. Finally. She tried to imagine where each of the families were going.

Were they all headed to New Brunswick? She looked for the families who boarded in Port Glasgow and tried to guess where they were headed. As she stood up for a closer look, John came into view.

"How're you feeling?" he asked looking directly into his sister's eyes.

Margaret was surprised at her rapid response to John's inquiry.

"Better, much better," she said. "How about some tea?"

John nodded. It was time to patch things up before the long journey, he thought. Margaret poured tea into two empty cups next to the kettle and the children sat down to enjoy the singing and dancing near the stove. As the night progressed, the two Murchie children let their fatigue take over and headed below deck. The young Pictou miners were still singing as Margaret made her way to the ladder. She was fascinated by their excitement and their laughter that was heard everywhere on the Eden.

"Why are they so happy?" she asked, assuming John knew their secrets.

"They're excited about their future," he said, superimposing his dreams on the miners. "That's my guess."

The bunk was more uncomfortable than it looked. Her brief nap on deck had taken the edge off Margaret's fatigue and now she was wide eyed and awake on the hard surface. Her stomach was still a problem so she curled up and faced the outside of the bunk. The ship groaned with creaking sounds as it headed south toward Cobh harbor. She tried to imagine where it was and what was under that deep water. Her thoughts eventually turned to dreams.

6

Cobh Harbour, Ireland

The ship entered the mouth of Cobh Harbour after dark with the passengers below deck. The crew dropped anchor south of Spike Island for safety. Navigating the River Lee was treacherous in the dark so they would weigh anchor at first light.

When Margaret awoke, she noticed the stillness of the ship.

"We're not rocking," she whispered to John.

After two nights of falling asleep to the ship's motion, the stillness was a surprise.

"We must be in port," John said. "I can't wait to see Ireland."

He jumped out of the berth, ahead of Margaret, grabbing some water for washing. The water felt good in his hands and better as he splashed it on his face. His mind raced to the six more weeks he would live on this ship. How did Papa handle it? How did they manage in these tight quarters?

Margaret followed John toward the ladder, anticipating the improved air she would smell on deck. As she stepped on the ladder, a sliver of the morning sun greeted her, forcing an increase in her pace. She felt the ship move as John steadied his foot on the deck.

"What's happening?" Margaret asked, unable to see beyond her brother.

"We've not reached port yet, that's all," John replied. "Hurry, let's watch as the crew take us there."

And with their eyes following the Irish coastline, the two Murchie children experienced the navigational skills of the crew. Only John noticed, Margaret was too busy looking around, examining this new country. These men are experts, he thought hoping their skills would keep the ship safe on the open ocean.

With the sun fully visible, more passengers climbed up the ladder and gathered on deck. Several groups would be leaving the Eden at Cobh, and they collected in one area without instructions from the crew. They seemed to know what to do. The remaining passengers were taking in the Irish surroundings. Cobh was it. The last brush with land they would have for several weeks.

John watched Margaret's reaction to the passengers as they prepared to leave the Eden. He was convinced she would not attempt an escape in Cobh. She had seen Port Glasgow and it terrified her. Besides,

Margaret was attached to Arran. She wasn't attached to Cobh or Ireland. He could let down his guard.

The Pictou miners were singing and laughing as they stepped off the Eden. The ship wouldn't be the same without them, John thought. Inside he wanted to celebrate with them. He shared their excitement, but his with Bay Chaleur.

Cobh harbor was bustling with activity. The noise and the number of people reminded John of Port Glasgow, but something was different. It seemed more established. The surroundings were also different from Scotland. The meadows were softer. Greener. Ireland wasn't that far away but it appeared like a different world.

As the ship unloaded the people and cargo bound for different ports, preparations were underway for the new passengers. Within an hour, the long queue of people started to move. The first steps were slow, filled with the hesitation of leaving their Irish homes behind.

The Blacknell family was in the queue, awaiting the crew's signal to board. The months of planning had turned into days of packing and now the finality of departure. Mother had filled the past few weeks with worry and concern. This decision would change their lives forever. There would be no going back. British North America must become the Blacknell's new home. Robert couldn't leave without her. If he left alone, she would never see him again. So, there she was, standing next to her son, awaiting a new chapter in her life and trying to hide her fear.

Her eyes caught the three young children as they listened to the crew's instructions and checked with Robert for confirmation. He was fulfilling Father's wishes, she thought. The moment fell over her as she fought back the tears of pride. Robert felt the pressure of his entire family firmly on his shoulders, but he tried to hide it with smiles and laughter. He didn't want anything to go wrong. They were so close to leaving Ireland.

Their ship, the Eden, had arrived from Port Glasgow early that morning with many families already on board. Like the Blacknells, these passengers were leaving their home in search of new beginnings in New Brunswick. Robert stared at the ship's masts. Soon the sails would be rigged over them and the Eden would head into the Atlantic. He knew he wasn't the first to board a ship to a far away place, but he certainly felt like the first. This was a big day for the Blacknell family and a pit was growing in his stomach, the longer he looked at the masts. It was a combination of absolute fear and the excitement of the future.

The signal to board was given and Robert reached for his mother's hand. She was trembling, so he held it tightly, leading her toward the Eden. Cobh's harbor allowed the ship to fit tightly next to the dock so they carefully walked across the plank to join the passengers already on board. As Robert scanned their faces, he noticed the fatigue, the look of excitement had dimmed. He glanced at his mother to see how she was taking it all in.

"Mother, watch your step, we'll be onboard in just a few more minutes," he said.

It would be a long voyage and he needed her to stay positive. Mother gave him a crooked smile but Robert could feel the tension in her hand. She relied on him and he knew it.

The crew assembled the new passengers on deck for instructions. It would have been easy to ignore it, but John and Margaret joined the new passengers to listen. Something new is possible, John thought, with the ship heading into the Atlantic. He was more surprised to see his sister remain alert as the First Mate delivered the rules.

"Families with children in the stern and individual male passengers in the bow," he said. "Stay below deck during the dark and stay out of the crew's way."

Nothing new. Margaret and John had heard it a few days ago. The passengers with cabins were instructed on their location. Margaret turned to watch the passengers head toward the cabins. This was new. She looked at John for a few answers.

"Why do these passengers have different sleeping arrangements?" she asked. "Are they special people?"

"Enough of your questions," he said, unaware of the rising tension building in his body. "Why can't you just enjoy the moment and prepare for the open ocean?"

As he was getting ready to blame his sister for their predicament, he stopped. John dropped his head and leaned over toward Margaret's ear.

"I'm sorry," he said. "I'm nervous about crossing the Atlantic and taking it out on you. I honestly don't know about the cabins. They must be for important families."

John wasn't sure if he would regret letting Margaret understand his fears. Would she use his honesty against him or become scared because of them? He didn't know. He was however, certain of one thing. He would find out over the next several weeks. Margaret wasn't good at hiding her emotions.

7

The Atlantic Ocean

Robert watched as the Eden crew weighed anchor and made sail. The harbor was filled with sailing ships so Captain Power's crew showed their skill as they maneuvered the ship toward the Celtic Sea in response to the Captain's crisp orders. He wondered and marveled as the crew readied the sails without difficulty. Was this an omen for the voyage? As the ship cleared the congestion and approached Spike Island, Captain Power requested the attention of all the passengers.

"Please assemble on the quarter deck," he called, in a voice loud enough for all to hear over the sails slapping with the wind.

John was eager to listen. Anything to push aside the fears building inside him. Over the past several weeks his first priority was getting Margaret on a ship to Bay Chaleur. Now the voyage was directly in front of them, freeing his mind to fill with other worries. He glanced at Margaret.

"Let's listen," he said, encouraging his sister to pay attention.

This part of the journey was different than anything they had done before. Living on an island forced them to respect the water, but that was the Firth of Clyde. Nothing had prepared them for a voyage across the open ocean.

John expected the Captain to start with his standard list, the one he delivered at Port Glasgow. Instead, he heard a different tone inside the message. A more personal tone. He heard the voice of a captain attempting to connect with the passengers.

"This will be a difficult journey," the Captain declared.

He looked down at the scared and tired faces staring back at him. Faces showing the fatigue of sleepless nights stamped in dark circles under their eyes. The Captain knew he had everyone's attention.

"I run a tight ship and have two priorities," the Captain said. "First is the safe passage of my ship and the second is the safe passage of all of you."

Captain Power wanted his passengers to understand their health and wellbeing would always be on his mind.

"I expect your cooperation while we head to New Brunswick," he said. "We're about to travel on dangerous waters. Has anyone heard the stories of other ocean crossings?"

A quiet murmur could be heard across the deck. Finally, a man with two young children by his side spoke up.

"I've heard them," he said. "Sickness, death and shipwrecks."

The murmurs grew louder.

"Any others wish to speak?" the Captain asked.

The murmurs stopped and when no one offered their stories, or spoke up, the Captain shared his experience.

"The light breeze we're enjoying within the Celtic Sea does not compare to the wind out on the Atlantic," he said, pausing for everyone to feel the air. "Yes, there are many stories of illness, shipwrecks and deaths. Storms are also an enemy of a safe passage."

The murmurs started again, not waiting for more wisdom from their Captain. A young passenger couldn't resist any longer.

"How can you keep us safe?" he asked.

The Captain nodded, recognizing the passengers had put their safety in his hands.

"The Eden is a great ship," he said, with the voice of respect. "She has sailed across the Atlantic many times with few incidents. The crew and I have learned the secret of a safe voyage."

He paused as though a question should be asked. Instead the passengers hung on his last word, almost expecting a mysterious answer.

"The secret is discipline," he said. "Discipline from all of you."

He made an arc with his arm starboard to port, emphasizing the responsibility belonged to the passengers.

Captain Power wanted to share the respect he had for this great ocean. He knew he couldn't give them his experience but he certainly could make them listen.

The Captain continued to describe the open ocean, the wind and the waves as dangers to the ship and all onboard. His voice became strict with pointed words.

"Orders will be followed," he declared. "You'll abide by the rules of my ship. If you do, we have the best chance of arriving safely on the shores of New Brunswick."

He remained silent for a long minute, allowing the significance of his orders and need for discipline to settle in.

"If the wind doesn't cooperate our journey will be longer," he said, emphasizing the role nature had in their voyage.

Many passengers nodded their heads, recognizing they were at the wind's mercy. They were confident a skilled Captain and crew could handle the weather. But they didn't know what to expect, not a single passenger had ever crossed an open ocean.

"My crew has crossed the Atlantic several times so we know the rigors of this voyage," he declared. "But anything can happen, and we'll need your help if the Atlantic gets rough."

This time, everyone nodded. Captain Power was making his point and the passengers wanted to listen.

"In good weather, everyone should be out of bed by 7 o'clock," he said. "Washed and dressed. None of this sleeping all day unless you are ill."

He glanced at Dr. Nichol for confirmation. Dr. Nichol nodded at Captain Power's words.

"We've a doctor onboard ship and he'll address any illnesses," he said. "If you're sick you must contact Dr. Nichol."

He pointed to the man standing next to the starboard rail. In turn the doctor raised his arm to identify himself.

Captain Power's words created a stir but he wasn't finished. The families who were uncertain about the voyage were more afraid, while others saw it as a challenge. The Captain had made everyone stop and think. The stories they heard about other ships were one thing. The passengers knew they were about to set sail and begin their own story.

"Meals will be at eight and one," he said. "Tea will be at six o'clock. Each family will receive the allotted provisions."

The Captain knew many families brought additional provisions, but leaving nothing to chance, he had secured enough food and water for an eight week voyage.

"The fires will be lighted at seven A.M. and ground out at seven P.M. Everyone in bed by ten. There will be no exceptions."

Fires were a concern for the Captain. An uncontrolled fire would put the ship in danger. He knew the galley could be managed by the cook, but the fireplace on the bow had to be closely watched by the crew.

"No open fires below deck, especially tobacco," the Captain said. "The Eden won't survive a fire."

It would be his last rule and the one he needed the passengers to fear.

"This is your ship too, at least for the next several weeks," he said and turned from his passengers to face the helm.

As he walked away, the passengers returned to their small groups, murmuring about what they just heard. Each family shared their worst fears and new responsibilities. The Captain had set the rules and the passenger's murmurs contained their acknowledged responsibility. Within a short time, frame, the Eden belonged to everyone onboard.

"Order and structure," Robert mumbled to himself as the Captain walked away. It felt right. He thought of the farm in Timoleague. Order and structure were necessary to run a farm that size. It was logical that a well managed ship ran in a similar manner. Robert was inspired by the Captain. He sounded sincere.

All at once, Robert was overcome with thoughts of his father. He tried to imagine Father on the ship, sharing family stories as the Eden made its way across the Atlantic. The adventure of their lifetime, Robert thought as he dropped his head to acknowledge the ache he felt for his father. He would make him proud, he vowed. Bay Chaleur would be better than Timoleague.

Robert headed toward the cabin with Mother expecting his brother and sisters to follow.

"Can we stay on deck with Sarah?" Thomas asked looking at his mother with the wide eyes of anticipation.

Mother looked at Sarah for confirmation. Thomas was known for dragging others into his requests.

"Is Sarah expected to stay out here?" Mother asked.

"I can," Sarah said, without hesitation.

It didn't matter to Sarah. She was a pleaser and would help her family.

"If Thomas wants to stay out on deck, I'm ready to stay with him," she said.

Mother smiled and gave Thomas the nod. Mother wanted to go back and settle into her transition home and Robert knew he had to keep her positive. She had said her goodbyes to Ireland when she left Timoleague and a farewell when she stepped onto the Eden. Mother was ready to look to the future and Robert didn't want that to change.

Most of the other passengers remained on deck watching the shoreline blend into the horizon and eventually disappear. There would be enough time to spend below deck, but not now. It was time to say goodbye to their country. They looked back over the stern as Ireland faded from view and the ship cut through the water. Now it was real. The Eden was their new home.

Margaret looked around and tried to imagine living on the Eden. Unlike Arran, it was an island with no escape. Arran was predictable. Nothing was out of place. Was this island as predictable? She couldn't run to the dory and row away for an hour. There weren't any rocks and gorse to hide behind. This was it. All out in the open for everyone to see. Or so she thought.

The first night was filled with music and dancing as families shared the songs they knew and loved. The adults told stories about the places and people they left behind. As the memories unfolded for others to hear, few could hold back the tears welling up.

Margaret turned to watch the children dance to the fiddles and the flutes. It was an escape from the sadness growing inside her.

When the ten o'clock hour arrived, the passengers headed toward the ladder for their first night below deck on the Atlantic. It would be a night like no other for most of the families. A night filled with conflicting sadness and optimism.

The footsteps into the dark hold slowed as the passengers traded the ocean air for the damp musty odor of steerage. Families with babies and young children filled every bunk, their voices and cries lamenting the late hour and the exhaustion of their departure day. Margaret covered her ears, attempting to block out the sound. Nothing improved. The sounds, the smells and the closeness added to the misery. Six more weeks might as well be a lifetime.

Passengers moved about all night, adjusting to the ship and dealing with the angst of sea sickness. By morning the smell of vomit was overpowering, forcing each passenger to accept the role of the Atlantic as controller of their fate. The air from the portholes provided little relief from the stench. It proved to be no remedy for the sickness onboard.

Margaret examined the floor before stepping out of the bunk, afraid of what she would see. With a path identified, she steadied both hands on the bulkhead and railings and headed for the ladder. The path disappeared in front of her as the rocking ship navigated each wave. Within a few steps, the debris and waste on the floor was heading toward her feet. A few more steps, she thought as she quickened her pace and stretched to reach the sides of the ladder.

Relieved to have each foot off the floor, she turned around and saw John not far behind.

The blast of fresh Atlantic air greeted the two, replacing any residual odor from below deck. Margaret winced at the coolness of the air against her face, but didn't complain. It felt good. At that moment, Margaret and John decided to spend as much time on deck as the Captain would allow.

The Captain's structure turned into a daily routine for the passengers. It seemed easy and made each day predictable. The Murchie children escaped up the ladder before seven each morning and spent their day on the deck. The two words, fresh air, became their signal, and up the ladder they scampered. The relationship between John and Margaret started to heal during the early days on the Eden. They needed each other.

On the fifth morning of the voyage, John noticed a change in the crew's behavior as he stepped on deck. The Captain's voice could be heard above the commotion.

"Furl the sails," he shouted to the crew. "The winds are shifting and getting stronger."

As John faced the morning sunrise, he noticed how the red glow extended far beyond the horizon. A bad sign, he thought, and rushed to collect a biscuit before heading below deck. Margaret followed along, not wanting to challenge the pending storm. The Captain wasted no time in securing the ship and warning the passengers.

"Lock down," Captain Power ordered. "All passengers must head to the bunks and cabins."

Within the hour, dark clouds appeared and a wind storm took control of the ship. The rain soon followed, when the clouds emptied its contents onto the ocean. The steerage passengers listened in darkness at the steady sound of rain pelting the deck. A rhythm of waves and shouting became the only recognizable pattern. The climbing wave, followed by loud voices and the Captain's orders were the prelude for the violent tossing of the Eden onto the Atlantic's troubled surface. In concert, the passengers tightened and released their grips on the bunk rails as the pattern repeated.

The Blacknell family found little advantage inside the cabin. Away from the flow of debris and waste but not far from the wooden ship's groans. It wasn't difficult to imagine the ship coming apart, Robert thought, as he gripped in anticipation for the next billow. He watched his mother steady her balance with the ship's rocking. He knew the conversation they would have after the storm passed. Mother's words would be harsh, he thought. Full of frustration and anger.

Below deck, a steady mumble of prayers filled the air. Fear had taken over, magnified by the constant darkness and the storm's fury. Margaret listened as promises for temperance and cleaner living were offered in return for safe passage.

"Will this storm ever stop?" Margaret asked, fear and hunger growing inside her.

Mr. McMillan in the next bunk spoke up, before John could answer.

"It will child," he said. "But not for many hours."

Nothing was safe unless it was tied down. Objects that had been set aside by the families were now part of a stream that flowed between the bunks. The slats were the only safeguard and the Murchie children held on, not wanting to become part of the stream running beneath them.

The storm rocked the ship for two days and nights until it reached calmer waters on the third day. They had survived their first storm, hours in the dark, damp steerage, with nothing to eat but hardtack bread and a little water. Whatever the chances for another storm, they had learned a newfound respect for the Atlantic and their Captain. A beautiful sunrise greeted Margaret as she climbed up the ladder and stepped onto the deck to breathe the much needed fresh air.

"Steerage smells worse than the animals at the end of the house on Arran," she told John.

He agreed shaking his head as they walked toward the fireplace. The footing was treacherous with the layers of salt spray covering the deck area and coating anything the waves touched.

"Quite a storm," he said, pointing to the salt resting above them on the masts. "After we get some fresh air, we must head below and help clean," John suggested.

Margaret agreed, even though the thought of heading back down the ladder was the last thing she wanted to do. She took a deep breath, trying to rid her lungs of the odor that encapsulated steerage. They would sleep in that bunk tonight, she thought, mindful of the mess floating on the floor at the bottom of the ladder. Without hesitation she followed John down into steerage, ready to clean her temporary home. A mature Margaret, John thought, satisfied the storm had created one positive outcome.

After cleaning the floors and organizing the storage area, the mood became festive as the passengers went topside and gathered around the fireplace for tea. They had survived the storm together, creating a new bond of kinship. It wasn't long before the instruments appeared and the dancing followed. The celebration continued until curfew.

The Atlantic had more storms for the Eden, but each successive storm was weaker than the previous one. The passengers learned how to prepare for each lockdown with less panic and fear as time progressed. They understood the importance of the words Captain Power had shared at the beginning of the voyage. They were better sailors, better passengers on the Atlantic.

When the second storm subsided, the rush up the ladder was measured. There was a sense of order instead of the gasping chaos of the first storm. Once again, Margaret followed her brother down the ladder for the clean up. After the floor had been washed down, the loose objects were placed back into the nearby bunks. As John placed a metal bowl on the corner, he noticed an old man still lying in his bunk. John wondered why the man hadn't moved since the storm cleared.

"It's time to climb the ladder," John said, gently pushing on the man's arm, in an attempt to awake him.

The old man didn't budge.

"Go get the doctor," he told Margaret, his voice rising in pitch.

When they returned, Dr. Nichol was quick to pronounce the man dead.

"It must be old age," Dr. Nichol said, at a loss for another explanation.

He looked at the two children and thanked them for summoning him. Margaret dropped her head, unable to stop the tears welling up in her eyes. Not since Duncan, had Margaret witnessed anyone die. It brought back too many sad memories. John set aside his own thoughts and immediately sent Margaret topside to get air.

The ship's crew took control, carefully wrapping the dead man in an old sail as the passengers looked on. The crew carried the body toward the side of the Eden for burial into the Atlantic as a hush fell over the ship. It was quickly replaced by prayer as Captain Power asked everyone to join him in celebration of the man's life. John and Margaret watched as the dead man gradually dropped out of sight. It was a sad day on the Eden.

The music that evening was mournful in respect to the lost passenger and his family. John thought about Duncan and the old man. He didn't know where their spirits went, but he knew they hadn't fulfilled their dreams.

There was light sleep in the Murchie bunk for most of the night. Vivid memories of Duncan and his death occupied their minds. John was quick up the ladder at sunrise looking to escape, away from his thoughts.

"Why's Duncan's memory fading so much?" Margaret asked John. "I can barely remember him."

Each time she thought of him, it was harder to put the whole story together.

"You'll remember once we're with Mama and Papa," he said. "You can ask Mama to tell you more stories."

"Do you think I'll forget Mama too?" Margaret asked bewildered with her emotions.

"Not a chance," he replied, smiling at his sister's thoughts. "You're tired now, and lucky to remember me."

Margaret smiled a half smile while reaching to hug John. It was a special moment for the two of them, almost a turning point toward their old relationship. It had taken several weeks to repair the lost trust, forcing John to wonder why trauma always brought people together.

When the ocean was calm, chores made the time go by. Cleaning, washing and trying to stay out of the crew's way kept everyone busy. Margaret spent time working with all the young girls on the ship.

It was a time for their imaginations to run free. They would create stories to offset the monotony of cleaning. Rebecca and Sarah Blacknell found this part of the day exciting. After the chores were done, they would watch for sea creatures. A whale, flying fish or a shark made an excellent addition to the next day's story.

The next morning, the Captain announced the ship was halfway to Bay Chaleur. He reminded everyone the arrival time could change. All it would take was another storm in the next few weeks, or heavy winds to keep the Eden in the Atlantic. You could hear the collective prayer among the passengers. Good weather was the small request. They had big dreams awaiting their arrival in New Brunswick.

8

Gulf of St. Lawrence

Robert spent time on the Eden's deck admiring the Captain and those who stood watch. He marveled at the crew's sailing ability and prompt adherence to the Captain's orders. With each nautical mile, the crew displayed a rhythm of expertise as the sails were trimmed to maintain the ship's course. Robert strained to listen as the crew shared the immediate challenges, their voices surprisingly calm as the howling wind passed through the rigging.

The Eden would soon arrive in the Grand Banks, east of the colony of Newfoundland, according to the crew. Robert heard excitement tempered by concern in their voices, signaling trouble was ahead. Cousin

Matthew had described the Grand Banks as filled with fish and fog. Fish so plentiful, every passenger could catch one by dropping a line into the ocean, he had written. Matthew also described how nature's gift of fish was wrapped in a blanket of fog. His description made Robert anxious to witness the danger the ship would encounter.

"We're east of Newfoundland," the Captain announced during the morning meal on day thirty.

"Newfoundland?" Margaret asked her brother.

John shrugged his shoulders and looked at the Captain for more information.

"It's a large island east of New Brunswick," Captain Power continued while staring into the puzzled faces of his passengers.

He didn't need to say anything more. The excitement of approaching land and New Brunswick was the news everyone wanted to hear. The Captain expected the excitement but had to share the upcoming perils.

"In the next few days, the Eden will sail into the Grand Banks," he said. "These are treacherous waters, with fog as thick as the morning porridge. All of you will need to be on watch."

The description of the fog didn't dampen the mood that evening. The music and storytelling had a different upbeat tone. It was time to celebrate the approaching land. Soon they would be off the ship.

The next morning, John and Margaret climbed the ladder convinced they would be the first to sight land, but they weren't alone in their quest. Most of the passengers gazed westward, looking for different shapes on the horizon, a darkness instead of the blue ocean, anything but waves and whitecaps. Around noon, they noticed the shape of a ship heading toward them. This wasn't the first ship they had sighted along the voyage, but none of the others had come this close. Out in the Atlantic, the ships were always off in the distance, sailing in both directions.

This sighting was different. The ship, Thetis, came close enough for the Captains and crew to share information.

"We're headed to Londonderry, Ireland," the Thetis Captain reported. "Left Quebec with a cargo of timber. The weather has been good with favorable winds," the Thetis Captain yelled toward the Eden. "Sail lightly, the fog is heavy on the Banks."

The Captain nodded and pointed toward the east.

"The pattern has been stormy over the past few weeks," Captain Power shared. "Nothing too severe but the seas were high and tossed us around. Might have lost a day or two fighting it."

John scanned the Thetis from bow to stern. The only people on the ship were the crew he thought as he moved to settle his eyes on her Captain. It didn't take much to imagine her cargo of people on the return trip to Quebec. A sense of relief gradually fell over him. He knew they were through the worst part of the voyage.

The Thetis was gone as quickly as she appeared. To many passengers, it seemed strange to talk to another ship in the middle of the open water, yet magical to see different people other than the passengers on the Eden. Music and dance filled the evening as the passengers shared their observations of the east bound ship. It would be part of their story, the story about their voyage across the Atlantic.

The Eden continued in a southwest direction toward New Brunswick with only her Captain and crew fearing the approaching fog. They would be joined in their concern early the next morning when the quiet rhythm of the waves was replaced by a continuous ringing of bells. The passengers raced to the ladder, unsure of what they would find topside.

John and Margaret joined the rush and faced a heavy grey fog as they stepped onto the ship's deck. There was nothing to see, the Eden was enveloped, with her upper masts invisible to anyone standing on deck. With nothing to see, they tried to make sense of the ringing bells by the crew.

"We're sharing our position," a crew member said, as many passengers stared bleary eyed toward him.

Soon more bells with different sounds could be heard as the Captain's voice filled the gap between each ring.

"Starboard," he directed, and the crew adjusted the sails. The passengers strained to see what the Captain understood but failed to identify any nearby vessels.

It was slow sailing with clanging bells announcing the presence of nearby ships and fishing boats. The loud monotonous rhythm of the Atlantic wind and waves was replaced by the high pitched cry of invisible brass. The passengers tried following the ringing without success. A bell heard from the port side would appear in a small fishing boat starboard, building a tension not felt on the open ocean.

Time stood still as the Eden sailed through the Banks, making hours feel like days and breaking the optimistic mood of the passengers. A sense of fear took over the Eden, under the layer of fog. It was a motionless fear, a fear forcing each passenger to strain their eyes for an outline or shape of a nearby vessel. The evening sunset intensified the passenger's anxiety as they moved below deck into complete darkness. John took Margaret's hand as they walked toward their bunk.

"The Captain will keep us safe," he said, expecting his words to be true.

"Will we drown down here if the ship hits something?" Margaret whispered, not wanting the others to hear.

"The rules are the rules," Captain Power said before John could answer. "Curfew doesn't change with the fog and we'll be out of this in a few hours."

John shrugged his shoulders and looked at his feet. There was little he could say to relieve Margaret's fear. That fear was shared among all the passengers as they listened with their eyes to the muffled sound of the clanging bells well into the early hours of the next day.

At dawn, the steerage passengers rushed up the ladder to witness a clear and beautiful sky. Smiles soon replaced the fatigue of a sleepless night as the islands and peninsulas of Newfoundland came into view. Land was near and soon they would replace the rocking Eden with solid ground. Cheers and whistles took over. They were close. Closer to the dream of a new life.

The excitement bubbled over into the evening mood changing the storytelling from the past to the future. Stories about land, new homes, the timber trade, a future without rents and the fear of eviction filled the air. A sense of optimism with the shoreline of British North America in sight. John eagerly shared his dream of owning a farm with plenty to eat and a few cows. Margaret was surprised at John's willingness to share the Arran story with so many strangers from Ireland.

"They're our Eden family," John said, in defense.

Margaret shook her head. She didn't see it that way. Family was family and the Eden passengers were just friends. Truth was, she ached for Mama and she wasn't interested in telling anyone. That wasn't for sharing, not even with John.

The celebration of the Newfoundland coast pushed past the curfew hour until the crew appeared and everyone rushed to the ladder to avoid the wrath of Captain Power. They had come too far to disappoint him now.

Margaret was slow to move, dreaming about Mama and Papa meeting the Eden. As she gazed at the rocks in the distance, she imagined how the arrival would be. A long embrace. It had been too long since Mama had held her.

As Margaret's thoughts drifted, a crew member grabbed her arm, pulling her away from her family.

"That hurts," Margaret said. "I'm heading to the ladder."

Instead of releasing her arm, the crew member put his hand over her mouth and pushed his face against her ear.

"Keep quiet or I'll tell the Captain," he said.

Margaret tried to turn her head to look at him. It forced him to tighten his grip, moving her arm behind her back.

"I've had my eye on you for a few nights," he whispered in her ear. "You look like a girl who I knew back home."

Margaret didn't know what to do or say. The sailor's hand was over her mouth and his hold on her arms was too tight. With all the strength she could gather, she bit down on his finger until he dropped his hand from her mouth. He hadn't expected a fight from a young girl, so he wasn't prepared when she kicked him while he was staring at his finger assessing the wound.

Margaret let out a scream from the bottom of her lungs, causing enough of a commotion to raise the Captain from his cabin. John heard the scream and charged up the ladder to find the Captain talking to Margaret and the young sailor. After a brief description from both parties, Captain Power asked John to take Margaret back to their bunk.

"We'll discuss the curfew violation in the morning Margaret," the Captain stated. He then sent the sailor to the brig to await his reprimand.

John gave Margaret a big hug and tried to soothe her tears. She was visibly upset so he didn't want to ask questions now, for fear of making it worse. Many of the families were awake and listening. This wasn't time for a lecture, it was time to be her older brother.

In the morning, John joined his sister in the Captain's quarters to hear her punishment. Captain Power was stern but fair with Margaret

"You've broken a rule and rules are important for the safety of the passengers," he said. "You'll clean the hold every day for the next five days."

Although Margaret didn't ask, the Captain also informed the two Murchie passengers of the sailor's punishment.

"He was flogged by the crew last evening," Captain Power said.

Margaret fell back on her heels when she heard the Captain's words. She remained silent, feeling guilty for the outcome. Captain Power watched her withdraw from the conversation and attempted to explain the punishment.

"On my ship, the crew are not permitted to have contact with the passengers," he said. "You both broke the rules, but a sailor who breaks the rules is not fit for the Eden."

The Captain stood firm. His ship would not tolerate an undisciplined sailor.

"He'll be placed on another ship as soon as we arrive in port," he added. "His behavior is not acceptable."

John nodded, remembering the Captain's words when the ship left Cobh Harbor. He understood the sailor's failure and was relieved by Margaret's level of punishment for missing curfew. He looked at his sister, trying to make sense of her poor decisions. She was nodding to Captain Power and ready to return to the hold. She understood her new duties and was ready to get them started.

John hoped Margaret had learned a valuable lesson. Possibly a life lesson. But Margaret was Margaret and all the lessons had a pattern. He wanted this one to be different. They were heading to a new land with too many unknowns.

The final days in the Gulf of St Lawrence were without incident. Margaret completed her punishment and told her story to any passenger who would listen. They all wanted to hear it. The sailor wasn't seen after the incident. He was forced to sleep during the day and out of sight when the passengers were on deck.

As the Eden approached land on her port side, the air was filled with stories about the futures. Most had plans to stay in British North America, in New Brunswick, but others would leave for the Boston States. Many relatives had left Ireland years earlier and headed to Boston. They had plans to join them as soon as possible and knew their journey was far from over.

Every inch of the deck rail had passengers next to it, staring at the rugged coastline. The rocky outline looked familiar, bringing memories of Ireland and Scotland forward as many tried to accept the new surroundings. It was their new country, forever to be compared with their former home.

The large green forests greeting the passengers was strange and different. The trees stood tall and close together, like militia protecting the land. Only the men with plans to work in the timber trade became giddy at the sight of the tall pines as wide as a small child. The others saw the trees as the task ahead.

The Captain relaxed the rules for the last night on board the Eden. The dancing and singing by the fire went into the early hours of the next day. There was no need to get a good night's sleep. They would be sleeping on land soon enough. Besides, it would be impossible to sleep. They had crossed the Atlantic, met her fury and now had the shore in their sights.

It was an end and a beginning. John looked at Margaret as she stared at the forests of New Brunswick. You could almost imagine her thoughts of Mama and Papa running to the dock to meet their little girl.

"I can almost see Mama and Papa," she said with a smile John hadn't seen in a while.

A sense of relief fell over John. He had fulfilled the promise he made to Papa several months ago. He brought Margaret to New Brunswick. Now he could focus on his own life and owning a farm.

9

Bay Chaleur, New Brunswick

The Eden entered Bay Chaleur at sunset with her passengers staring at the endless forest against a bright orange sky. The trees seem to cover every acre of land in front of them, barely giving form to a town or a village beneath the canopy. There wasn't anything to compare this with. The forests in Ireland and Scotland had been harvested hundreds of years ago. It was a new land.

As the dock came into focus, the crew prepared to furl the sails and ease the Eden into the harbor. She had carried her passengers of Scottish and Irish pioneers to their new home. It was time to give her sails a rest.

Robert stared at the trees with the other passengers. Cousin Matthew had warned about the forests and the size of the trees. Land improvement would be part of the grant he had written, but Robert brushed it aside. Now it stood directly in front of him. The magnitude and scale were daunting. A moment of doubt was immediately dismissed. The Blacknell family was not going back to Ireland. He looked back toward the Gulf of St. Lawrence in an attempt to reduce all doubt. He turned to see Bathurst Harbor. The future was so close.

Bathurst Harbor was a horseshoe shape, demanding a slow and purposeful navigation toward the dock. The passengers grew restless watching the painstaking actions of the crew. They were ready to step on the soil of their new home. But first, they needed to get off the ship.

"Is this the wilderness?" Margaret asked John, wondering how they would find Mama and Papa.

John nodded, unsure of how to answer. He feared arriving at the wrong harbor but never thought it would be all forest.

"Look at those trees Margaret," John said, trying to change the subject and bring a smile to her face. "Have you ever seen a tree so straight and tall?"

Margaret looked at her brother and shook her head, remembering the conversation with John back on Arran. Yes, the trees were tall and everywhere.

"But how can we live among these trees?" She asked innocently.

John thought about it for a minute before replying.

"We'll clear the land by cutting some trees," he said. "Papa must've started that work right after he arrived."

Finally, the anchors were dropped and the ship came to a stop. The excitement that followed the ship into the harbor didn't drop with the anchors. It continued, growing as the passengers anticipated their first steps off the Eden.

The Captain stood at the helm, attempting to be heard over the excitement.

"Attention," the Captain said.

The passengers turned to listen to their Captain. The respect he commanded was now strengthened with admiration. They owed much to this man for his skillful sailing of the Eden across the Atlantic.

"We've arrived earlier than planned but too late in the day for passenger processing," Captain Power continued. "We must stay onboard one more night. It's too dark to complete the paperwork this evening."

The smiles and laughter that filled the air less than five minutes earlier immediately disappeared. The only sound that could be heard between the Captain's words was the wind in the rigging as the furled sails adjusted to their anchored state.

"The doctor will be here in the morning to examine everyone," the Captain continued. "I ask all of you to follow the rules."

The Captain looked at the disappointment in his passengers. It was written in their faces, they couldn't wait to debark and leave the Eden behind. He knew the rules must be followed and after one more night, they would set foot on New Brunswick soil. To the Captain, Bathurst Harbor was only a midpoint. He would leave with the Eden and head back to Ireland in a few days.

"You may stay on deck all night, if you prefer," he added, relaxing the curfew one more night. "We'll start at sunrise tomorrow."

He headed back toward his cabin feeling the weight of each passenger's sadness in his steps. He was confident it would change with the sunrise.

John could hardly contain himself.

"This is Bay Chaleur," he shouted. "We made it. I was so fearful we wouldn't."

John was excited and couldn't stop talking, revealing more of his feelings to his sister.

"I kept my promise and brought you here," he said. "Papa will be so proud of me."

Margaret looked at John, surprised that he wanted Papa's attention.

"Could we jump off the ship?" She asked. "We're so close and have only a few things to carry."

John laughed, surprised but not shocked by the words coming out of Margaret's mouth.

"No, we'd be in trouble," he said. "They could send us back and I don't want to go back."

Margaret thought it over for a minute. She didn't want to go back either. She could wait one more night to walk on solid ground.

"I can't wait to see Papa and Mama," Margaret declared. It had been far too long.

John wrapped his arms around his sister. It was more emotion than Margaret had seen in John for quite some time. Positive emotion, the emotion she would need over the next few weeks.

Margaret knew Papa would have words for her when the family was together. She would be given a scolding, the type only a father can give his daughter, but the desire to see her parents was stronger than anything Papa could say. She would listen as only Margaret could.

John and Margaret stayed on deck for a few more hours gazing into the night's sky, while looking at Bathurst Harbor. Tomorrow, John thought.

"Can we go to the bunk?" Margaret asked, tired from the day's excitement.

John was relieved by her request. He nodded and down the ladder they went. Their last night on the Eden would be spent below deck.

As the sun peeked over Bay Chaleur, the passengers grew impatient waiting for the doctor. The level of excitement from the previous day was laced with eagerness and frustration.

"The doctor will be here soon," Captain Power announced, without knowing the exact time.

He wanted the passengers to settle down. Any demonstration of anger would not be tolerated by the doctor.

"Please assemble in a queue so the process will be fast," he advised. Without hesitation, the passengers gathered near the plank, anticipating their final minutes on the Eden.

Around ten o'clock, the doctor came on board and talked to the Captain and Dr. Nichol while making notes in his small book. He turned to face the queue of passengers and started a detailed inspection of each person. There hadn't been any medical incidents during the journey but the doctor was required to follow the immigration process.

A busy dock awaited the families when they finished with the doctor and left the Eden. As John stepped off the plank, he searched the faces for someone familiar. Back and forth, scanning all the people meeting family or friends. But he didn't see Papa. Anywhere. He had written before they left Arran, certain the mail would have arrived before the Eden, but he didn't know. He only knew he couldn't see Mama or Papa on the Bathurst dock.

John looked at Margaret and tried to contain his fear. A flurry of bad thoughts raced through his mind. What had gone wrong? In a few hours, the evening would be upon them and he had no idea where his family lived. Margaret's eyes started to well up as John grew quiet. She had put them in this situation and had no idea how to make things better.

"Where's Papa?" she asked, not expecting an answer. "He should be here. What if something happened to their ship and they never made it?"

Many days and nights had passed since they left Arran and now, they were stranded, in a wilderness filled of forests.

"Where can we stay if Papa doesn't come?" Margaret asked. "I don't want to go back on the ship."

Without family to take them away, there were few options for the Murchie children. Walking was possible, John thought, but which way?

"Let's ask at the Harbor office," John said, realizing walking was their only option. He left Arran with little to no money or means to pay for an overnight stay. Their luck had run out.

"Maybe we can start walking after we get directions," he said, hoping Margaret would agree.

He wasn't sure where Archibald lived and didn't expect the man inside the office to know either, but he had to ask. They could start walking in the morning, after he found a place to sleep for the night.

"I'm scared," she finally admitted aloud to John. "I can't sleep in the forest. It's too dark."

John headed toward the office, trying to appear confident. He didn't want anyone to take advantage of their situation. As he opened the door, he heard Robert Blacknell describing the Eden and Captain Power to the man sitting behind the large desk. After a few minutes of accolades, Robert left the small building, giving room for John and Margaret to approach the desk.

Cousin Matthew was waiting on the dock to meet the Blacknell family as they debarked from the Eden. Mother was the first to recognize Matthew as she stepped onto the dock. Without speaking, she abruptly grabbed Robert's arm and started to wave it. Surprised by his mother's action, Robert scanned the dock to see if anyone was waving back.

"It's Matthew," Mother said, pointing his arm to the left.

It had been ten years since Matthew left Timoleague with his family and Robert wasn't sure he would recognize him. Thankfully, Mother did and wasted no time in seeking Matthew's attention.

Matthew reached for Mother, embracing his aunt with love and the respect for the journey she had endured. She wrapped her arms around him, they had made it to Bay Chaleur and he was solid proof.

Robert waited patiently for his mother to release her grip on Matthew. He knew he couldn't push her, but he wanted his own time. When Matthew left Timoleague for New Brunswick, Robert lost the cousin he had looked up to. The person outside his immediate family he had shared everything with. Now he wanted to share all that had changed.

When Matthew turned to Robert, they could barely contain their emotion. The young child Matthew left in Timoleague had transformed into the tall man standing in front of him. Robert reached for Matthew with a ten year hug. It was good to be together. Laughter soon followed as the two picked up where their relationship had stalled, Matthew the elder and Robert, the eager student. The younger siblings looked on with a vague memory of Matthew. Robert's stories and the letters had kept him alive in their minds, but everything else had erased with time.

The trunks and furniture were loaded into the carriage as Mother described the voyage and the great Captain Power. Robert was pleased to hear his mother's kind words about the Captain so he remained silent wanting to hear more. Mother was never much to give compliments. She was hard to please, lending more meaning to her positive words.

Mother had found an audience to share an animated conversation about the storms and the fog, forgetting she wasn't the first emigrant to cross the Atlantic. Rebecca turned away from the story she had just experienced and noticed Margaret and John alone on the dock. She knew something must be wrong. Why were they alone? Where was their family? Rebecca pulled on Robert's arm to get his attention and pointed toward the Murchie children.

Robert lowered his head to hear concern in his sister's soft voice. He agreed. The two should be with their family by now and not standing alone. Without hesitation, Robert left Mother in the middle of her story and headed toward John and Margaret.

John wasted no time in describing their predicament, his voice increasing with fear the longer he spoke.

"Let me ask Mr. Blacknell if he can help," Robert offered, knowing the two were abandoned and scared.

He didn't know if Matthew's family had room for two more, but he would ask. He was certain the two children shouldn't be left to wait, especially in the New Brunswick wilderness.

John watched Robert pull Matthew aside and gesture toward them. He noticed how Matthew was slow to respond at first, but as Robert continued to talk, Matthew changed from listening to nodding. Before Robert had finished, Matthew motioned for John and Margaret to join them.

"Would you care to stay the night at our home nearby?" Matthew asked, catching John with his direct question. "We're cousins of the Blacknell family and Robert is concerned for the two of you."

Matthew realized he needed to develop trust with this young man within a five minute conversation.

"It wouldn't be a problem," he added. "Are you expecting family to arrive soon?"

John was flustered at first with all the questions but he answered as best he could. The evening was closing in and there were few options so he had to move past his worries about Matthew. He seemed nice enough, John thought. And Rebecca's family was with him.

"Yes, sir," he answered. "My family was expected. I'm not sure where they are."

They walked over to join Robert's family next to the carriage and jumped in the back with their small bags. As the horse pulled away from the dock area, John continued to scan for faces, a single face he knew. With each scan, the disappointment continued, the dock had only strangers.

On the ride to the settlement of Stonehaven, Matthew reminisced about his arrival in New Brunswick.

"It was pure wilderness back then," Matthew said. "A land waiting for people to make it their home."

John winced thinking it was still pure wilderness. Was he missing something? He made eye contact with Margaret and she gave him a half smile, still trying to assess the new mess they found themselves in. As Matthew described the animals living in the forests, John realized the walk to find Papa would have been a terrible mistake, maybe impossible. His fear grew when Matthew told stories about killing the forest animals for food. It was clear the walking option was out when Margaret's stared at John and rapidly shook her head.

The carriage left the Bathurst dock for Stonehaven with Matthew describing the settlement the pioneers had built along Bay Chaleur. They fondly named the area, the Capes of New Bandon, knowing the name would give the newcomers comfort. It was a settlement of Protestant Irish families, mostly from Munster Province, many from Bandon Town.

The carriage ride was a welcomed change for the passengers, the constant rocking of the ocean was replaced by a road made from tree logs. At least Matthew could control the pace when the wheels met the rotting wood. They were heading east with Bay Chaleur in constant view, the mountains forming a grand new landmark.

The house in Stonehaven was comfortable with two fireplaces and a second floor with rooms for sleeping. It was a very large home by Arran standards yet similar to the Blacknells' farm back in Timoleague. The big difference was its construction.

John and Margaret had never seen a house made of wood before and tried not to look surprised at everything inside. Pioneer living might be difficult, John thought, but he liked what he saw.

Matthew's wife, Sarah Jane was surprised to see two additional guests for the night, but adjusted the sleeping arrangements with ease. She had learned to be flexible. Living in a new country, filled with daily surprises, built that skill.

"Matthew's family are New Brunswick experts," Robert declared once everyone was settled around the fireplace.

Matthew blushed and pointed out his dream was the same as the one both Robert and John shared.

"The promise of land is invigorating," he said. "And when you start clearing the land, that excitement starts to wear off."

Robert smiled while nodding his head, knowing he had much work in front of him. Matthew explained to John how his family took the voyage across the Atlantic to settle in Stonehaven with several other Irish families.

"This area was settled by Irish immigrants over the past twenty years," Matthew said. "A group of families from Bandon, Ireland decided it was time to leave."

John was surprised to hear the role religion played in the decision to emigrate. He hadn't given any thought to different religions. On Arran, Papa said, religion didn't define anyone. Everyone was the same. From Matthew's stories, Ireland sounded quite different.

The conversation made John realize how little he knew. For sixteen years he lived in one area, on one small island. Now he had crossed the Atlantic with people from other parts of the United Kingdom. He could only imagine what he would learn in the upcoming months.

At the right moment, John openly shared his appreciation for the kindness both Robert and Matthew had shown them. He also shared the story of why they were traveling alone. John softened the part where Margaret took off from the ship. There wasn't a need to shame her now. They had made it to New Brunswick.

"So, you see, we're not orphans," he said with a nervous laugh. "It looks that way, and more so since our parents didn't show up at the dock. But we're not."

Truth was, John didn't know if they were orphans. They hadn't started out that way boarding the Eden. But they had no way of knowing if Papa made it to New Brunswick. It was a great deal to think about, so John chose to ignore the possibility.

"How would my father know when a ship was due to arrive?" he asked innocently, hoping Matthew would know.

"I told Papa the ship would arrive this week," he said. "Maybe he'll be waiting if we head back to the dock."

John kept talking in an attempt to reassure himself while keeping his sister calm. Maybe Matthew knew about the Arran settlers and where they lived. Without hesitation, he described the families from Arran who came to Bay Chaleur around the same time as Matthew, also settling along the bay.

"They sent letters back, describing this beautiful country so my father decided leaving was the right thing to do," he said.

Matthew listened intently, nodding when John described the letters back to Scotland. They had all done it. Encouraged others to follow. Matthew abruptly stopped John.

"There's a few settlements farther north along Bay Chaleur," he said. "The parishes of Colborne and Dalhousie have a number of Scots."

John was hopeful. Should they head north or back to the dock, he wondered.

"Many Scots settled in Northumberland County too," Matthew continued. "But that's further inland."

That night, the emigrants slept in their new country for the first time. It was a peaceful sleep without the whining sound of wind in the rigging or sails snapping against the masts. Both John and Margaret slept well past 7:00 the next morning.

Margaret was first to rise and nearly jumped out of bed when she saw how bright the sun was in the window. She headed down the stairs, expecting to see John waiting impatiently for her. Surprised he wasn't up yet, she started a conversation with Rebecca's mother, Mary who was washing dishes.

"Are you happy to be here?" Margaret asked.

"I'm happy to be off the ship," Mary replied. "It was a long voyage. A voyage I only took because of Robert."

Margaret was surprised to hear she wasn't the only person who didn't want to leave home.

"Me too," Margaret added. "I didn't want to leave. I wanted to stay on Arran."

The conversation was interrupted by John finally making his way to the kitchen.

"Good morning," John shouted. "It is great to be here. On Bay Chaleur and off the ship onto dry land."

Everyone could see and hear his enthusiasm. It entered the room before he did. The detail of finding his parents didn't seem to bother John today. He appeared ready for any adventure.

Margaret was quiet, taking in her brother's new found enthusiasm. They were finally in Bay Chaleur and just as she had worried, Papa and Mama were nowhere to be seen. Now what? Her head was creating all sorts of worries and her brother appeared to be carefree. Arran was everything they knew and now they were surrounded by nothing they knew.

"Well Maggie, we have an adventure today, looking for Papa," he said. "We can find the other people from Arran if we head north."

He sounded so sure. Sure, that everything would work out. So far it hadn't. In a few short months, her life had completely turned upside down.

She resented John's excitement. The more she thought about it, the more she realized he had his wish of reaching New Brunswick and she had nothing.

The mess she had created didn't seem to have an end. What if she had held Mama's hand back in May? What if she had simply kept her mouth shut? Papa always said her impulsive behavior would get her in trouble one day. Now here she was in New Brunswick, without Mama and Papa. She had John but he was ready to move on.

Her thoughts were startled by Matthew's voice.

"My apologies, I was daydreaming," she said. "Can you ask me again?"

"What do you think about New Brunswick?" he inquired. "I know it's only a few hours since the ship landed but you must have some thoughts about your new home."

The timing of the question couldn't have been worse. It was more than Margaret could bear and she started to cry. The tears rolled down her face and she quickly covered her eyes with her sleeve. John reached over to console her.

"It's been a long journey and our family was supposed to be at the dock in Bathurst," John explained.

He was trying to find the right words to make Margaret's crying acceptable. He also didn't want anyone to pity Margaret. She didn't respond well to pity.

After Margaret pulled herself together, the discussion turned to Colborne and Bathurst Harbor.

"It'll be impossible for me to take you today," Matthew said. "The farm will not wait another day for me. I've too many chores to complete."

Robert jumped in ready to take the children all the way to Colborne in the carriage, if Matthew would let him. Mary agreed almost before he offered.

"Robert can help," she said. "We know how important family is and we want you to find your mother and father as soon as possible."

Robert knew he could put off his business with the grant for a few more days and assist the Murchie children. Margaret looked at Robert, embarrassed by her tears but more eager to find her parents. She nodded acceptance of his offer as John shook Robert's hand. They now had a plan, a plan to bring them closer to Mama and Papa. Margaret and John would be leaving Stonehaven shortly and head to Colborne. But first they would stop at the Bathurst dock.

10

Colborne, Gloucester County

Margaret climbed into the back of the carriage, leaving Robert and John up front for the ride north. She listened as John filled the air with constant talk and laughter, a nervous reaction to the day's potential outcome. She watched Robert as he focused on the map Matthew had drawn.

"This road will take us back to Bathurst Harbor," Robert announced. "If your family isn't there, this north road goes toward Colborne," he continued, while pointing to a line on the paper.

"Soon, very soon," John kept saying, while glancing at his sister and smiling.

They turned onto the road and the carriage wheels began to wobble with the uneven logs.

"Trees are used for everything," John said, feeling strange in his new country.

"The settlers must use the cleared trees to build these roads," Robert replied. "But why?"

He shrugged off the question and gazed across the bay. The small waves on the water reminded him of the inlets along the Irish coast. Memories, he thought as one of the wheels sank into a rotten log, grabbing his attention. This wasn't the time to reminisce and stare at the ocean.

"Matthew was right, it will take us an entire day to make it to Colborne on these roads," he said. "So much to see, and avoid."

Margaret liked being alone in the back, listening to the conversation between John and Robert. They shared stories about Arran and Timoleague. Robert described Bay Chaleur and what he knew from letters Matthew had sent. Sounds like Archibald's letters, Margaret thought. But Robert seemed to know and share so much more than she heard from John or Papa.

"Matthew's family moved here when it was difficult for Protestant families in Ireland," Robert explained."

John admitted he didn't understand the problem, so Robert shared some of the history and the challenges between the Irish Catholics and Protestants over the years. He described the business failures in Bandon and the family's long term safety as the Blacknell's reason for emigrating.

"Arran had different challenges," John told Robert, sharing the changes in the farms and the clearances of the people.

Robert nodded, recognizing the differences and similarities each family had.

"Grants by the British Government is our common thread," Robert added. "The dream of a better life and the prize of farmland."

John listened intently not realizing Margaret was taken by the conversation. She was puzzled, trying to place her life inside the story unfolding in the carriage. She had lived on Arran, unaware of so many things. Money and religious issues were two big ones. And now, in the past few months, she was growing up faster than ever. Before the whisper voices, she knew everything. At least everything she needed to know on Arran. Now she was in a totally different far away world. A world she was not yet comfortable in.

Margaret was deep in thought, as the carriage headed down the road to the dock, the conversation moving past Arran and Ireland to the challenges ahead in New Brunswick. The tension in John's voice increased as the dock came into view. He wanted to see his father and settle his immediate future.

At the dock, they saw the Eden. She was one of three ships in the harbor, and today she looked like a completely different ship. A ship with new cargo for the return trip to Ireland. The crew was busy loading large tree logs into the hold where, the Murchies had slept only a few days ago.

Margaret's eyes scanned the Bathurst dock, leaving the Eden behind for good. The dock was filled with men working to load the ships, so Margaret strained to look between the logs and men for familiar faces. It was a quick scan and came up empty. Suddenly, she saw John jump out of the front seat.

"Papa, Papa" he yelled. "We're here. Over here."

He made so much noise that even the crews loading the cargo stopped and stared back at John. Papa finally turned toward the carriage and his face lit up. Margaret had never seen such a smile on her father before. She jumped out of the carriage, following her brother as fast as she could. In that moment, she forgot everything, everything about not wanting to leave Arran. It was a rush to feel her father's embrace.

"Well, it's a sight to see the two of you," Papa said, holding his children for several minutes.

He couldn't believe his luck. So much could have gone wrong, yet the two of them were in his arms.

"The dock officer told me the Eden arrived yesterday," he said releasing his children from a tight embrace while looking directly at John. "Even the immigration officer didn't know where you were."

Margaret kept her arms around Papa, refusing to let him go. The past several weeks easily collapsed in on her releasing a flood of tears down her cheeks. Papa wasn't a sentimental person, but after seeing his two children, and Margaret's tears, his emotions got the better of him. There was a sense of completeness. Tears welled up, forcing Papa to wipe them away with the back of his hand.

"Your brother did a wonderful thing," he told Margaret, his voice breaking up.

John blushed and looked at Robert, trying to validate they weren't orphans. He was nodding at Robert while motioning his head toward Papa, silently stating, we have parents. At that point, John realized he hadn't introduced Robert.

"Papa," John blurted. "This man helped us when we couldn't find you, after we arrived in Bathurst."

Papa reached for Robert's hand and gave it a confirming shake. Robert smiled, feeling Papa's strength and the calloused hand of a hardworking man.

"It's a pleasure to meet you," Robert said. "You've —"

John interrupted, filled with the excitement of finding his father.

"This is Robert Blacknell," he said. "Robert's family invited us to stay in Stonehaven last night." John's excitement continued to take over the conversation.

Papa released Robert's hand while John explained Stonehaven and the ride back to the Bathurst dock.

"And we came back to find you," John said.

There was much more to tell but it would have to wait for another day. Papa knew Robert had done something special for his family.

"Thank you," Papa said. "My family will find a way to repay your kindness. Today I can only thank you with words."

The Murchie family had barely settled in New Brunswick and relied on friends for more than Papa wanted to admit. They had little money, just enough to get by. It was a truth Papa couldn't deny.

"Your appreciation is enough," Robert said. "There isn't a need to do more."

Papa insisted. He was emotional and thankful.

"We must remain in touch," he said. "Do you have an address, where mail can be sent?"

"My family will be moving to Eel River Settlement shortly so you can address any correspondence to the local post office there," Robert said.

Robert sensed it was time to leave the family alone in their celebration.

"I must get back to Stonehaven," he said, smiling at John and Margaret. And with a wave, he was gone.

As he left the dock and turned east toward the bay, something told him the Murchie family would succeed in reaching their dream. The tenacity of the two children was evidence enough.

11

Murchie Farm

The excitement of having his children in the carriage was quickly overshadowed by the road conditions between Bathurst and Colborne. The Great Road hugged the rocky coastline and demanded Papa's full attention. It was treacherous travel, with whole sections of the highway washed out by the bay's wave action. They would be home soon enough and then he could enjoy his family.

During the straight sections of the road, he shared a few stories about the new farm, with a tone of optimism similar to the days on Arran. The hard work and wilderness had done little to change Papa's mind about living on Bay Chaleur.

The remaining daylight dwindled as the carriage arrived in Colborne and Papa signaled the horse to turn down a small lane. They approached the clearing as Papa prepared his children for their new home.

"That's our farm," he said, pointing toward the building and a field with tree stumps. "It's not much, we're still getting acquainted with this big country."

The house seemed strange by Arran standards. It was made of tree logs laying on their side.

"Archibald and the other families from Arran helped build the house," Papa said proudly.

John and Margaret nodded, trying to take it all in. Their lives had been transformed in the past few months and now they were staring at an unrecognizable building. Before they had time to collect their thoughts, shouts and screams came out the door, followed by Mama and the girls.

"John, Margaret, you're here," Mama yelled, running toward the carriage with both arms in the air. As she reached her children, a smile took over her entire face.

"John, you're a wonderful son to stay and bring our stubborn girl here," she added.

There it is, Margaret thought. The first mention. Papa had avoided talking about Margaret's behavior, but not Mama. She didn't waste any time.

Mama reached for Margaret and pulled her tight against her body, releasing a tension that had built since the fateful day in Lamlash. They both sighed, feeling the warmth of their overdue embrace. Too many sleepless nights had passed since the last hug. For Mama, they were nights filled with an emptiness of worry, and a fear of another loss.

Margaret instantly became a little girl inside her mother's arms. The tears and chaos of the past two months melting away. She pushed aside her fear of a scolding. It didn't matter, she felt her mother's love.

When the time came, she would listen. The words would sting but she knew their pain would pass. She would listen to the anger and frustration knowing the happiness of having the family together on Bay Chaleur would prevail. She had little choice.

Mama moved from Margaret to John, pulling her only son toward her with a strength buried deep inside. Mama didn't think the day would come when Margaret and John would stand in front of her, but now she could touch them both. Her dream had become a reality.

Liza and Janet surrounded John as everyone walked toward the log house following Papa. Margaret fell in line, reaching for her mother's hand. It was clear the two sisters were seeking answers to the chaos over the past few months. John smiled and shook his head. He wasn't about to break the spell of the Murchie reunion right now.

"There are many stories to share, later," he whispered to Janet.

Janet looked into John's eyes and acknowledged a future conversation would cover more details. The truth would come out, soon

They stepped into the small log house to find wooden walls and floors surrounding them, the small windows no match for the evening's darkness. A few candles lit the main room dwarfed by the burning embers in the fireplace. Mama was quick to point out the sleeping rooms at each end of the house.

"The girls sleep in this room," she said. "John, you're next to them."

All the unimportant stuff was done. It was time to catch up and learn about the voyages and their new home on Bay Chaleur. The conversation flowed as Mama and the girls prepared supper. Margaret avoided Janet's glares while she tried to fit into the established routine. Nothing had changed between the two sisters. A jealousy rooted in the competition for Mama's attention. Tonight, Margaret was the main attraction. Janet would keep her words inside.

Emotion carried the evening as storytelling and laughter lighted the small room. The family had endured. Mama could set aside the fear of losing Margaret and John. They were home. She closed her eyes, barely believing how the events had turned out. This day should never end, she thought, as she reluctantly headed to bed. It was time for sleep and to dream about the future.

At dawn the next morning, Mama was awake and ready to start a new day.

"It's time a young girl is up," she said, pushing against Margaret's arm to wake her. "There's much to do."

John was sharing the stories of the Eden's journey across the Atlantic with Janet and Liza listening intently. He described Port Glasgow with all the people and the miners heading to Nova Scotia. He wanted to know if their ship had stopped at the same ports.

"Not many families can compare their Atlantic crossings," John said, with a nervous laugh.

"No family should have more than one," Mama said, stopping the conversation. "There's no need to talk about it anymore."

She was reluctant to talk about the voyage. Her memories of the first few days were horrible and weighed heavy. In a split second, she lost her youngest daughter and only son. To Mama, the Atlantic was more than waves and wind. It had separated the family making her feel vulnerable and empty. That feeling was erased as Mama gazed at John and Margaret sitting across the table from her. The tension and worry evaporated as Mama touched both their arms, confirming they were real.

Margaret sensed that the conversation could turn toward her bad behavior so she tried to change the topic.

"What's it like here?" she asked. "Have you seen Archibald? Is this better than Arran?"

Her questions, at their blistering pace had the desired effect, turning Mama's face brighter.

"It was difficult at first," she said, dropping her shoulders as the emotion of the early days in New Brunswick returned. "There was so much to learn and get done."

John sensed the burden of starting a farm on Bay Chaleur was resting on his mother's shoulders. It was easy to see how much work the family needed to do. The cleared land was filled with stumps awaiting removal while the house stood cold and dark under the canopy of the remaining tall trees. At that moment, Papa entered the house and turned the conversation toward Archibald.

"Archibald opened his home to us for several weeks," Papa said.

"The McKinnon family has been so graceful," Mama added. "Archibald comes by every day to help Papa with the clearing. Without John to do the heavy work, we needed the extra hands."

Papa was about to add to Mama's compliments when, almost on cue, Archibald opened the door and stepped in with a large grin on his face.

"So here they be," he said in a voice that could be heard in the next county. "John got the lass and made it here safely."

He reached over and patted John on the back.

"A fine young man," he added.

Archibald quickly described for Margaret and John the advantages of living in New Brunswick. As he talked about his farm and the land, Margaret's thoughts drifted back to Arran. Back to the fields surrounding their small house. It seemed like a long time ago.

"Are you listening lass?" he asked, expecting her full attention.

"Your family's been worried sick about the two of you," he said, not sparing Margaret from a scolding.

He frowned, expecting Margaret to look at him with admiration. When he didn't see it, it turned from a scolding to a lecture.

"It's time for you to give your father and mother the respect they deserve," he said. "It's time for you to give me a little respect too."

Margaret knew it was due, but wasn't sure why Archibald was the first to deliver the reprimand. She had acted foolishly back on Arran and deserved everyone's anger. She looked up at Archibald and slumped in her chair.

"Yes, I'm listening," she said. "I know it was a terrible mistake to run away," she said, trying to soften the lecture. "It was wrong."

Mama abruptly stood up and stopped everyone.

"We're all here in one piece," she said, brushing the front of her dress with both hands.

It wasn't like Mama to stop a good talking-to.

"Let's start thinking about the good things ahead," she added and sat back onto the chair.

Archibald understood and smiled back at Mama.

"Well, she's your daughter," he said. "Just glad, she's not mine."

With everyone ready to move on, Papa pushed another difficult subject.

"The winter's our next challenge and fear," he said, trying to look scared.

It was the word Archibald needed, and he didn't hesitate to describe what was in store for the new immigrants.

"A cold that fills your bones and makes you ache all over," Archibald said. "This isn't Arran, it's a bitter cold and if you're not prepared, a family can freeze to death. The McKinnons were not completely prepared for our first winter, but we survived. You must listen."

He paused, waiting for a reaction. The Murchie family remained silent, not knowing what to say. The challenges of having their own farm kept mounting.

"The leaks between these logs will need fixing, if you want to stay warm," Archibald added, pointing toward the walls of the house.

The fear in Papa's voice became clear. Archibald had the experience of many winters behind him and the Murchie family needed to heed his advice. John was convinced Archibald's experience would keep them from freezing.

"There'll be plenty of snow," Archibald said. "We've a few months to prepare, you mustn't delay."

Archibald expected the Murchie family to be ready. He encouraged James and Elizabeth Murchie to emigrate with their children to Bay Chaleur and now their first winter was approaching. He felt responsible for their survival, yet knew talking would not prepare them. The only choice was hard work by everyone.

John claimed he was ready for the challenge, asking Archibald to describe their first spring planting.

"What about the stumps?" John asked, when Archibald didn't mention how he removed the unsightly tree remains. "How'd you get rid of them?"

Everywhere he looked, there were tree stumps surrounding Papa's new house.

"Ah, the stumps," Archibald said. "They must be burned."

John shook his head and looked at Papa. There was much to learn about farming in his new home.

"Several life lessons await you in the coming months, young fella," Archibald said, looking past John's eyes with his own. "Farming on Bay Chaleur is just one of them."

12

Stonehaven, Gloucester County

Robert made his way back to Matthew's farm with only his thoughts as a companion. He hadn't been alone since the ride to Cobh, and his needs were quite different then. Now it was time to plan for a new life in Eel River Settlement.

He thought about the next few days. A trip to the nearby county office to complete the grant, and a visit to the Settlement would fill one of those days. His heart raced with the thought of his new farmland. What would it look like?

He yearned to walk the land and assess its potential. It was one thing to view a rough outline of a grant drawn on a map, and a completely different experience to stand on the actual ground. He wanted to feel the earth beneath his feet and in his hands. At the county office he would arrange the official survey then head directly to Eel River Settlement.

Robert thought of his ancestors and how they must have felt arriving in Timoleague centuries ago. How was the farmland selected? Did they have the same sensation of responsibility, shouldering the dependence of the family? His thoughts went to his father. Would he be proud? Proud of the decisions he made and how he had convinced Mother to travel?

His work was just beginning. It was time to show everyone why New Brunswick was the place to live, instead of Timoleague. He imagined it would be a bigger challenge than crossing the Atlantic.

When he pulled into the Stonehaven farm, Matthew was busy in the barn so Robert set the horse in the pasture and stepped inside the house. Rebecca and Thomas were reading while Mother and Sarah were helping prepare the food for supper. Mother was startled when she turned to see Robert walk in.

"You're back early," she said. "I thought Matthew said it would take all day to travel to the place up north."

"We stopped at the Bathurst dock and their father was waiting to collect them," Robert said. Mr. Murchie seemed a little bewildered when they all saw each other."

"Interesting family," Mother said. "Must've been a terrible thing to have two children stay behind. And that episode on the Eden—"

"That episode was the sailor, not Margaret," Sarah interrupted.

Mother shook her head. She could only imagine what it would have been like if Sarah or Rebecca had stayed in Ireland or disobeyed curfew. They are much better behaved, she thought.

"She's a feisty one, that Margaret," Mother said.

Robert was surprised at Sarah's willingness to stand up for her new friend. It wasn't like her but he knew how righteous Mother could sound.

He felt a kinship for John. Over the past two months, John shared many of the same responsibilities Robert had with his mother and siblings. At least in John's case, he had his father. The responsibility of taking care of Margaret was only temporary.

It would be fate if their lives crossed again in this large province, Robert thought. He didn't know how or if it would happen, but anything seemed possible. But those thoughts were for another day. The priority now was completing the grant survey paperwork and preparing the land for a farm. There wasn't time to think about anything else.

Robert spent the evening listening to Matthew's advice on land clearing, and house building. The trees on their Timoleague farms had been cleared centuries before Matthew and Robert were born, providing little experience for the two men. Bay Chaleur was different, unlike anything they knew in Ireland and Matthew had much to share.

When the ideal cutting techniques had been described, the two men turned their attention toward Robert's mother. She must stay in Stonehaven with the children until a proper house could be built, Matthew advised. At first Mother would have none of it, but as the evening and the argument wore on, she grew convinced it was the best option for all.

Almost resolved, Robert thought, as he listened to Matthew describe the winter and the wilderness surrounding the Eel River Settlement. Having Mother with him while the land was cleared wouldn't work. She needed better living conditions and the comforts available in Stonehaven. Finally, she agreed and Robert headed to bed knowing he had secured an open timetable of one year to build a house.

Rebecca and Thomas could finish school in Stonehaven while Sarah developed her home making skills with Mother and Sarah Jane. They would be far better off, Robert told himself, especially with Matthew's experience.

Early the next day, Robert rode to the county office in Dalhousie to finish the grant details. As he traveled north along the coastal road dotted with settlements, he wondered which one was named Colborne. He wanted to ask the first passerby, but no one shared the road with Robert that day.

Arriving in the town of Dalhousie, he found a few shops and office buildings including a local sawmill. The ships anchored in the harbor reminded Robert of the voyage across the Atlantic. He stared at their masts, wondering where the wind would take them, then quickly looked away. There wasn't time to dream. He had important business to attend to.

He located the county office and arranged for the survey, completing the final step to ownership. A sense of anticipation started to build inside him. It was time to visit the settlement and walk the land.

"Which road will take me to Eel River Settlement?" Robert asked, wondering if the man behind the desk was also a recent immigrant.

"Take the south road and turn right after the sandbar along the cove," he said. "The road follows the river."

Another official with few words, Robert thought, deciding not to ask any more questions. He left the office and followed the man's directions, traveling along the coastal road and retracing part of his earlier ride. He headed inland along a narrow path, keeping the Eel River on his right. It wasn't a well traveled road, Robert thought, unsure of what he would find the farther inland he went.

After a few miles, Robert found a cluster of houses and farms and was confident he had arrived. The area was heavily forested so he pulled out the map to find any identifying marker. The river appeared as a dark line and several grants were identified with lighter outlines. Once he pinpointed his location near the river, he headed toward the area labeled "Blacknell 200 acres".

It was a proud moment to see his family's name on the official document, but he still needed to confirm the land's potential. On the map, the Blacknell 200 extended along the north west branch of the Eel River, following its meandering path for about a half mile. Water access was important for travel and farming, Robert thought, acknowledging his good fortune.

A close look at the map revealed how the settlement road divided the Blacknell grant into two parcels, providing easy access to the farm. But which parcel should he build the house on? It was time to walk the ground and decide, so Robert tied the horse to a nearby tree.

A feeling of satisfaction fell over Robert as he stood on his new farmland for the first time. He took a deep breath, inhaling the sweet scent of pine and fir, filling the air around him. This was his. It was his prize for crossing the Atlantic.

The time for celebration would come. Celebrate when the house is built, he thought. Celebrate when Mother and the children can move here. Now it was time to decide if the boundary lines needed to change and where to put the house.

Robert stared at the map. He knew these decisions carried more weight than a mark on a piece of paper. He walked toward the river, taking in the size of the trees and calculating the work ahead. The underbrush was thick, forcing Robert to make a jagged path to the water.

He arrived at the river's edge and looked down to the water flowing ten feet below him. Safe from floods, he thought. It was at that moment Robert decided the ideal location for the house. He would build it on the north side of the river, between the bank and the road. On the path he had just walked. There was also plenty of land to build a barn next to the house.

He continued along the northwest side of the river until he reached the proposed border. Should he push the river access or leave it as recorded, he wondered. A quick walk north was all it took for Robert to realize the water access was a necessity. The farther inland he went, the more brush and marsh he encountered.

Robert picked up his pace as he walked back to the carriage, holding the map tightly in his hands. He imagined a finished house and barn along the Eel River. The future farm for the Blacknell family.

He headed back to Stonehaven with a head filled with ideas. The one thing he was certain of, was keeping quiet about the amount of work the farm required. His mother didn't need to know. She would ask too many questions and Robert wasn't in a hurry to answer them. He needed time to get started. Anything could change.

13

Colborne Winter

Margaret settled in Colborne with her two sisters. Only a year separated each of them, forcing three unique identities to demand the attention of Mama and Papa. Three girls, three different spirits and personalities. To a stranger, it was difficult to imagine they came from the same family.

The rhythm of arguments picked up where it had stopped on Arran. Nonetheless, Margaret found it comforting for everything to feel so normal. Liza, her oldest sister, was very close to Mama, always quilting and sewing at her mother's side. She followed Mama's rules, frequently requesting her sisters to do the same.

Janet found her identity in the space outside those rules. A risk taker at heart, she frequently pushed the boundaries established by Mama. Margaret was a blend of both girls, a little creative with a hint of risk taking. She found a way to top it all off with a free spirit that no one in the family could match.

Several days after Margaret's arrival, Janet suggested they explore the shoreline and nearby wooded area.

"There are a few interesting places worth looking at," Janet said.

In actuality, Janet didn't find any of it interesting, she only wanted to prove her knowledge of Bay Chaleur to Margaret. Leaving Arran behind would not change their ongoing tension and rivalry. Today, Janet wanted the upper hand.

Early the next morning, after breakfast, but before Papa called them for chores, the girls headed down toward the bay. The cool salt breeze met them as they turned to face the water.

"Archibald calls this the east wind," Liza said.

"Fear the Bay Chaleur east wind," Janet added in a voice mimicking Archibald.

The three girls laughed at Janet's imitation and picked up their pace toward the shore.

"Why does he lecture us all the time?" Margaret asked, following in the footsteps of Liza.

"He's an old expert, according to Papa," Liza answered. "He should be able to tell us what to do."

The giggles continued at the thought of old Archibald. He was close in age to Papa and neither should be considered old, but to young girls, everyone was old.

As they made their way around the trees, creating a trail of footprints where the underbrush gave them space, the salt air and the forest's sweet aroma surrounded them. It took their full attention to avoid the low tree limbs and the sprawling sapling branches stretching to grasp the nearest sliver of sunlight.

A thin cloud of small black flies followed their every step, forcing the girls to brush their necklines as the insects pierced the tender exposed skin. The flies were annoying, leaving small welts as reminders of their tiny, yet harmful bites.

The dark forest was the perfect location for Janet to scare Margaret with stories of the animals living among the trees and fields nearby.

"Bears with claws and moose as tall as a barn live in these woods," Janet said, trying to sound ferocious. "It starts with these pesky little flies."

Margaret shrugged her shoulders, telling Janet she didn't care. Without plans to venture too far into these woods, what did it matter, she thought. Janet laughed and rushed ahead of her sisters. When Liza and Margaret caught up, Janet was ready with more tales of monsters. The pattern continued until they made it to the water's edge and the east wind off the bay blew the black flies inland.

As Margaret approached the water, she thought of Bennan. Bay Chaleur's rocky beach was like Bennan, but on a bigger scale. The rocks were the same dark grey and black color and everywhere. She paused thinking how easy it was to compare everything to Arran. Bay Chaleur was too new. It wasn't home yet.

"Do you miss Arran?" she asked her sisters.

"Of course," replied Janet. "We grew up there, but when Papa decides to move on, it's time to move on."

Janet's voice grew tense, showing her frustration with her sister.

"Why did you want to stay on Arran?" Janet asked. "Do you know how awful that was?"

Margaret was sorry she asked the question and knew Janet had more to say.

"Mama was sick for weeks on the ship crossing the Atlantic," she said. "We were worried she wouldn't make it.

Margaret looked at the ground, not knowing how her actions had hurt her own mother. There wasn't anything she could say.

"We all had issues leaving Arran, but none of us were selfish and acted out like you," Janet continued.

Margaret needed to change the subject, the conversation was not in her favor.

"Let's find a new landmark," she said. "Something like Holy Island. What about that mountain with the steps heading into the clouds?

Janet looked across the bay and nodded.

"I wonder how far away those steps are?" Janet asked. "One day we'll walk up to the top of that mountain and look across to Colborne. Once we find out how to get there."

They all laughed and attempted to outdo each other skipping stones across the calm water.

"Six skips," Janet claimed.

Liza was still thinking about the mountain steps while Janet was claiming victory.

"It's too far," Liza said. "Those steps in the distance are too far. The island in front of us is much closer."

Janet stopped and looked at Liza, staring at the land in front of them.

"You want to go there?" Janet asked pointing across the water.

"We could get a dory and row over," Liza suggested.

It was like the days on Arran. The three sisters away from Mama and Papa, finding new treasures or secret places. Making escape plans they would never take. Even Liza was trying to misbehave, planning trips to an island offshore.

The girls decided their new home wasn't anything like Arran. The forests, the mountain steps across the water and even the flat island in front of them. Only the color of the beach rocks seemed familiar.

"It feels like we're the first people walking here," Liza said. "Nothing's disturbed."

An eerie quiet came over the three. They had heard all the folklore and stories about Arran. The ones about the battles, the spells and the stone circles on Machrie Moor. Would New Brunswick have the same scary stories too?

"Do you think we're the first?" Margaret asked.

"It's possible," Liza answered.

It was something Liza wondered since the family arrived, but was too afraid to ask. The forest was so dense.

"Can we go back?" Margaret asked. "Those stories always scare me."

They turned toward their newly made forest path, confident they could retrace their steps. The morning had been a time to connect. A morning when the three girls weren't chopping wood, knitting, quilting or getting ready for the winter. That would be waiting when they got home.

Mama insisted a final year at the Colborne school would suit her youngest daughter, forcing Margaret for forgo her daily chores. Margaret didn't argue, she could contribute on the weekends while meeting other children and reuniting with a few Arran friends.

When school started and the long shadows of fall took over, the beauty of Bay Chaleur became visible. The mountain steps across the bay were ablaze in reds and yellows. It was difficult to ignore but the view took second place to the preparations for winter. Archibald's reminders of the peril of a first winter were never far away.

"January's the toughest month," he warned. "It'll be bone aching cold."

When the Murchie family's first Bay Chaleur November arrived, a few small snow storms blanketed the ground. By the end of the month there were several inches of snow covering everything.

"This isn't so bad," John said. "What's Archibald talking about?"

"Not sure why he thinks this is difficult," Papa said, agreeing with John.

It would be another few weeks before the true New Brunswick winter made its appearance. The inches of snow turned into feet while the bitter wind off the bay swept the snow into drifts covering the path between the house and the barn. By early January, breathing the cold air brought tears to John's eyes when he headed outside to clear the snow. Now he knew what Archibald meant and an overwhelming sense of concern came over him. Would they survive the winter?

The next few months became a series of cold days, colder nights and powerful snowstorms. To keep warm, the fireplace was in constant need of wood, forcing the Murchie children to take turns moving wood from the barn into the house. It was the worst chore by far and each child tried to put it off without success.

"The sun will set in the late afternoon," Papa would warn.

It didn't matter. The next day would bring the same reminder and a reluctant child heading to the barn for an armload of wood.

John was expected to load the fireplace with wood before the family went to bed for the night. As the wood burned, everyone slept with their socks and jackets on, covered by the heavy quilts the girls had finished weeks earlier. At sunrise, no one wanted to leave the warmth of their beds. But someone had to. The first one out of bed was expected to get the fire started. Another difficult chore, but this one usually fell to John and Papa.

The Murchie family now understood what Archibald had been telling them. Winter was cold and it was difficult. The snow flurries in November didn't equal the biting January wind and freezing temperatures of February. But winter's challenges didn't change their minds about living on Bay Chaleur. It was their own farm covered in several feet of snow.

The months of snow eventually gave way to April and memories of the cold nights started to thaw. Laughter was finally heard on the Murchie farm. It was a winter that forced everyone together for the common purpose of staying warm. When spring started its renewal, the Murchie family reminisced about their year. They were a different family from the one who left Arran. They had a new way of life and a closer bond.

14

Blacknell Barn

As the Murchie family readied the farm for winter, Robert gathered the necessary tools from Matthew's barn for the grueling task awaiting him in Eel River Settlement. The grant was complete with the river frontage he requested. It was time to clear the land.

The goodbyes started as Robert loaded the carriage and hugged each of his siblings, not knowing when he would see them next. At nineteen years of age, he had never been away from his family, but for the next year, he would be completely alone. After Matthew promised to make regular visits, Mother relaxed and gave her son a hug with a tenderness Robert hadn't expected.

He headed north on the coastal road once again, passing through the now familiar small settlements along his journey. The road was becoming recognizable, yet the location of Colborne wasn't. One of these trips he'll find another traveler and ask, he thought. Until then, he could only guess.

Matthew had arranged boarding accommodations for Robert with the Harrisons, an Irish family who moved to Eel River Settlement several years prior. They were familiar with the challenges facing Robert and ready to share their knowledge and experience. Robert was thankful for their guidance and the prospect of having a warm bed and regular meals, while he turned the forest into a home. In the coming months, Robert would spend many hours with the Harrisons, asking questions and seeking advice.

After the first breakfast at the Harrison home, Robert made his way to the land, anxious to confirm the outline on the chart. The decisions about the house and barn sites had been made. Today he could explore more of the Blacknell 200.

Robert headed west against the flow of the water, searching for the marked cedar tree described in the grant. With each step the excitement grew, tempered only by the underbrush and dense forest. The distance was thirty chains, according to the chart, not quite a half mile but the limit of today's exploration. The weight of the work ahead was too much, forcing Robert to turn back.

He returned to the house site and grabbed the axe Matthew had given him. Walking over to the tree closest to the road, he knew the process would be orderly. Cut and clear, he thought as he took a deep breath and steadied his feet.

Whack! Whack! The axe moved through the tree with the strength of Robert's body. After several minutes of constant striking, the tree fell. Robert leaned the axe on the ground, wanting to celebrate the beginning. Instead, he stepped over it and adjusted his weight toward the next one. He had to keep cutting. There would be many more swings, and felled trees to come.

For the rest of the day, Robert continued to clear the area, letting his mind drift when he wasn't swinging the axe. The barn would be built first, he decided. It would be faster, with fewer inside walls and it could hold a temporary room. A room large enough to accommodate a stove, and a place to sleep and read. It would be simple living and remove the burden of walking back and forth to the Harrison home.

Supper with the Harrisons the first night was cordial with storytelling about Ireland and Bay Chaleur. Their house was comfortable, not too fancy, allowing Mrs. Harrison to keep everything tidy and in its place. Robert excused himself after the meal, and made his way to his room. He was ready to collapse from the day's work.

Tomorrow he would start again, with the men Matthew had organized from the local church. It was their gift to new immigrants, Matthew described. Their way of helping others adjust to life on Bay Chaleur. Robert smiled when they arrived shortly after sunrise with tools and ample physical strength. He accepted their help without hesitation. Every muscle in his body ached from the previous day.

One of his new neighbors, Alphonse Arseneault, was part of the group, so Robert approached him as the men finished their work. The conversation flowed between the two, as Alphonse shared his family's story and the early days of the Settlement.

"Our roots go back to New France, many years before the province of New Brunswick existed," Alphonse told Robert. "Acadians we are called, arriving here when the British exiled us out of our homes near the St. John River."

For Robert, the British had always been a positive influence, a benefactor guiding his family with grants for a new life. This was a different Britain for Alphonse and the same Britain despised by many of the Irish Catholics.

"That must've been difficult for your family," Robert said.

"Ah, yes," Alphonse admitted. "It was hard on the older people, but we are resilient and have learned to love this community near the Eel River."

It would have been easy for Robert to nod and walk away from Alphonse's story, but he didn't, there was more to learn.

"It was safer on Bay Chaleur than the St. John River," Alphonse added. "And now, new families from Scotland and Ireland are joining us."

"The Blacknell story is very different," Robert replied. "My family arrived here from Ireland and my ancestors settled there from England."

Robert's thoughts drifted to how different their lives had been. Alphonse nodded, accepting that difference, as he listened to Robert describe a simpler, less stressful journey to the farm in Eel River Settlement.

"My ancestors settled this part of the world in the late 1600s," Alphonse added. "They were fishermen and trappers."

He looked at Robert with a wide grin. A man proud of his heritage.

"Perhaps I've gained a little of their knowledge," he said laughing.

Robert smiled and nodded. There was much to learn from his new neighbor. It would be good to understand the struggles between the French and English in New Brunswick, he thought. The history of Bay Chaleur was new to him and he wanted to hear more from Alphonse. His would continue to ask questions. Questions that would help shape Robert's knowledge and appreciation for the Acadians.

Alphonse was eager to share the stories of the Arsenault family. In addition to bringing tools and relatives to help in the clearing, Alphonse brought stories of the past. Stories that Robert looked forward to hearing at the end of each work day. Robert's appreciation for Matthew and Alphonse continued to grow. The Blacknell farm would not have been possible without them.

As the sunlight hours grew shorter with each day, the forest prepared for the winter ahead, displaying its last gasp. Every leaf turned bright yellow, orange or red, the warning of the cold to come. The men continued to cut and clear with the warning colors in front of them. When the last of the colorful leaves settled on the forest floor, Robert could only imagine the cold ahead.

The barn structure was up and livable by December. Robert told the Harrison family he would return if the weather became impossible. They nodded, expecting to see him in a month once the bitterness of winter set in.

The bitter cold of January kept Robert inside the barn for several days. After the first night, he thought about joining the Harrison family but it was too dangerous to venture out into the wind. He remained by the fire, awaiting an improvement in the weather. Each night, the howling wind would wake him from a light sleep and test his decision to live on Bay Chaleur.

Robert resolved he wasn't going to let Mother Nature change his mind. She made him more determined. After staying inside for three days, Robert headed out of the barn. It was the moment he realized the placement of the barn door had saved his life. The snow drifts from the storm reached the barn's roof on the river's side. Had the door faced the river, he would have been inside the barn for weeks, unable to push aside the snow. He could hardly believe his luck.

The pattern of storms started to change by the middle of February, allowing the men to increase the pace of clearing. Robert experienced the worst a Bay Chaleur winter had to offer. He vowed to be better prepared for the next one and to never tell his mother about his close call.

Matthew reported on life in Stonehaven during his visit at the end of February, giving Robert a view into his mother's adjustment to life outside of Timoleague. For his part, Robert sent Mother monthly updates in the mail about the farm and his progress. Mother, however, was better at keeping Robert informed. He would find several letters waiting for him when he walked to the local postmaster's house in the settlement. News about Thomas and Rebecca at school and Sarah's chores at the Stonehaven farm filled the pages. The Eel River Postmaster smiled when Robert stopped by. He was anxious to meet the rest of the Blacknell family when they moved in.

Toward the end of March, prior to the snowmelt, Robert decided to take time away from cutting trees and visit Stonehaven. It would be faster than a spring visit on the log roads, so off he went with Alphonse's sleigh wagon at first light.

Robert had been in the settlement for seven months, only departing for business or to purchase the necessary supplies in Dalhousie. As he turned south toward Stonehaven on the coastal road, the frozen bay welcomed him with a biting east wind. He stared across the bay to the snow covered mountains, on the opposite shore. Snow and ice, as far as his eyes could see. He wondered when Mother Nature would release her hold on the Bay Chaleur winter.

Robert arrived in Stonehaven around dusk as the family was preparing supper.

"Well there's a sight for sore eyes," Mother declared when Robert walked into the house.

He hadn't expected such a warm welcome but took it all in.

"Wonderful to see all of you," Robert said.

Thomas, Sarah and Rebecca came running into the room to see their brother. Mother smiled as the children embraced and excitedly shared their stories.

With everyone circled around him, Robert decided he had his own story to share and carefully unfolded the progress on their new home.

"Our home in Eel River Settlement will be ready in the fall," he said.

Mother was surprised and disappointed.

"I thought you were coming to tell us it was time to leave Stonehaven," she said.

Robert stared at his feet trying to avoid his mother's glare. He hated disappointing her and now he had created a second problem by suggesting when the house would be ready.

"There's much work to be done," he said. "In the fall, the inside of the house will still need work."

Robert didn't want his mother to think the house would resemble the Stonehaven home. They were years away from the comforts Matthew and Sarah Jane enjoyed.

After supper and stories about the winter, everyone went to bed. Tomorrow Robert would head back. It would be a long cold ride with the weight of a new promise on his shoulders.

15

Colborne Spring

Spring swept the bay with departing ice floes, melting snow and the thawing earth. The Restigouche River released its ice to the bay, announcing the early days of the shipping season. But the warming sun and the green shoots on the soil mattered the most to the Murchie family. They had survived the cold Bay Chaleur winter and it was time to farm again.

Colborne came alive as the men returned to the fields to prepare the soil for planting. The women found time together at the Colborne church, displaying their handiwork, and creating gossip to share over the summer months.

After one of the gatherings with the local women, Mama announced to Liza and Janet she found work for them with two local Arran families.

"The Cook and McPherson families are looking for domestic help," Mama said, with the expectation of a happy response.

Mama decided for her girls. There was little doubt in her voice, yet her two daughters reacted as expected. Liza smiled, wanting to hear more and Janet went silent, clenching her hands into tight fists.

"When do we start?" Liza asked, anxious to escape the winter monotony inside the Murchie home.

Janet didn't bother to ask any questions, she knew it was too late. Mama never changed her mind, especially when a commitment to her friends was involved. It was too embarrassing.

"Next week," Mama answered. "Each family is expecting you next week."

It was all worked out. The girls would overnight with the families during the week, caring for their children and return to the Murchie farm for the weekend. Janet kept her thoughts to herself, revealed only by her hands. Without a secondary education, she knew there were few choices. On that day, Janet vowed, Mama would never decide for her again.

Along with Janet, Margaret was also silent. She watched, wide eyed, as Liza grew excited over the domestic work and Janet grew sullen and angry. Margaret was thankful she had school to finish over the next few months. There was much to learn watching her sisters.

The Murchie household adjusted to an evening with John and Margaret during the week and a full house on the weekends. John usually went to bed early, after a day of constant work. A day of farming or clearing the land for future crops. They knew the growing season was short and every day counted toward the preparations for the next winter.

Mama's hand was also meddling in John's future. The Stewart family, early settlers in Colborne, started dropping in for tea or Sunday afternoon visits. Mama and Mrs. Stewart seemed to have a plan and Catherine Stewart, their daughter had her sights on John.

"She's a lovely girl," Mama would tell John after each visit. "From a good Arran family too. It's time you get to know her."

Before long, John was visiting the Stewart farm and courting Catherine. It was a short walk up the road and John made excuses to visit.

"The Stewarts are experts to learn from," he said. "Experts on Bay Chaleur and the short farming season."

Papa knew better than to challenge John. He saw the change in John when he talked about Catherine. He saw a younger man, when he looked in John's eyes. It was the man who courted Mama back on Arran.

Margaret knew he would eventually marry Catherine and move to his own home. They seemed made for one another. She was exactly like John. Very deliberate and practical with bursts of excitement. Catherine adored John. After Catherine's father gave his blessing, the couple decided to marry when John turned nineteen. It was a little over a year away.

Papa decided he would divide the farm for John and Catherine and started the paperwork process with a solicitor in Dalhousie. John would have his own land and farm, making his Bay Chaleur dream a reality. Papa planned to carve out a section near the main road, allowing access for both farms. Mama pushed Papa for a different parcel. She wanted John closer, but finally agreed when Papa suggested John needed to grow.

"It will be a short walk," Papa said. "John and Catherine will be nearby and on their own."

Papa wondered if departing Arran without two of the children still bothered her. She shouldn't be worried about a few hundred feet, he thought, but Elizabeth Murchie had a tendency to worry.

Nearly a year had passed since the family settled in Colborne Parish and despite the differences with the winter, their new home felt like Arran.

"It's like we never left," Mama said. "Most of the family names in Colborne are Arran names."

Colborne had become Arran. At least one hundred families settled along the bay, many of them near the Murchie farm. The tradition of helping each other continued as new immigrants arrived and joined their former Arran neighbors on Bay Chaleur.

Over the next year, Papa planned to help his son build a new home and farm. Papa knew his decision to leave Arran was good a year ago. Now with John getting his own farm, it turned out to be brilliant.

Margaret was fully immersed in her final year at the Colborne school, a one-room schoolhouse with twenty four students. With a range in age from seven to fourteen, Margaret was one of the oldest. The Parish school had convinced Miss Brown, a Scottish immigrant living in Halifax, to move to Colborne to teach their children. She took the opportunity, knowing she could live among familiar traditions. Margaret enjoyed Miss Brown's stories and work as a teacher. To stay on her good side, Margaret always completed her studies ahead of schedule.

As an immigrant, Miss Brown told her class to remember where they came from, but Margaret didn't need any reminders. Arran was how she compared everything.

Miss Brown boarded at the MacAlister home just down the road from the Murchies, so Margaret tried to walk home with her every afternoon after school. Miss Brown pushed Margaret to read, sharing her love of books, and reminding Margaret her formal schooling would soon be over.

"You can still read," Miss Brown said. "It doesn't need to be for school."

For Margaret, the walks were magical and she listened to every word from Miss Brown. Most of the other children found the teacher strict but lively, keeping a comfortable distance. Her teaching style was engaging but no one liked her reaction when they fell out of line, or didn't complete their work.

"Mama says that Miss Brown is just right," Margaret told her school mates, not realizing her actions and words made her the teacher's pet.

"We need to do our work," she said, more righteous than any other eighth grade student.

The weekends were full of conversation and distraction when Liza and Janet came home. Liza was full of stories, and excited to share her week with the family. She enjoyed the work and the children she cared for. For Liza, it was a stepping stone to marriage. Mama smiled, listening to Liza describe the Cook household. It was Mama's way of learning about the Arran families without asking them direct questions. Perhaps more gossip stories.

Janet, on the other hand, found domestic work trivial and decided it was a path to nowhere. Definitely not a stepping stone. She wanted to become a nurse but without the money for school, she needed the earnings from the McPherson family. She remained quiet, tending to the children and saving. She had a plan and it wasn't marriage.

Margaret was thankful for the school days, escaping to the classroom and then the stories on the walks home. Being alone in the house with Mama in the afternoon and evening wore on Margaret. The day always ended with Margaret angry at her mother.

"Did you finish your school work tonight?" Mama would ask on a typical day.

"Yes, it's complete and you can look at it," Margaret would reply.

The same questions and answers over and over. Margaret wanted her sisters in the house. Strange how she pined for the arguments with Janet. It was banter. It was a different issue for each argument. It wasn't her mother nagging or telling her what she should do. Margaret missed the insight from watching her sisters and getting their advice.

When the next weekend came around, Margaret asked Janet for her help. It was an unusual request but Janet took it in stride.

"Look, if you want her off your back you need to give her something else to do," Janet said. "Why not share some of the books you're reading?"

Margaret thought Janet was clever and started leaving the books on the table for her mother. Within a few weeks, the conversation changed from school assignments to the characters in the books. It was obvious there was more to learn from her sister Janet.

Ahead of the summer months, the paperwork for John's farm was ready to sign. Papa headed into Dalhousie with John, knowing a dream would soon be realized. They finished quickly at the solicitor's office and headed back to Colborne, excited and ready to celebrate.

As the carriage turned toward the Murchie home, they were met by Malcolm McCormack and his son. Malcolm seemed agitated, so they stopped to listen.

"John, John, you must head to the Stewart farm immediately," he said.

John looked at Malcolm, a little bewildered at how the happy occasion became a panic, but set out toward Catherine's home. As the carriage approached the farm, it was obvious something was completely wrong. There were several carriages and wagons next to the house. It looked as though all of Colborne Parish was at the Stewart home.

Papa followed John inside the house, looking for Catherine. When they finally found her, she was sitting at the table, next to her mother. The two women were holding each other's hands. Neither of them noticed John, their eyes filled with tears and bodies shaking from uncontrollable sobbing.

"What happened?" Papa whispered to the man standing in the doorway.

"Heart attack," he said. "Went quickly. We're waiting on the undertaker now."

Papa headed toward John to give him the news before he faced Catherine, but it was too late. As he walked into the kitchen, he saw John consoling Catherine in his arms.

Grief took over the Stewart family under a fog of sadness in Colborne. The entire parish attended the wake at the farmhouse, bringing food and sharing stories about Catherine's father.

Time stood still for the Stewarts after the funeral. Catherine's mother barely functioned and before long, she settled into a deep depression. She was lost without her husband.

Catherine accepted the responsibility of caring for her siblings, her mother and the farm. Within a few weeks, she was completely overwhelmed, forcing John to rethink their marriage date. He didn't find an argument, both families agreed the Stewarts needed John. The farm also needed a man and John left the Murchie farm immediately. He finally fulfilled his dream. It wasn't quite the circumstances he envisioned back on the Eden, but John now had a hundred acre farm.

Papa took the situation in stride, setting aside the legal papers until the Stewart estate was settled. Mama wasn't sure how to react. It was only a short distance away, but John could have been back on Arran. Margaret also missed him and his constant nagging about her impulsiveness. A short walk would get his opinion when needed. They had sealed a special relationship on the voyage across the Atlantic, but John had other priorities now. Margaret knew she wasn't one of them.

16

Eel River Farm

A sense of accomplishment and pride washed over Robert as he turned his gaze from the barn to the farmhouse standing in front of him. A short time ago, this land was covered in trees and now it held the future home for his family. He stared at the basic farmhouse, smiling as he imagined his mother's reaction. A two story building with sleeping rooms upstairs and two large rooms on the first floor. A shadow of the house they enjoyed in Ireland, but a house filled with optimism.

Robert thought about the men who worked alongside him to make the house a reality. They shared in this accomplishment, their handiwork visible inside and out. Because of neighbors and new friends, the house was now ready for his family.

But it was Alphonse's experience and guidance Robert appreciated the most. Without Alphonse, Robert would never have cut the trees in the winter when the sap wasn't running or moved the logs to the local sawmill along the stable frozen roads.

After the March visit to Stonehaven, Robert returned to Eel River with an eagerness to bring his family home. Mother Nature cooperated with an April snow melt to power the silent sawmill to life. The logs were sliced and cut into shingles and boards, now covering the Blacknell house. The Eel River forest had changed its purpose. Instead of standing guard over the river, its wood protected the Blacknell family from the Bay Chaleur weather.

In early November, Robert headed to Stonehaven to collect his family. He left early one morning as the overnight frost ignored the rising sun. Perhaps this trip he'd pass another traveler along the coastal road and ask about each settlement.

Despite spending close to a year without his family, Robert was never alone. The Harrisons, Alphonse and the church families had kept Robert company, filling more than the family void. Former strangers were now friends with a shared experience of creating the Blacknell farm.

He arrived in Stonehaven, shortly after supper to the delight of everyone. Mother had anticipated this day and rose from her seat as Robert walked through the front door. Robert was smiling, knowing he had fulfilled his promise. He knew his father would've been proud.

"The farm's ready," he told his mother, speaking before anyone greeted him. "It's in need of your hand, your fine touch on the inside."

Robert showed a rare level of emotion, wrapping his arms around each of his siblings. He saved the final hug for Mother. It was an embrace to celebrate, the Blacknell family was together again.

Before Robert released his arms, Matthew asked if Sarah could stay on for the remainder of the school year. It was a request both Mother and Robert couldn't deny. Mother was first to give the nod and Sarah didn't argue.

The next morning, Robert loaded everything into the cart, careful to place his mother's treasured furniture where it wouldn't break. Thomas and Rebecca climbed in, navigating around the small tables and the spinning wheel. Everyone knew the sentimental value the items held for their mother. It was an essential part of getting her on the ship, Robert thought. A small price to pay.

On the ride to their new home, the family filled the cold air with small talk about Stonehaven, New Bandon and the Eel River Settlement. When the latest news was complete, Thomas and Rebecca decided to share what they learned about New Brunswick, their new province.

"It started in 1784," Thomas said, proud to tell his elder brother.

"You know more than I do about our new home," Robert told him. "You'll be expected to teach me."

All agreed and for the remainder of the trip, the two children asked questions while Robert and Mother tried to answer. Robert threw in a few questions about the Acadians, hoping to hear what the children had learned about Alphonse's ancestors. Thomas immediately responded. He was eager to meet Alphonse's family.

"The French were on Bay Chaleur before the British," Thomas declared.

Robert nodded, pleased with Thomas' studies.

"We learned about the Mi'kmaq too, they were here before the French," Thomas added. Mother looked at Robert, puzzled.

"Mi'kmaq?" she asked.

"Yes Mother, the natives, the people who lived here first," Robert said. Thomas smiled, pleased with his schooling advantage.

The conversation moved to the fall leaves and the natural beauty of the bay. It was Mother's first trip north along the coastal road of Bay Chaleur and she marveled at the mountains across the water. The trees had past their peak of color, replacing the red, orange and yellow leaves with brown or nothing at all. It was Mother Nature's announcement of another approaching winter. An announcement they had learned to respect.

Before long the Blacknell family turned west on the cove road following the Eel River. Robert's excitement grew as the carriage approached the new farm.

"This road's new," Mother claimed, as the carriage wheels labored over the large ruts.

"Yes, until recently, the river was the only access to the settlement," Robert replied.

He knew his mother would find wilderness living a challenge, but it was too late for any change.

"This isn't Timoleague or Stonehaven," he continued, anticipating a disappointment. "It's all new."

He was concerned Mother would compare their new farm to more established communities. This won't be easy he thought.

As they turned off the road into the farm, Robert glanced at his mother, bracing for harsh words. She kept a straight face as she gazed upon her new home.

"It's nice," she said, trying to remain positive. "I was expecting something more like Matthew's house, but this will do."

Robert had prepared himself for her first reaction and didn't respond. At least she didn't say anything negative about all the tree stumps surrounding the house, he thought.

"There's plenty to do inside Mother," Robert said. "The house needs a woman's touch."

Mother was right about one thing. The house will do. It had to.

"What's it like inside?" Rebecca asked.

"It's simple," Robert claimed. "But with all of us together, we can make it a home."

He knew the house didn't meet his family's expectations, but no one could take his sense of accomplishment away. Deep inside, Robert would let their first reaction eat away at him. On the surface, he stood tall.

Thomas was the first to enter the front door and immediately changed the mood. Delighted in seeing the large stove in the middle of the main room, he couldn't hold back.

"You did this?" Thomas asked, amazed at his older brother. "You built all this?"

"Yes, with the help of neighbors and friends," Robert said. "Let me get the fire started while you unload the cart. We'll all feel better in a warm house."

Before long, the family huddled around the stove, delighted in the blanket of heat created by the burning wood. It was good to have everyone here, Robert thought. Good to be together inside their new home before the winter set in. A second winter would test the farmhouse and Mother's resolve for Bay Chaleur.

"My bones feel cold," Mother complained. "It's a damp cold, different from Stonehaven."

There was nothing Robert could say to change her mind. Mother was convinced living in Eel River was colder than Stonehaven.

"We'll need to be strong," Robert said.

He couldn't change the weather. He just needed to let his mother complain. They had endured the journey to Bay Chaleur, and as far as he was concerned, nothing would send them back to Ireland.

The stove kept the house comfortable and Mother started to add her touch to the four rooms. Basic household chores took time, keeping everyone busy and reduced the time to complain. At least that's what Robert thought.

January proved to be the most difficult month for cold temperatures, forcing the family to stay indoors as much as possible. The snowfall came in waves during the month of February, drifting as high as the roof by the beginning of March.

As the weather warmed and the wind stopped creating squalls of snow, Thomas and Rebecca found sledding as the perfect escape. The steep bank to the river was exhilarating on the way down but a slow walk back to their starting point. Giggles turned to laughter each afternoon when the two children grabbed a few extra shingles from the barn and headed to the bank. The shingles made a perfect sled adding to their mischief and giggles.

On a warm day in April, the children's laughter could be heard down the river, all the way to the cove. But suddenly the laughter stopped, creating a silence soon followed by screams. The screams bellowed from Rebecca as she watched Thomas slide over the thawing ice and fall into the cold Eel River. She reached for his coat, anything to grab, but he was well beyond the length of her arms. Without thinking, Rebecca laid down on the thinning ice and inched her body toward the hole Thomas had created. She reached into the icy water, pulling her brother out with a strength that appeared from nowhere.

The two cold, wet and exhausted children made their way up the bank toward the house. Thomas shivered as Rebecca burst through the door and yelled for her older brother. Mother heard the commotion and moved toward the children, knocking over a small table as she turned.

"Dear Thomas," she cried. "What happened?"

As Rebecca described the details, Mother removed Thomas' clothing.

"Heat up some water, Robert," she said. "We need to warm up his body."

The remainder of the day at the Blacknell household was focused on Thomas. He recovered from the trauma of the day, but never forgot his first winter in Eel River.

17

Murchie Daughters

Mama stared at John's chair for weeks after he left for Catherine.

"He's not coming back here to live," Papa told her. "He's down the road at the Stewart farm.

It didn't matter, Mama didn't have her boy to talk to every morning. It was more than an empty chair in the house, it was a hole in her heart. John occupied a special place and no one, but no one could fill it. Papa didn't see it that way. He missed John's help in the barn and out in the fields since the work had doubled with John's departure.

With John on his own and Mama preoccupied with sadness, Liza and Janet discovered lives beyond the

Murchies. Donald Campbell, a neighbor on the east side of the Cook farm, became a regular visitor. Donald found Liza interesting enough to stop by the farm every day. Like clockwork, Liza patiently waited for Donald to walk into the kitchen for a cup of tea or a glass of water around mid morning. She wouldn't dare tell her mother about her new interest. Liza didn't think Mama would understand. Despite keeping it quiet, it wasn't long before Mama was asking questions about the Campbell family, especially when Liza was out of the house.

"He's the young Campbell fella from Arran," Papa said, annoyed with his wife's questions. "He's a nice boy. The family farmed in Shiskine."

Papa shook his head, trying to forget how much his wife meddled in everything. Mama knew they were from Arran, but that wasn't the point. She wanted a nice Arran boy for Liza and didn't know Donald's family very well. She needed to learn more about them and it was clear she wouldn't be getting the information from Papa.

Life was unraveling for Elizabeth Murchie. Her son was living down the road, and now her two oldest daughters were courting young Colborne men. Donald Campbell was the easy problem compared to Janet's interest. According to Mrs. McPherson, one of their Irish farmhands, Edward Good, was spending far too much time flirting with Janet. Mrs. McPherson's report sent Mama into a frenzy, increasing the hand wringing and worry. Papa was expected to discourage his daughter from Edward.

"What's it matter if he's Irish?" Papa asked, brushing the request aside. "If he treats Janet well and can provide, what difference does it make if he's from Ireland?"

It was time to meet more Irish people, he told her. Time to do more than worry and stare at an empty chair. She was acting foolish, their daughters would find their own way. Hadn't she? He grew frustrated with her constant hand wringing. The farm needed her attention more than her daughters.

Margaret watched the arguments and courting with open eyes. As long as Mama was focused on the others, she left Margaret alone. Alone to read or visit Miss Brown at the MacAlister farm. That was all well and good, but she couldn't ignore her father's plea for help, and gradually without prompting Margaret picked up some of John's responsibilities. Papa was right. The farm could use more hands in the fields.

As the summer approached, a new family from Arran arrived in Colborne and Papa invited them to stay on the Murchie farm until their house was ready. Archibald had helped the Murchie family and now it was their turn, he told everyone.

The Taylor family was from Bennan and brought word about Isabella and Neil to Papa. The family situation had changed and the MacNairs would be leaving Arran in a few months. Just in time for winter, Papa thought, but it didn't matter, he was happy to have Isabella realize her dream too.

When the Taylors landed at the Murchie farm, Mama was completely occupied with Mrs. Taylor. Mama was the expert now, sharing her knowledge of Bay Chaleur and the adopted Arran customs. It was the right distraction for Mama. An empty chair had been filled and Mama had someone to talk to.

While the two women were developing their new relationship, Mama failed to notice an attraction growing between James, the Taylor's eldest son and Margaret. It wasn't long before she sensed James was spending far too much time staring at her daughter. James couldn't help himself, he was drawn to Margaret's red hair, blue eyes and enthusiasm. There was something special about her, he thought.

James had more challenges than Mama however. His father expected all of his children to help with the house, so each morning he walked his children up the coastal road to their new farm. Clearing, cutting and filling the gaps between the logs, the cycle of building a pioneer home continued.

At supper time the hunger competed with the exhaustion from the day's work. A few polite words after the meal, signaled the upcoming well deserved sleep. James always found time to wink or stare in Margaret's direction during supper, while Mama kept an eye on his every move.

One evening after the supper meal had finished, James casually approached Margaret.

"Meet me in the barn," he said, walking toward the door.

Margaret blushed and looked away, not wanting James to see the redness in her face. She couldn't believe she'd have a chance to talk to James alone, without her meddling mother. Margaret thought James was the most handsome boy she had ever laid her eyes on. She waited until Mama wasn't in sight and slipped out the door.

Margaret raced to the barn with the innocence of a young girl. The darkness inside didn't slow her anticipation as she tried to find James after opening the door.

"Are you looking for James?" Mama asked, moving toward Margaret.

Margaret felt the blood drain from her face at the sound of her mother's voice and the sight of Mama holding James by his right ear.

"Mama, why are you here?" she asked, afraid other words would escape into the night's air.

"I've been watching the two of you for several days now," Mama said. "It must stop. James, you'll be expected to stay at your new farm. You're not welcome here any longer."

And with those harsh words, Mama marched James back to the house. Margaret stood in the dark for a painful few minutes, trying to decide what to do next. She couldn't understand why her mother was so upset, so she hurried back to find out.

"There'll be time for boys," Mama said, as Margaret walked into the kitchen. "You're too young."

Margaret still didn't understand why her mother was waiting in the barn. She was certain it was more than meddling, but didn't know why. Over the next few weeks she avoided the subject and spent time helping Papa in the fields. It was the perfect escape from her mother.

The Taylors were disappointed in James, and accepted his banishment to the Taylor farm without argument. For the church women in Colborne it was gossip, something to talk about. Elizabeth Murchie had banished the young Taylor fella they all said, wondering what happened. Eventually the story was replaced by other gossip but it left a soft mark on the Taylor family.

At the end of October, Isabella and Neil arrived with their four children pushing the limits of the Murchie house. The Taylor farm wasn't quite ready but Mrs. Taylor took advantage of the opportunity to leave. She continued to feel the sting from James' behavior and knew the distance would help the two families resume their former relationship.

Margaret also welcomed the change. The tension had increased since the barn episode and Mama needed a new distraction. Isabella would bring new stories about Arran and change Mama's mood. At least that was Margaret's wish. The family was constantly changing and she wanted her old mother back. Not the meddling and worrying one.

It would be different with the MacNairs in the house, they were family. Papa's family. Excitement filled every room the first weekend after Liza and Janet came home. They expected their arrival but it was still a surprise when Isabella was found standing in the kitchen. The bedtime hour came and went as the women in the house shared stories about the past several months.

Margaret listened with both ears as Isabella described the recent departures from Arran. More families were leaving she told Mama, leaving for Upper and Lower Canada too. Margaret thought about wanting to stay on Arran. She realized she would never go back. Arran had changed too.

As the fall weather displayed its last gasp of beauty on the bay, the MacNair family surveyed their new farmland. There was much work to be done but Papa knew the weather would not cooperate.

"Wait until the hard frost," he told Neil. "The frozen ground is easier to work on."

Neil took Papa's word. He had little choice, Papa had the expertise Neil needed.

John and Catherine visited the farm the following Sunday afternoon. Word had quickly spread about the MacNairs in Colborne and John wanted his aunt to meet Catherine. There's more to this visit than meeting Isabella and Neil, Margaret thought. They must have news to share, since John hasn't visited in months and the family barely saw him since the marriage. It was as though they had traveled from Arran when Mama and Papa greeted the two newlyweds at the door. Mama was excited to have her boy back in the house, barely containing her emotion every time John spoke.

Margaret waited for John to mention the barn episode, knowing he would remind her of the Eden and the issue with the sailor. But the afternoon passed without a word. Maybe John didn't know about it, she thought dropping her guard to watch her mother's reaction to John's stories about the Stewart farm. Catherine sat patiently, politely nodding when the conversation turned to her. Mama always kept her eyes on John, never looking directly at her daughter-in-law. It wasn't evident if she liked her and chances were good, she harbored negative feelings for taking her son away.

Everyone shared stories of the past few months. John captivated Papa with stories of his new farm and the harvest. Mama finally asked the question everyone wanted to ask.

"When will you have a child?" she said.

John blushed and looked at Catherine.

"We're expecting a baby now," he said, reaching for Catherine's hand. "We wanted you to know, so we came to tell you before the church ladies shared the news."

Mama stood up and hugged both of them.

"How wonderful," Mama said, smiling and trying not to cry. "How wonderful for all of us."

This would be the first Murchie grandchild and if Mama could have her way, there would be more.

The conversation was all about babies after that point. Liza and Janet had no trouble sharing their recent experiences being domestics. Margaret had little to contribute. She tried to change the conversation, but no one heard her or bothered to listen. For the first time in a very long time, she was an outsider.

18

Mother Blacknell

The first harvest in Eel River was a celebration for the Blacknell family. For Robert it was more. The new potatoes and oats were proof of the rich soil the farm was built on. It was also the bounty of Robert's hard work over the past two years.

Sarah was home, arriving at the beginning of the summer with Matthew and his family. Mother had her oldest daughter by her side and an opportunity to entertain. No one could tell Mother wished for her old home in Timoleague, as she proudly showed her visitors Robert's accomplishments.

The family settled into the routine of farming with the addition of sheep, goats and a few cows. Robert balanced his time between running the farm and clearing the trees. The commitment to improve the land was still a promise of his grant.

The leisure time the family enjoyed in Ireland wasn't a part of their regular day. There wasn't time. Establishing the farm took every waking hour.

Mother was proud of Robert and knew his father would be too. He had become the man his father expected. A man who cared of his family. But she had concerns about Robert giving up his own future. He needed his own family, she thought. It wasn't right. She had to do something about it, but how to find a nice Protestant Irish girl in this new community. She decided to inquire at the next church community gathering.

It didn't take long for Robert to learn about his mother's actions. Sarah whispered in his ear about the church ladies and he grew furious.

"Mother, I don't need the burden of a wife," Robert said, trying to remain calm.

"Burden?" Mother said, pretending to be shocked.

"Yes, a burden," Robert calmly replied.

He knew better than to raise his voice. The conversation would end quickly if he added an octave to the sound coming out of his mouth.

"I've Rebecca and Sarah to care for," he continued. "I want to be here for them until they're married and on their own."

Robert expected to provide for his sisters, filling the role of their father.

"I've no time for picnics or dances," he said.

In his own mind, his goals were clear and a wife would be a distraction.

Robert politely asked his mother to stop interfering. Mother nodded but knew it was out of her hands. The church ladies were in motion and many of the young local women were actively seeking his attention.

"Why can't you be open minded about this?" Mother asked. "There are several women you should meet. Why not attend a few church social events with me?"

Robert could feel his body temperature increase. He didn't want his mother to know how upset he was getting, so he lowered his voice.

"There's too much to do on this farm," Robert said, trying to change the focus of his disinterest.

Mother was persistent. She had promised a few of the church ladies and didn't want it to reflect poorly on her.

"It's important to me," she said. "What harm could come to enjoying the companionship and attention of a young woman? Just enjoy yourself. You've been working so hard, for so long."

Robert reluctantly agreed, he was tired of arguing with his mother. She wouldn't stop.

"Alright, I'll go to the next dance," he said. "But that's it. You must stop."

He didn't show Mother his anger. She had agreed to the voyage, and the simple house. She had given up a pleasant life in Ireland. He could manage this.

The monthly church dance was a few weeks away giving Robert time to think about his promise. This was absolutely not in his plan. He knew he had too much responsibility with his family and the daily farm chores. Robert needed an excuse or a way to avoid the pressures of attending the silly dance.

The time passed quickly and before long, Robert was facing the church dance the next day. Over the past week, he tried to avoid the topic with Mother but she was insistent.

"You need to find a wife," Mother declared at breakfast, not giving up. "You need to think about your own future," she would say in the evening after the late meal.

When she was more thoughtful, she would thank her son with words, but never changed her focus on the dance.

"You've taken care of all of us for so many years, not only here, but back in Ireland," she said the night before the dance. "Now it's time for Robert."

Robert was not interested, but Mother didn't stop. Why was she so adamant? For the second time, he agreed to go, tired of the constant nagging. It was difficult to say no to Mother and he felt obligated. As a son, he hadn't developed the ability to stand up to her, at least not yet. Perhaps a stronger man would have prevailed, he thought as he headed off to the community hall in Charlo, a settlement near the cove. He planned to leave an hour after arrival, satisfying both his mother's demand and his own need for sleep.

The evening in Charlo unfolded beyond Robert's plans. The hall was filled with most of the single men and women from the surrounding area. Robert wasn't aware of the number of young people living in the communities around Eel River. It became as clear as the Bay Chaleur night sky, he had been working without looking up and around.

The evening was filled with flowing conversation and polite introductions. Scotland and Ireland were the homelands, Robert learned. Many were from the Isle of Arran, the home of John Murchie, the young man from the Bathurst dock. He wondered if he would see John among the group.

He looked around the hall with John in mind and was distracted by what he saw. There were several attractive women attending and he was drawn to a few familiar looking faces. He thought how Mother would enjoy hearing about all the young women, so he focused on their appearance. Mother was certain to ask questions the next morning, so he worked on his response. As he scanned the room his inner thoughts were elsewhere, thinking about all the work waiting for him the next day. The stumps that needed removal and the barn that needed cleaning. It never ended.

Once Robert felt the time was right, satisfying his mother's request, he decided to leave. As he headed toward the door, he noticed a young woman, a familiar face. He paused.

"Is your family from the Bandon area in Ireland?" he asked.

"Yes, my family's from Kinsale and I know your sisters," she replied. "Connelly is my family name. You may know my father, Matthew."

Robert was surprised. He didn't know the Connelly family had decided to leave and journey to New Brunswick. It was yet another sign of keeping his head focused on the farm.

"Yes," Robert said. "I know your family and your Kinsale farm. It's nice to meet you—I'm sorry I didn't get your name."

"It's Mary," she said. "It's wonderful to meet you too, Robert. I was hoping to see you here, at the dance."

Robert smiled and continued to move toward the door. Mary started to move toward him.

"Please stay," she said. "We must have a dance before you leave."

Robert was polite and waited for the music to start again. He took Mary's hand and they headed to the dance floor. Mary couldn't believe her luck in seeing Robert. She had her eye on him back in Ireland and now she was on the dance floor next to him. So much to take in.

The music ended and Robert walked Mary back to her seat. Once she was seated, Robert thanked her for making the evening so special and excused himself.

"I must leave," he said. "The farm is waiting for me and the animals don't take to my dancing and staying out late."

It reminded him of cousin Matthew and his inability to take the Murchie children to Colborne.

Mary smiled and thanked Robert for the dance. She knew better than to ask for more of his time. Robert was a special man, according to the church ladies.

Outside the dance hall, Robert headed toward the horse and carriage, oblivious to someone calling his name. Eventually he turned to see Samuel Dixon standing in front of him.

"Samuel," Robert declared. "When did your family land on Bay Chaleur?"

"A few weeks ago," he answered, excited by the chance meeting. "I was hoping to find Sarah here, but it wasn't to be."

Robert and Samuel stood by the carriage for several minutes exchanging information about their families. For his part, Robert kept it brief, not knowing how

Sarah felt about him since the departure. That was not the case for Samuel. He was flowing with stories and updates, eager to see Sarah and pick things up exactly where they'd left off.

Robert headed home filled with thoughts about the evening. The list of chores was temporarily pushed aside for his sister and the conversation with Samuel. He would tell Sarah everything and let her decide. It might stop Mother from encouraging these dances, he thought, smiling as he rode along the cove. He would leave out the part about Mary Connelly. Something was different about their dance. He felt a strange attraction for Mary he couldn't describe.

19

Expanding Settlements

Over the next two years the Colborne and Eel River Settlement communities continued to grow. Fewer settlers arrived from Arran than in previous years, closing a chapter in the island's migration history. But Bay Chaleur became home to a new group of immigrants. Large numbers of families from Ireland, the ones who chose to leave as conditions on the island forced many Catholics to emigrate.

The new immigrants and families found their way to Bay Chaleur as the economy boomed with the province's timber trade. A great fire along the Miramichi River a decade earlier, forced shipbuilding and logging to move north along its shores. The Bay

Chaleur forest stood tall, inviting tradesmen and immigrants ready to work.

The Murchie family also added to the growth in Colborne with the birth of James, John and Catherine's new baby. John remained true to the Arran tradition of naming his first son after his own father. Mama was pleased with a second James Murchie in the family, proudly mentioning it in every conversation. Mama became the perfect grandmother, finding ways to help without getting in the way and making regular trips to the Stewart farm. The name of the farm was a constant question for Mama.

"Do you think the farm will ever be known as the Murchie farm," she asked John.

"Does it matter?" he replied.

John was too busy to worry about things he considered trivial.

"It would be nice," Mama stated softly before dropping the topic. She knew John had his own farm and that's what mattered.

John had no intention to create problems over the name of the farm. It would always be the Stewart farm to him.

In Eel River Settlement, there were few changes to the Blacknell family. According to Mother, Samuel Dixon wasn't worthy of Sarah's attention and shuddered when she heard he was living on Bay Chaleur. Mother was reluctant to let Sarah become a young woman, claiming Sarah was still needed at home.

Sarah received monthly letters from Samuel not long after his conversation with Robert. The distance and difficulty in travel made it impossible for the two to meet, but Sarah knew the day would come. Perhaps the next social dance, she thought after collecting the most recent letter at the Postmaster's home. Instead of arguing with Mother, Sarah kept performing the household chores expected of her. The letters were her secret.

Things were about to change as the farm was taking shape and no longer needed the continuous pace of clearing and improving. There were over twenty acres cleared and the crops were more than enough for the Blacknell family. Mother decided it was time for her children to enjoy a social life, similar to the one they had in Timoleague. Social activities, beyond the monthly church gatherings, would signal the Blacknell farm was doing well.

Along Bay Chaleur's coastal road, the number of farms revealed a growing population from Dalhousie to Bathurst. After several years of painstaking work to build houses and improve the land, a glimmer of free time appeared. Without trees to cut and logs to take to the sawmill, the families found time between the planting and harvesting seasons for social gatherings.

Despite this growth, the Colborne families continued to share their pastor with the communities around Bathurst. Reverend Caldwell travelled regularly up and down the coastal road, holding monthly services based on his schedule.

As the Colborne community of Arran settlers grew, talk of having their own pastor grew with it. The local church was built in 1834 as the home for monthly services but it was empty most of the time and suited for services, not events.

The freedom from clearing pushed the families to want more, more than an empty space. They wanted their own pastor and a place to regularly meet and celebrate. The wanted a hall. A place for everyone to gather for events beyond the pastor's sermon.

The sentiment rose as the families found more time to spend together. Reverend Caldwell met with the community the following summer and agreed to take their request back to the church officials. There wasn't a need to worry about the land, the community told him, the McLeans had offered part of their farm for the building.

At the November sermon, the congregation hung on every word Reverend Caldwell spoke, waiting for news about the church ruling. Toward the end of the hour, he paused.

"Oh yes, I almost forgot to mention," he casually said. "The officials of our great church have agreed to build the Colborne Community Hall."

He watched as a wave of excitement rippled from the pulpit to the back pew.

"And the kindness of the McLeans will make this possible in the coming new year," he said with a wide grin.

The words hung in the air for a minute before the congregation erupted. Everyone thanked each other and sought out the McLeans for their generosity. The Reverend wasn't done and continued to speak after everyone settled back into their seats.

"We'll need to work together to build this great hall," he said.

The Colborne community knew the church didn't have much money and everyone was willing to contribute their labor.

"The building will require more than your time," he told the congregation. "May I suggest an afternoon dance with the surrounding areas to help raise additional funds?"

Not a naysayer could be found. Mama volunteered along with Mrs. Taylor to start planning the event. Margaret should help too, Mama thought. No one seemed to notice the Reverend hadn't mentioned anything about a full time pastor. There was too much excitement over the hall and the upcoming dance.

And so, the planning began. Mama thought it would be the perfect event for Margaret. She could meet new families, and find one in need of a domestic.

"Why'd you think planning the event is perfect for me?" Margaret asked, after her mother introduced the idea at breakfast.

Mama was in the middle of an explanation when Margaret interrupted.

"Why not Janet or Liza?" She asked. "They need to meet new people."

Janet was never involved in family activities over the past several months and Margaret wanted to remind her mother of her sister's absence.

"Liza and Janet have avoided all family events for the past year," Margaret declared, looking directly at her mother.

She decided to include Liza, to increase her side of the argument. Mama would have none of it and pushed the conversation.

"Janet's leaving for some type of nursing, some training in the winter," she replied, knowing the tension would rise with this announcement, but it was time for Margaret to hear it.

"She won't have time and Liza is helping Donald with his family," she added. "It's time for you to do more."

The truth was out. Janet would have her way and become a nurse. It had been in the whisper voices for the past few weeks.

"Why can't you just speak up when things are changing?" Margaret asked her mother. "Why's everything a big whisper?"

Mama knew Margaret always compared herself to her older sisters. It was natural in a household of girls. She wished they could send Margaret to secondary school but it was not possible.

"We whisper because no one knows how you'll react," Mama said. "It's time to stop acting like a child."

Margaret stood still, unable to find the words to answer her mother. She didn't think she was behaving like a child. In her own mind, she was acting like a young woman. She asked questions, tried to learn more, confronted problems. What was she missing?

Mama turned toward the stove, suggesting the conversation was over. But Margaret didn't want it to end. She had just heard about Janet, but that didn't matter. It was Mama's words that mattered. They cut deep and stopped Margaret. Mama remained quiet, another signal for Margaret to stop talking.

Margaret headed toward the door, the fresh air always brought fresh thinking. As she closed the door behind her, it dawned on her. Janet had saved enough money to attend school. Janet had made nursing school her own reality. It wasn't Mama holding her back.

The next morning Margaret approached her mother with a new attitude. If Mama wanted her to do something, she would do it. That included the planning activity she asked about yesterday. She had seen her sisters behave this way and was frequently surprised by her mother's response. It was time to stop arguing with Mama.

"Mama, I was thinking about the May event overnight," Margaret mentioned as she walked into the kitchen. "I'll help you if that's what you want."

Mama wasn't sure what happened, standing over the stove and staring back at her daughter. Margaret is so fickle, she thought, accepting the offer without question.

"Wonderful," she said. "I'll tell Mrs. Taylor today."

Margaret left the room smiling, yet wondered why it worked so well. She didn't know it then, but planning for the May event was exactly what Margaret needed. Her social circle had been small, consisting of family friends, school mates and Miss Brown. She would have the opportunity to meet new friends from outside Colborne.

The first meeting was scheduled two weeks out at the McLean farm. As Margaret walked into the kitchen, she recognized Sarah Blacknell from the Eden immediately.

"Aren't you Sarah Blacknell?" she asked.

Sarah looked across the room and smiled at Margaret.

"Yes, how've you been Margaret?" Sarah said, recognizing the red hair and piercing blue eyes. Margaret inquired about Rebecca and her adjustment to life in New Brunswick. Sarah shared the past few years, trying as best she could to hit the parts that would be of interest to Margaret.

"Rebecca keeps the books for the farm," Sarah said. "She has excellent arithmetic skills and Robert let's her do it all. You remember my brother Robert?"

How could anyone forget Robert, Margaret thought.

"Your brother saved us," Margaret claimed. "My family is indebted to him."

Sarah blushed as she heard Margaret's claim.

"Indeed, Robert is special," Sarah replied.

As they finished sharing the events of the past, James Taylor entered the back door and walked over to join them. Sufficient time had passed since James' barn episode and the Murchie family had accepted his apology. Everyone makes mistakes, Mama claimed, putting the issue to bed.

"Margaret, may I have the pleasure of an introduction to this attractive young woman?" he asked, examining Sarah Blacknell's fine features.

"This is Sarah Blacknell from Eel River," Margaret replied. "Her family crossed the Atlantic with John and me."

Margaret felt a pang of jealousy that started in her arms and ran through her entire body. Why was James making a fuss over Sarah, she thought?

"Nice to meet you, Sarah," James said and quickly got to the point of his visit. "I'm here to collect my mother. Do you know where she might be?"

The girls pointed to the sitting room and he started to walk away.

"You must save me a dance Miss Blacknell," he said. And with that request, he disappeared into the sitting area, leaving Sarah, barely able to speak.

Sarah blushed not knowing how to respond. She wanted to see Samuel at the dance and now James Taylor was making her blush. This was all new.

Margaret tried not to let James' words bother her, but it was too late. A strange pang of jealousy overcame her thinking. Margaret didn't know what to say to Sarah Blacknell.

As the planning meetings inched closer to the event, the excitement continued to rise. A date had been selected for May. The perfect month for Bay Chaleur. It was too cold to plant but warm enough for an afternoon gathering.

When Reverend Caldwell spoke in February, he thanked the committee and set the stage for an afternoon for all the families to enjoy.

"There's much to be thankful for," he said. "And we'll celebrate soon."

Margaret counted down the days to the event. She would soon get a chance to dance with James Taylor but something bothered her about his attraction to Sarah Blacknell. Her thoughts went back to the barn incident. Did Mama know more about James than she shared that day?

20

Outside Work

The New Brunswick timber industry continued to attract immigrants from across the Atlantic in search of work and a better life. Ships similar to the Eden regularly sailed with their timber cargo eastbound and paying passengers heading west. For a time, it was the perfect business for any ship owner.

As the market demand shifted towards finished wood products, northern New Brunswick was ready. Sawmills appeared along the many rivers and streams flowing into Bay Chaleur. The rivers proved to be the perfect conveyer, bringing the cut logs from deep inside the forest to the nearest mill. The water's work wasn't complete until it powered the giant saw changing the timber forever.

Many Colborne farmers liked the idea of working at the sawmill, especially during the spring timber drive. The mills paid well and the extra money went a long way for each family. Fishing on Bay Chaleur was another option for additional money, but few ventured out into the water, due to the potential for storms. Perhaps the Atlantic crossing was too fresh in their minds.

Unlike fishing, no one talked about the dark side of the sawmill. Their voices only shared the positive. When Archibald reminded everyone with stories about injuries to his son from the local mill, his words fell on deaf ears.

"Charlie lost two fingers cutting logs last year," Archibald told anyone who would listen. "There aren't enough safety concerns."

Archibald wanted his friends and neighbors to know. He wanted them to hear about the dangers.

"Charlie's not the only one," he added. "He told me many stories of men losing fingers and arms from the machinery."

No one stopped to listen. They wanted the extra money and to reduce their dependence on farming. Many of the men went to the sawmills with the full knowledge of the dark side, and chose to ignore it. They could manage their own safety, they told Archibald when he started another story.

The mill was a place like no other. It was noisy and filled with a fresh smell of sawdust. And it had a sense of teamwork. Strong masculine men working together, changing trees into planks. Transforming nature with their hands and a water-powered saw.

The sawmill in Bell Dune tugged at John. He inquired about working and was hired on the spot. After a few short weeks at the mill, John found an excitement he didn't have on the farm. There was camaraderie among all the men. They looked out for each other and kept everything positive despite the challenging and difficult work.

The mill was hot in the summer, but the draw to be with the other men was compelling. John found himself working three days a week while farming. The Stewart farm was doing well enough to have a few hired hands so John was confident nothing would fall apart at home while he was at the sawmill. He also brought home more money working just three days a week. More than the farm gave the family from selling their excess hay or turnips.

Eventually Papa decided to try the mill. John had encouraged him to work at least one day a week with him. It would help the family, John insisted. Margaret was old enough to work the farm with her father and she had a mind for it, he reminded Papa. He saw her entrenched at home, so he knew she would welcome a day without Papa ordering her around.

Papa immediately felt what John enjoyed about the mill. All the men became friends. They operated like a large family, a family of boasting strong men. Soon John and Papa were sharing mill stories at every family gathering. Generally, they were stories about new mill workers and the mistakes they made.

"Why do you make fun of the young men," Mama asked not understanding how men behave together.

Papa just shook his head.

"It's what everyone does," he said. "It's a ritual when you join. Each man has to prove himself."

Papa looked at John and they both broke out laughing. No one else in the room understood what they were laughing at.

Margaret looked at the two men and started to laugh.

"Mama, you should be laughing too," she said. "I haven't heard Papa laugh this hard since we arrived here."

Mama cracked a smile but didn't laugh. The rituals didn't make any sense to her. What did they prove?

Margaret thought about her mother's reaction later that evening. When everyone had left and Margaret was alone with her mother, she tried to understand.

"Why didn't you laugh this afternoon?" she asked.

"I'm worried about Papa," Mama said. "The mill's hard work and he isn't getting any younger."

Margaret was confused.

"Farming's hard work," she said.

Mama nodded, accepting that both the mill and the farm required the same level of labor from Papa.

"I know, but this seems different and your father's working with a bunch of young fellas," she said. "And it makes him act younger and stronger than he really is."

There was something to Mama's worry, Margaret thought. Since John and Papa started working together in the mill, things definitely changed. They had a different relationship. It wasn't father and son anymore. But Margaret couldn't quite describe it.

21

The Afternoon Dance

The anticipation surprised everyone as the dance grew closer. All along the bay, it was the main topic of conversation. The nearby communities of Eel River and Dalhousie also had it on the tips of their tongues. For many families it was simply a time to celebrate the results of their hard work over the past few years. Others saw it as time to get together with friends and neighbors. The young ones saw it as time away from chores and farming.

Whatever it meant, the idea that started as a way to raise funds for a new hall, had become the celebration of the year. At the time of the announcement, it seemed straight forward. Invite a few families, get the local boys with their instruments, bring a special recipe to share and have a good time. It quickly became bigger than all of that. The families had transformed the Bay Chaleur wilderness into farms and the afternoon dance became a welcomed diversion. An escape from all the hard work and a chance to share new stories.

Everyone agreed, May would be the perfect month. For the farmers, the event was a guilt-free day. The soil wasn't ready to be turned for planting. It was mud season and only a foolish farmer would plant in the earth still wet from the winter thaw. The day was a break from the routine each family had come to accept since their arrival on Bay Chaleur.

As the day grew closer, the sun cooperated with its high angle and longer hours. Finally, the day arrived and Reverend Caldwell stood proud as he greeted everyone on their way into the barn. A steady stream of families dressed in their worship clothes arrived from all over Bay Chaleur.

"Welcome to Colborne Parish," Reverend Caldwell said, as he greeted each family. "Thank you for bringing your special food and a donation for the future hall."

There were popular dishes and recipes from Arran, reminding the former islanders of events back home. The Irish families shared breads and sweets made from homeland recipes placing them on tables set up for the event. Years of cooking traditions and baking expertise blended together in a single afternoon.

"It's nice to try something new," Catherine Murchie declared after eating a few of the Irish breads. She tried to get John's attention by pointing at all the food, but he was too busy chasing baby James to notice.

The hum inside the barn increased as more families arrived to share their food and tales of the past few years. In all, fifty families attended the event, creating a special day for Colborne Parish.

Margaret entered the barn with one purpose in mind. She wanted a dance with James Taylor and rapidly scanned the open area of the barn the minute she entered. As she searched left and right, she paused when her eyes came upon friends she hadn't seen in a while. She kept looking, there would be time to catch up after her dance.

When several scans, didn't reveal his dark hair among the crowd, she weaved her way to the far end of the barn with her two sisters following. Turning to face the entrance while standing among friends from school, she waited. Liza and Janet tried to make sense of her weaving through the crowd.

"What're you doing?" Janet asked her sister. "This is silly, we're walking all over the place without talking to anyone.

"Don't you want someone to ask you to dance?" Janet asked, trying to point out that Margaret wasn't courting anyone.

Margaret marveled at her two sisters and how settled they were with their lives. They weren't looking to dance with anyone, knowing their young men would soon join the party. Their lives were complete.

A few changes were on the horizon with Janet's training in Dalhousie alongside midwives and nurses. Everything in her life was falling into place, exactly as she planned it.

Liza, was completely different. She was waiting to get married, putting in the time as a domestic with the Cook family. Boring, Margaret thought. Why would anyone wait to get married? She would never wait, it didn't make any sense. There was more to life than domestic work and waiting.

Donald arrived first and gradually made his way toward Liza, smiling as he approached her. Margaret thought he was a nice man. He cared for Liza and they made a nice couple. But there wasn't much excitement between them.

Janet was putting Edward through his paces and he went along. She loved nursing and he loved her. That was that. Edward would see Janet when she had time for him. With the domestic work and a future in nursing school, they rarely saw each other. Mama might get her way on this one, Margaret thought.

She continued to scan the crowd for James, while pretending to be in a conversation with Donald. She looked directly over his shoulder as he talked about something she didn't bother to hear. She nodded when he finished, hoping that was the correct response.

As she swept her eyes across the barn for another scan, she came across a face that was so familiar, yet she couldn't place him. He was tall with light brown hair and standing next to an older woman who also looked familiar. Where had she seen them before? They were animated in conversation with the family next to them but where or how did she know them? Arran? Who could they be?

She tried to place them in her familiar settings. If it wasn't Arran, then where? Suddenly it dawned on her, and she broke out smiling. It was the Blacknell family from the Eden. She had sailed across the Atlantic with them. It was Robert and his mother. But where was Sarah? If Sarah had been standing with them, it would have been obvious. Margaret looked everywhere around Robert. Would she recognize Rebecca? It had been five years since the voyage. Margaret continued to scan the hall. Settling her eyes on two well dressed and attractive women walking towards Robert. One was definitely Sarah. And Rebecca? Oh, how she had changed.

Without hesitation Margaret moved away from her sisters and headed toward the young women.

"Are you Rebecca?" She asked before standing next to her.

She was too excited to wait for an answer.

"I'm Margaret Murchie, from the Eden," she said. "Do you remember me?"

Instantly, Rebecca gasped and answered in a loud shriek that bounced off the barn's rafters and fell upon the families standing below. The barn went silent and everyone stood still, not knowing what was next. When they saw the two young women embrace and giggle, the conversation started as quickly as it had stopped.

"Yes, yes I am," Rebecca said. "I hoped to see you here. Sarah told me about seeing you at the meetings."

She stood back, holding Margaret's hands by her sides.

"You look so lovely Margaret," she said. "All grown up and all. Come with me, you must see Mother and Robert."

It happened so fast, and before Margaret realized what she had started, both girls were pulling her towards Robert. When Robert laid his eyes on

Margaret, he couldn't believe what a beautiful young woman she had become.

"Margaret, it's a pleasure to see you," Robert said, pausing with each word. "My how you've changed since our voyage. Is John here and your family? I would enjoy meeting your sisters and mother too."

Robert was surprised at how the words kept flowing out of his mouth. He glanced over at his mother and tried to pull her into the conversation.

"Do you remember Margaret Murchie?" he asked. "Look at how she has grown up," Robert said.

Mother wanted Robert to spend his time with the young Irish girls she had her sights on. A conversation with Margaret Murchie would not do. She tried to be polite, knowing Robert would be upset if she wasn't. Mother smiled and gave Margaret a nod.

"Lovely young girl, you've become," she said. "Now if you'll excuse me, I must talk with Elizabeth Connelly. Robert, please join me shortly."

Robert was embarrassed by his mother's abrupt words. He had no intention of joining her now or later in the afternoon. Pushing aside his mother's behavior, he engaged in a longer conversation with Margaret, He wanted to learn everything about their farm, Colborne Parish and the family's adjustment to Bay Chaleur. Margaret for her part, was surprised how much she enjoyed talking with Robert. As she told the Murchie story, she realized how she much had changed and how Colborne was now her home.

"Do you miss Ireland?" she asked Robert.

"There are many things I miss about Ireland," he told her. "But there is little time to think about what I left behind."

Margaret thought it was a sensible answer.

"I missed Arran when I first arrived," she said. "It's become a distant memory now."

The words almost startled her. A distant memory after five years, seemed impossible, she thought.

There wasn't time to think about Arran as Robert continued to share the Eel River winters, the blizzards that prevented going outside and the bitter cold wind.

"Archibald told Papa about the winters, but we didn't understand what he meant until the snow and wind arrived," she said.

John joined the small group, excited to see Robert and introduce his young family. There was much to share since the day on the Bathurst dock and both John and Robert filled the air with stories about their farms. John listened but was soon distracted by Margaret as she stared at Robert, hanging on his every word. For once, she wasn't focused on herself.

A few minutes later, James Taylor entered the barn and spotted Margaret's red hair. He headed toward her recognizing Sarah Blacknell standing beside her. The entire group appeared to be telling stories. This will be easy, he thought. Margaret has little patience for boring conversation. He approached the group and interrupted.

"May I have this dance Miss Murchie," he asked, staring into her blue eyes.

Margaret looked at James and smiled, forgetting her original purpose.

"I'm sorry James," she replied. "I'm in the middle of a conversation with the Blacknell family from Ireland. It'll have to be another time, thank you."

James wasn't sure what to do next, and for a minute he looked at his feet. After he pulled his thoughts together, he made eye contact with Sarah and tried his question again. Sarah blushed, and walked to the dance floor with James. Mother was busy with Mrs. Connelly and didn't notice Sarah leave the group. Robert smiled knowing there would be questions later when Mother spotted her daughter.

Sarah left James Taylor and returned to the conversation as Samuel arrived at the barn. She immediately waved to catch his attention, turning bright crimson when he approached her. James shrugged his shoulders and moved to another group. He wasn't sure what happened to Margaret but it didn't matter, there were other young women to dance with.

The afternoon came to a close, despite everyone's wishes for the day to continue. Margaret didn't want to leave the enchantment she felt when the event was over. It was all new to her. Despite missing the dance with James, she thought it was the best afternoon in her life. James Taylor didn't matter.

Before leaving the barn, Robert had the opportunity to meet the rest of John's family. Mama could hardly believe she was meeting the man who saved her children.

"I'm finally getting to meet you," she said, not knowing if she should hug him or shake his hand. "The Murchie family is forever indebted to you."

Robert acknowledged the appreciation and tried to brush it off.

"You would've done the same," he said.

Papa nodded, realizing Robert was right. It was time to move forward, but not forget.

The grey clouds over the Bay didn't change the mood on the ride home or slow the conversation from Margaret.

"Maggie, where are these words and feelings coming from?" Mama asked.

"This is the first time I don't miss Arran," declared Margaret. "There were so many people to see and talk to. For the first time, I realized Colborne is home."

"It wouldn't have anything to do with that man Robert, now would it?" Mama asked, knowing her youngest daughter too well.

Margaret blushed and went quiet for the first time.

The journey back to Eel River was long, but the Blacknell family was giddy from the day's event. Mother was the only person not talking. She was pouting because Robert hadn't danced with any of her chosen Irish girls. Sarah and Rebecca saw their mother's behavior and smiled to themselves. Rebecca leaned over to whisper in Sarah's ear.

"Does Mother think she can choose for Robert," Rebecca said.

"Choose what?" Thomas asked, unsure of the conversation between his sisters.

"Shush," Rebecca insisted.

The two girls laughed at Thomas, then returned to their stories of the afternoon.

"Samuel," Rebecca taunted. "Hmmm…"

Sarah blushed and looked away.

Robert turned around and noticed Thomas shaking his head.

"Girls," he said to Robert. "What's wrong with them?"

Robert didn't try to answer. He was thinking about the afternoon and how beautiful Margaret Murchie had become. He noticed the scowl on Mother's face and smiled to himself. This will be a challenge, but if she wants me to find a wife, then she needs to let me do it on my own. At that moment he realized, convincing his mother about Margaret could be more difficult then persuading her to leave the Timoleague she treasured.

22

Domestic

The McPherson family needed a domestic. Before long, Janet would leave for her training and Mrs. McPherson was already in a panic. She stopped by the Murchie farm to ask for Margaret since her children loved Janet. Mrs. McPherson thought Margaret was the perfect replacement.

"I can't manage these wayward children alone," she complained to Elizabeth Murchie. "I need help. Can you have Margaret come to the farm?"

Mama always wanted to help the other Arran families so she immediately agreed without asking Margaret. Mrs. McPherson left the Murchie farm, filled with a sense of relief knowing Margaret would soon be at her doorstep.

Margaret shook her head, hardly believing the words coming out of her mother's mouth. Then a fear of the challenge fell over her. She knew the McPherson children and house were a mess. She had listened to the stories from Janet about their wild behavior. This wasn't good.

Mama would have none of Margaret's argument. Mrs. McPherson was her friend and Margaret was available. It was settled, Margaret would replace Janet the following month.

Domestic work wasn't the job Margaret wanted but what else could she do? There wasn't anything else. A young woman in Colborne had very few options. She felt trapped in her mother's decisions.

For the past several months, Margaret tried to be more accepting of Mama's decisions and it seemed to work in her favor. The planning committee for the event turned out better than she expected, reducing tensions in the house. Now Mama was at it again, and Margaret didn't have a choice. At least she had the memories of the afternoon dance.

The event left Margaret floating. She was easily distracted by day dreams about her conversation with Robert. She replayed the conversation over and over in her head, planning her words for the next time. James Taylor wasn't on her mind after that dance. She had moved on with new thoughts. Thoughts she would need to survive inside the McPherson home.

Margaret made her way to their farm, creating a nightmare in her mind of the six children and the disasters awaiting her arrival. Her feet grew heavier with each step, slowing her pace as she walked down the road. The ill-mannered children ranged in age from four to twelve, three girls and three boys. Brats, Janet would say on the weekend.

Janet claimed their behavior was set a while ago. They didn't listen. They screamed at each other and the older boys didn't help their younger sisters. Janet called it an upside down family. If only the girls were older, they could help with the young ones. But that wasn't the McPherson children. No one wanted to take care of each other. They only fought.

Margaret thought she would lose her mind that first day. School was out and everyone was home in the messy house. The children would hide when Margaret needed to round them up. She went to bed wondering how Janet survived this chaos. At least her bed was in a quiet place, so she could sleep. It had taken all of her energy to keep the children in line and out of the cupboards. Her worries seemed to be coming true and she was failing at her first job.

She slept soundly for a few hours and awoke early, her mind twisting ideas and solutions to the children's bad behavior together. When it was time to step out of bed, she had a plan.

"Everyone will have a job," she announced to all six children after they appeared for breakfast. "We'll pretend this house is our ship and we're sailing across the Atlantic."

The children stood still, their mouths open, trying to make sense of Margaret's request. Daniel, the oldest took a chance and broke the silence.

"Miss Murchie," he said. "We don't remember the voyage."

It was an innocent comment but one that gave Margaret insight into the McPherson family's conversations. She thought about Captain Power and how he kept a tight ship. She clapped her hands together to signal it was time to listen.

"Don't worry Daniel, we'll make it up," she said.

She wasted no time in getting things in order. The second day would not be a repeat of day one.

"The McPherson ship will set sail immediately," she said. "When I clap my hands together, you'll need to queue for assignments. Anyone who steps out of line will be flogged and sent to the brig for an hour," she added.

A silence fell over the room. A silence Margaret cherished.

That evening when Margaret laid her head on the bed, she didn't have time to dream about the dance. She was asleep within minutes.

Margaret was surprised how much she enjoyed bossing the children around and teaching them how to fend for themselves. She also had the bonus of living away from Mama and Papa. The day was filled with activity, make believe and cooking. It was during the cooking times that Margaret found herself dreaming of possibilities. Cooking became her thinking time.

She shook her head realizing how much time itself had changed her. Her thoughts never went to Holy Island and the Arran she left behind. Her thoughts were about the future. Would she end up like John and find herself with another family? Or would she manage the Murchie farm?

Janet was away and Liza was close to marriage. Donald was slow about asking for Liza's hand,

Margaret thought. Was there more to it? She would find out this coming weekend. It didn't make sense, they had been courting for quite some time.

The more she thought about managing the farm, the more she knew she wasn't prepared. Mama trained the girls on the importance of keeping a clean home, but Papa only spent time on the basics of farming. She knew how to milk a cow, feed the chickens, but not how to keep the books. There was more to running the farm she needed to learn. Now her weekends could be busy too.

On Saturday morning, Margaret approached Papa at breakfast.

"Why haven't Liza and Donald set a date for marriage?" Margaret asked. It was a logical question since they had been courting for more than a year.

"It's not your concern," Papa replied without hesitation.

"What do you mean, not my concern?" Margaret pushed.

She didn't understand why her father answered so quickly to shut the conversation off. Mama shook her head as she looked at the two of them.

"Margaret needs to understand these things," Mama declared.

Papa moved to get out of his seat but Mama came over to the table and stood next to him, preventing his escape.

"Donald is not ready to support our Liza," Mama said. "He doesn't have his own land and his father is reluctant to divide the family farm."

Margaret looked at the two of them surprised at the answer.

"What does this mean," she asked. "I don't understand."

Mama didn't wait for Papa to answer.

"We cannot expect Liza to marry someone who can't support her."

"But she loves him and Donald loves her," Margaret said. It seemed so obvious.

"Maggie, I would've expected you to understand that love can't feed Liza," Papa said.

Now she knew. Papa wasn't letting Donald marry Liza. As they finished the conversation, Liza walked into the kitchen.

"Has everyone decided to talk about me without me in the room?" she asked.

Margaret rushed to her sister's side.

"It's my fault," she said. "I started the question about you and Donald. Now I understand."

Liza wasn't angry, she was hurt. Hurt that her family didn't wait until she awoke for the conversation. Margaret saw the hurt and tried to change the subject to her other weekend interest. She would talk to Liza later to mend the mess she started.

"Papa, I want to learn more about farming," she declared, ready to move on.

Liza looked at her sister and started to laugh.

"You certainly can change the mood in a hurry Miss Maggie," Liza said.

The tension in the room immediately changed to laughter. Papa had a new helper and he would take advantage of his daughter's interest.

Later in the day, Margaret waited for quiet time with Liza.

"What are your plans then, with Donald," she asked, after she apologized for the morning conversation.

"He's saving for land," Liza replied. "Can I trust you not to tell Mama?"

Margaret was stunned. This is not the Liza she knew. This is a new Liza. Was New Brunswick changing Liza too?

"Why are you staying quiet on it," Margaret inquired.

"Donald and I have a plan to move away from Colborne," she added. "We need to be away from the families that control us."

There were no words to describe how Margaret felt after her conversation with Liza. John was gone, Janet was leaving and now Liza had plans to move away. She saw her future trapped in Colborne, alone with Mama and Papa. A future she didn't relish.

Margaret returned to the McPherson farm with new plans, to save for school. She wouldn't be the only Murchie daughter living in Colborne.

The days and weeks started to blur into one another and before long, the McPherson children went back to school. It had been a summer of Captain Murchie and her sailors, an adventure none of them would soon forget. She agreed to stay on for the next few months but only in the afternoon after school.

The fall harvest was around the corner and Papa needed her. The priority was the farm. If she was trapped in Colborne, she would become a skilled farmer.

23

The Evening Dance

Robert awoke the day after the Colborne event to a farm ready for work. There wasn't time to savor the feelings he experienced the previous day. He needed to prepare the ground. The Bay Chaleur farming season waited for no one. Robert knew there was a short window to lay down the seeds, so he left the house after breakfast. As he worked, he thought about Margaret. There was something about her. Something that made him pause. Was it the same pause he had after the dance with Mary Connelly? He wasn't sure.

Mother continued to push Robert to meet the young Irish women in Eel River and Dalhousie. It was a short five mile ride into town and Mother found every reason to make the trip.

"The Anglican Church women are having a tea," Mother declared. "I would like you to take me."

"I can but need to come straight back to the farm," Robert replied, suspicious of her request.

"That won't do," she said. "I'll have to wait for you to return."

It pained Robert to drop everything and try to please his mother. He knew her motive, so he kept his ground.

"The farm won't wait, so you'll have to," he said. And with those words, Mother set a new course to find Robert a wife.

They would come to him, she thought and immediately started a series of afternoon tea socials at the house in Eel River. She would arrange the social on the days she expected Robert to finish early from the barn. Mother managed to guess correctly a few times, forcing Robert to sit for tea with the young women. It wasn't long before he found extra work to do in the barn, and the teas became uneventful for Mother.

Late one afternoon, Mary Connelly sat patiently with Mrs. Blacknell sharing stories as Robert remained in the barn. Mother expected to surprise him, but six o'clock came and went and there wasn't any sign of her son. As Mary politely said her goodbye, Robert entered the house, covered in the residue of the day's work. It was a surprise and an awkward moment for everyone. Robert felt his temperature rise but recovered enough to politely leave the room. It was Mother's last afternoon tea in Eel River Settlement.

Robert couldn't explain to his mother, the importance of establishing the Blacknell farm in the settlement. He was a young farmer among more experienced men. A wife would not help him demonstrate his worthiness, he thought. He saw the other farms with their growing pastures and thick oats and wanted to claim equality with the hard working men from New France and Scotland.

With the seed in the ground and the warm temperatures of summer, the plants started their march toward the bright sun. Robert recognized the Bay Chaleur summer as the best time of year on the farm. The benefits of hard work appeared in every field. Visible to anyone or everyone to see. Before long, the harvest would be upon them. The time when the farming community raced against Mother Nature.

Robert had improved almost thirty acres since day the first walked the Blacknell farm. It started with clearing for the barn, the house and finally for the gardens and the hay fields. He stood at the front of the barn and gazed across the acres in front of him. It was something to behold. Something to be proud of.

Almost a year would pass before Robert saw Margaret Murchie again. The Blacknell farm would complete the harvest and settle into the dark days of another Bay Chaleur winter. With little farming during the cold months, Robert found time to think and let his mind drift back to the Colborne event, and the social where he met Mary. Maybe his mother was correct. Was it time for a wife? It seemed possible now, but in the spring his work would start again.

Robert asked Sarah about the next social gathering. It couldn't hurt to attend and it would keep Mother happy. Sarah was surprised at Robert's question but shared what she knew about the March event.

The Colborne afternoon dance was an impossible event to follow. Months later, young and old alike, were still talking about it. Still sharing their favorite moments or reminiscing about the food.

The planners decided March had to be different and selected a large hall in Dalhousie. The weather wasn't favorable that time of year with the potential for late winter storms. A major snow storm could change everything, so the planning group wanted the event indoors.

Liza decided to participate without any prompting from Mama. Margaret thought it was strange and wondered about Liza's plans for the future. Without a farm, Donald could move to town.

"Did you spend time in Dalhousie to plan this event?" Margaret asked, suspicious of her sister. "What's it like?"

Margaret hadn't spent much time in town and thought Liza would share her observations. She might also share what Donald's plans were, but needed to be careful. Liza avoided talking about her future.

"It's quite different than the farms," Liza said. "The houses are close together and the general store is only a short walk. Not like the walk in Colborne."

Margaret decided to stay silent on Donald. She would watch her oldest sister, and learn. Liza would never reveal her secrets by answering questions anyway. If Margaret wanted to learn more, she needed to pay attention.

After a series of meetings, the March event was scheduled for a Saturday evening. A collective gasp could be heard up and down the coastal road. The young ones had overruled and decided. Fortunately, no one complained. It was agreed, the young men and women of Bay Chaleur needed their own social time.

"It's for adults not families," Liza reported before Margaret could ask. "The barn wouldn't do for March and nor would an evening without heat."

"Lighting?" Margaret asked. "What about food and music?"

Liza looked at her sister and shook her head.

"What's this about?" Liza asked. "This is not like you Maggie. When did you ever ask about food?"

Margaret immediately blushed and tried to change the subject.

"Just thinking about the dance, that's all," she said.

Liza wasn't swayed. She saw Margaret at the last dance with locked eyes on Robert.

"Why does this dance have your heart?" Liza asked, barely able to keep from laughing.

"I've a soft spot for Robert," she admitted. "Do you remember him?"

The giggles that followed made Margaret blush more. This was a strange feeling. The giggles and the blushing. Now she understood why Liza smiled when she talked about Donald.

When the day of the dance arrived, the young people across Bay Chaleur were excited. This was an event made especially for them. Once Margaret heard it was an evening dance, she became the perfect daughter. She didn't want anything to go wrong. No punishments would keep her home. Mama and Papa enjoyed this new Margaret, frequently asking for extra chores. Margaret readily complied. Nothing would keep her away from the dance.

She had no way of knowing whether Robert would be at the dance, but Margaret hoped she would see him. She was so anxious to get to the dance she begged Liza to leave a little early. A few of the young men from Colborne were taking their carriages to the dance. They would meet anyone leaving for Dalhousie at the church and head into town. Margaret gladly joined Liza and Donald on the first carriage.

The sun was setting in the cloudless sky as they headed up the coast. Everyone had their winter coats on and huddled together to stay warm. You could feel the camaraderie in the carriage with the songs and storytelling. It didn't matter if the tune was off, everyone would laugh and sing louder. The carriage approached the hall, as David Connacher was in the middle of his story about the ghost of Bay Chaleur. When David told everyone to look for the ghost ship on the bay, they looked up, only to realize they had reached the hall.

Everyone jumped out of the carriage laughing and headed inside, not waiting for the ending.

"David, you have a gift of storytelling," Liza said. "We were hanging on each word and didn't notice the carriage had stopped."

David smiled and headed inside.

"More on the way home," he said. "Let's meet at ten at the front door."

Once inside, the laughter continued. The expectation for the evening was high. So much time had passed since the last social event, raising everyone's expectations for this one. Margaret left Liza and Donald when she saw Annie Hamilton, one of her friends from school. While it was good to see Annie, she really wanted to see Robert.

"Annie, how've you been?" Margaret asked. "It's been too long."

Annie told of her upcoming marriage to Peter Steele and Margaret described her ordeal with the McPherson children. They laughed at how time had changed both of them. Annie hadn't kept up with Miss Brown but knew she was still in Colborne teaching. There was so much to share, but the conversation stopped when Peter arrived.

Annie caught his attention when he walked into the hall, and motioned him to join her. After polite introductions, Margaret excused herself, giving Annie the time to spend with her beau. She scanned the hall for Robert or the Blacknell girls. She knew the evening would not be complete without talking to Robert. There were many familiar faces, but no Robert.

Without Robert, everything seemed to grind to a complete halt. The conversations were words she didn't hear. The smiles in her direction were faces not people. Margaret couldn't believe the feelings she had. Was this a crush? Imagine feeling like this all the time, she thought.

Margaret needed someone to talk to. A distraction. Someone to take her mind off Robert, so she headed toward Liza. Liza was standing next to the refreshments table with Donald and Janet. Just as Margaret poured a drink of punch, Janet slapped her on the back.

"Well, well," Janet said. "If it isn't my baby sister, the new McPherson domestic."

Margaret laughed while giving Janet an evil look.

"If you hadn't left them in such a bad way--" Margaret started to say before Liza interrupted.

"Girls, stop we are at the dance," she said. "No more. Be civil, at least in public."

With that, Janet made one last comment and walked away from the refreshments area, swinging her arms in triumph.

"Margaret thinks she's better than all of us," Janet whispered loud enough for her sisters to hear.

No one followed Janet. There was no need to encourage or respond. Margaret looked at Liza for an explanation.

"You must've known how Janet feels," Liza said. "She's tired of following me and being compared to you," she added.

Margaret shook her head in disbelief. How could she have been so blind to Janet's feelings? Suddenly a sense of relief came over Margaret. At least she wasn't thinking about Robert. This is sister stuff, she thought. We'll work through it. As Liza tried to apologize for Janet's hurtful words, Margaret motioned for her sister to stop.

"It doesn't matter," Margaret said. "Janet doesn't always say the right thing."

Annie Hamilton joined Margaret just as Janet walked away.

"Now, where were we?" she asked, and picked up the conversation exactly where they had stopped.

"I need to hear more about these McPherson children," she said.

Annie was caring for her brother's children and found Margaret's stories far more entertaining. It was harder to laugh about family. Annie couldn't, but Margaret didn't have a problem laughing at the stories Annie shared about the Hamilton children.

Annie was the free spirit Margaret couldn't be. She was the youngest in a family of six and had learned to be carefree from her brothers and sisters. Annie's family had moved from Arran a year after Margaret's family. Annie thought Margaret was a kindred spirit because of her bolt from the first ship. Among many of the young people, Margaret was a celebrity.

In all the laughter and stories Margaret didn't notice Robert entering the hall. Unlike Margaret, Robert had no trouble telling his sisters he was looking for Margaret. He trusted Sarah and Rebecca to keep a secret from Mother. They had many special agreements and the personal interests of a sibling was one of them. Robert protected them and acted like their father but he also knew his place in their lives. Their appreciation made this special agreement.

Robert politely called her name when he approached her. Margaret was deep in conversation and barely heard the voice, almost ignoring it. As she turned around, Robert was standing next to her. She jumped and immediately felt her pulse race. The color of her skin turned from pale white to red in a matter of seconds. Oh, how she wanted to be in control yet this strange feeling kept interrupting and taking over. Her inner voice told her to let go. There wasn't any sense in fighting it.

"How've you been?" he asked, looking directly into her eyes.

Margaret opened her mouth to tell him about the last several months and but only one word came out.

"Fine," she said.

Robert immediately sensed her nervousness. He was nervous too. Something was different between them.

"You look well and it's wonderful to see you," he said.

Margaret started to laugh. At first it was a nervous laugh and then she relaxed.

"Robert, it's wonderful to see you too," she said, letting her shoulders drop enough to relieve the tension in her body.

She had thought about this moment, deciding what to say and how to say it. But when the time came, her mind went completely blank. The words she had practiced were nowhere to be found. Instead of saying the wrong thing, she had nothing to say. Finding her voice, Margaret thought she would try again.

"How's the farm?" she asked. "Your sisters? You?"

She could feel her lips tremble with excitement as the words left them.

"Everything about the farm is good," Robert answered. "The harvest was more than we needed."

Robert was interested in hearing about the past several months, wanting to put the pieces of this young woman together so he could understand her. He found everything about Margaret intriguing. Even the impulsiveness of her youth seemed charming, but he knew so little. Tonight, he would ask more questions and learn about Margaret Murchie.

Their conversation covered family, the farms, and anywhere the words flowed. Margaret didn't want the evening or each moment to end. She had Robert to herself and didn't want to share him. There was something magical that happened when he was next to her. She listened to every word, wanting it to last longer than one evening a year.

"I truly enjoyed our conversation Robert," she said, trying to extend the hour to another day. "Would you care to visit at our farm in Colborne?"

Margaret wasn't waiting for the protocol of the day. She had an opinion and never struggled to let it be known. Robert was pleasantly surprised with Margaret's forward request. He was not shocked. He had seen Margaret's assertiveness before.

Robert wanted to see more of Margaret too. A desire surrounded in challenge as Mother was not supportive of Margaret. Mother fiercely stood for tradition and Margaret was anything but tradition. His thoughts turned to a list of challenges his mother would present. As quickly as they appeared, he shut them down. It wasn't the time to think about his mother, it was time to enjoy the company of the young woman standing next to him.

The hands on the clock turned faster than normal that night in Dalhousie. Robert and Margaret spent time on the dance floor and sat together at one of the small tables. The conversation flowed all evening.

The young Irish women Mother had paraded by Robert were miffed. They expected Robert to ask them for a dance and it didn't happen. Even when Mary Connelly walked over to Robert, he politely greeted her and went back to his conversation with Margaret. They wanted to know who caught Robert's eye so Mary approached Sarah.

"Who's the young woman Robert's dancing with?" she asked. "He's certainly captivated by her tonight."

Sarah knew better than to give anything away.

"Oh, they met on the ship from Ireland," Sarah answered. "They're old friends," she added.

Mary nodded and thanked Sarah. Sarah watched as she walked back to her friends. As she approached them, they leaned toward her trying to hear the newfound information. I must prepare Robert, Sarah thought. Mother will hear about this from the church ladies.

Before long, Liza and Donald were looking for Margaret so they could head back to Colborne with David Connacher. Janet was boarding in Dalhousie, so she could leave on her own time. They found Margaret and motioned her to head toward the front door where David stood waving.

Margaret knew she had no choice but to say goodbye to Robert.

"Will you call upon the farm?" she asked, in a voice between a question and a statement.

"I promise," he answered. "I can't tell you when but I'll call on a Saturday afternoon. Be well Margaret and I'll see you soon."

Margaret looked in his eyes and saw her own feelings. She said goodbye and headed to the door towards Liza and Donald.

The cold ride from Dalhousie to Colborne was filled with stories of the evening. The food, the music and all the excitement of being young and sharing laughs with friends. They all agreed, Bay Chaleur was a great place to live. David Connacher finished his ghost story while the moon left a trailing reflection across the calm Restigouche River.

"And on a night, such as this, you can see the ship on fire," David said, in a voice shaking to add to the fear.

The carriage went silent while everyone looked across the bay, expecting a ship to be visible. The silence was finally broken after a few miles when Liza and Donald talked about the event. Margaret kept a quiet voice. She let Liza and Donald talk about their evening. Margaret had nothing she wanted to share with the world at this moment. She wanted to savor every word, every dance and every laugh she had earlier that evening with Robert Blacknell. She was keeping it all to herself.

24

Courting Games

The next morning, Robert unknowingly set the stage for a showdown with his mother. He intended to change her opinion of Margaret without an understanding of Mother's entrenched position. He innocently shared brief excerpts from the dance, one at a time, forcing his mother to stitch each one to the next. It was a patchwork quilt and she wanted the whole story at once. The finished product. There were promises to keep and church friends to thank and Robert wasn't cooperating.

Sarah and Rebecca stayed away from the conversation, smiling and nodding when asked. Robert would answer for them when possible. Sarah stared at her feet, avoiding eye contact with Mother and blushing when Samuel's name was mentioned. Rebecca headed to the barn when the topic came up. She had allegiances with both Robert and Margaret. She wouldn't pick sides.

Robert was acting odd. Before the dance, he had little time for social events and now he couldn't stop talking about a dance. Mother knew he was up to something but let him think she was listening. She had been young once and courted by his father. Her eyes welled up thinking about the early days. So much love and hope for the future.

After church the following Sunday, the church ladies pulled her aside. The whisper voices turned into loud conversation as they described the dance in gossipy detail.

"He only danced with a young Scottish girl," they told her. "He never left her side."

Mother appeared to grow taller as her posture aligned with her determination. Margaret Murchie would not stand in the way of the future she had in mind for her son, she thought. He would follow as his father had done and marry the woman his family chose.

She forced a smile while feeling her temperature increase. Didn't Robert understand she was already evaluating the available women in Bay Chaleur? And Margaret Murchie was not one of them.

It was clear, Robert didn't know how to pick a wife. His behavior at the dance proved that. She would have to intervene. All the women she introduced him to and still he only wanted to spend time with Margaret. She walked to the carriage shaking her head while refusing to discuss it with her daughters.

Robert brought the carriage to the front of the church and Mother climbed in without saying a word. He had witnessed the women all huddled around her and tried to keep a straight face, knowing how angry she must be. The ride to the farm was quiet, only Thomas asking his usual questions and trying to find out why everyone else wasn't talking.

After a month, Robert announced he was going to visit the Murchie farm the following weekend.

"It's a short ride to Colborne and I'd like to pay the family a visit," he said.

Mother decided to challenge. She couldn't believe her ears.

"What's going on with the Murchie family that you need to visit?" she asked, expecting a mumbled answer. "It's that young redhead isn't it? She's nothing but trouble Robert. Mark my word. A strong willed woman will be difficult."

There, it was out. She felt better because Robert needed to hear it. But her mouth wouldn't stop.

"I can't tell you what to do, but I can tell you Margaret Murchie isn't the woman for you," she added.

Robert took it all in, knowing his mother had to share her opinion. It was a clear warning wrapped in love and concern from her. She would eventually change her mind, he thought. It would take time. She had changed her mind about emigrating, she could change her mind about Margaret.

Robert smiled and knew better than to argue.

"Margaret's a fine young woman," he said. "A strong will is an asset in our new homeland."

He motioned toward the door, touching her shoulder on his way.

"We can discuss it later, when the chores are done," he said.

He left his mother little time to respond, heading out the door to the barn. Alone in the barn, he could prepare for his upcoming conversations with the Murchie family and Margaret. But first he must think about Mother's conversation. Were there any weak spots, he could take advantage of? Weak parts of her argument, she wasn't committed to. She will soften, he thought. It happened before after she had proof. Now she needed proof of the woman Margaret has become.

"Maybe I should come with you," Mother said, walking into the barn. "A visit to the Murchie farm would be good."

"A fine idea," Robert answered.

He was calling her bluff. She always had plans for Saturday and would not give them up so quickly.

"I will make arrangements and adjust my plans," she replied.

Robert was shocked. It was completely unexpected. He said nothing.

Later that evening Robert approached Sarah about Mother's reaction to the Murchie farm visit. He wanted to know what Mother was up to.

"I've been meaning to tell you," Sarah said. "Mary was asking about Margaret at the dance last month. I told her you were old friends from the Eden."

Sarah looked at her feet, hoping Robert would not be upset with her for not telling him, untll now.

"That's a good answer," he said. "Was Jane there too?

"Oh yes, and they both were gossiping about you," she replied.

Sarah knew her brother was the bachelor the young women talked about. He was handsome and aloof, naively encouraging their affection.

"Not sure that's enough to stop all the women from appealing to Mother," Sarah said. "Mother opened that door with the afternoon teas."

Robert knew instantly what to do. They both could play this game. He knew Mother wasn't alone with this, so he needed to find out more about the women. All the women Mother was pushing his way. And he would enlist the help of his sisters.

"I'm going to need your help," he said. "Can you persuade Mother that all these women are unsuitable for me?" He asked.

"I'm not sure I know how to do that," Sarah replied, totally innocent to the complexity of life. "But yes, if it'll make you happy," she continued.

"It will and I know how you can do it," Robert declared.

And with that, Robert and Sarah made an agreement to discover shortcomings in each of Mother's selection.

"Think of the things Mother wouldn't like," he offered. "Pointing those out are our best option. Things necessary for homemaking. You know how important they are to Mother."

Sarah hesitated, she liked many of the women and didn't want to say bad things about them.

"Not bad things, Sarah," Robert said, sensing his sister's confusion. "Just things that make them unsuitable for me. Women who want to be taken care of, for example. I don't have time to take care of a woman. She needs to be more like you and Rebecca."

"Oh, now I understand," Sarah replied. "You need a farmer's wife, not a town girl."

"Yes, that's it," said Robert. "A farmer's wife."

"Give me a week or two," Sarah requested, knowing there was work to do.

The next day, Robert approached his mother and shared the details about the trip to Colborne.

"We'll leave around ten o'clock, if you are still planning to travel to the Murchie farm," he said.

"Yes, I'm planning to join you," she replied. "Shall I bake some bread or a cake to take with us?"

"What a wonderful idea," he said. "Yes, please."

Robert was convinced his mother would enjoy the visit. This will work in my favor, he thought. Once she gets to know Margaret, she will see the true person.

25

The Murchie Farm Visit

Since the evening of the dance in Dalhousie, the McPherson children spent little time in the brig for bad behavior. Captain Murchie was distracted and a few infractions slipped by. There were no complaints from the children, they liked this new Margaret. A Margaret with extra smiles and a lighter hand.

Margaret noticed the difference too. She wasn't trying to control her emotions. Especially the emotion of floating on the clouds. Sleep was a different issue. Falling asleep took hours and when she awoke, there was boundless energy. Robert was always on her mind and the memory of the evening dance not far behind.

It didn't make sense to Mama when Margaret told her about the upcoming visit by Robert. She decided to ask Liza what happened at the dance.

"There's magic between them," she said. "An attraction when they're together."

Someone attracted to my Margaret, thought Mama. And Robert? This didn't make any sense to her. Nevertheless, she would be on her best behavior when Robert came calling. Margaret was her problem child and finding a willing suitor for this daughter was something she welcomed with open arms.

The letter arrived with a short note announcing the visit would be the upcoming Saturday. One short sentence noted Mrs. Blacknell would be joining Robert. That didn't matter. The visit was real. The letter was all Margaret needed to see. It wasn't a dream, she thought. Robert would visit the farm and she would have him all to herself.

When the day finally arrived, Margaret couldn't contain the excitement, waiting by the door for nearly an hour before the Blacknell carriage arrived. As it made its way up the road, Margaret ran out to greet Robert, standing near the barn where he would leave the carriage.

Robert smiled as he watched Margaret run out the door. This was exactly what he expected. Full of life and bursting with energy. Margaret didn't look at Robert's mother in the carriage, she was too busy looking at Robert. As Robert helped his mother step onto the ground, Margaret acknowledged her.

"It's nice to see you again Mrs. Blacknell," she said. "May I help you with anything?"

Mother shook her head and gingerly made her way toward the house holding Robert's hand. Margaret sensed Robert's mother was not fond of her, but she wasn't going to let anyone ruin the day. Robert was in Colborne.

Robert took his mother's words and tone in stride. He would have time on the ride home to discuss it with her. He hoped her gracious personality would come to life inside the Murchie home.

Margaret bubbled with excitement as she shared the past several weeks with Robert. The words streamed out of her mouth, barely pausing for a breath on the short distance to the door.

Once inside, Mama and Papa rushed to greet Mrs. Blacknell.

"Welcome to our home," Mama said, surprised Margaret hadn't mentioned Mrs. Blacknell would join Robert.

Robert sensed the omission and jumped in to answer.

"It was a last minute decision," he said.

"What a wonderful surprise." Mama said, knowing a discussion with Margaret would come later. "It's nice to have both of you here. We still feel indebted to your family for helping our John and Margaret."

"Let me get some tea," Mama offered. She rushed to the stove, grabbing the kettle, nearly dropping the lid in her haste to fill it with water.

Everyone moved into the sitting area near the fire as Mama poured tea and cut Mrs. Blacknell's cake into slices. The conversation was slow to start but once the topic of winter came up, no one held back. They laughed at how naive they were when they first arrived.

"I'm not sure emigrants would leave Ireland or Scotland if they knew the truth about the cold winters," Papa insisted.

"No one told me about blizzards so thick your hands disappear in front of you," Robert added.

It was a common thread. As recent immigrants they had newfound knowledge and shared experiences.

"This must be the coldest place on earth in January," Papa declared, taking pride in surviving that first year.

Margaret shared stories of that year on the farm without taking a breath. Papa would interject to add his point of view, leaving everyone laughing at how dissimilar a father and his daughter viewed the events. At one point, Margaret took a deep breath and declared she was done.

"That's all I remember," she said, her loud laughter filling the house.

Robert wasn't afraid of the energy displayed in front of him, but it was clear his mother had concerns. As the conversation slowed and the afternoon wound down, Robert saw Mother tighten with every burst Margaret shared.

"It's time for us to leave," he announced. "It will be a few hours to get home. The corduroy roads are rotted out in several spots between here and Eel River."

The afternoon was everything Margaret had wanted. As she watched Robert turn north along the coastal road, she wished she was riding with him. Then she thought of Mrs. Blacknell and how mean she seemed today. She knew there would be no Robert without his mother's agreement. Margaret vowed she would find a way to change her opinion.

The corduroy roads added the perfect rhythm to the conversation on the ride home to Eel River Settlement. The ups and downs of the wheels spurred the questions and answers in the carriage. Mother had little problem starting and sharing her opinion, once the Murchie farm was out of sight.

"How can you manage that amount of energy?" she asked. "Will she ever be calm?"

Robert tried to take the questions one at a time, then gave up, waiting for his mother to grow tired of questions without answers.

"It's impossible to manage another person's energy, Mother," he started. "What does calm mean?"

At the halfway point, Mother had exhausted her objections and turned complimentary toward the Murchie family.

"They're a nice family," she admitted. "A pleasure to visit."

Robert relaxed his shoulders, relieving the tension that was building in his back. Progress was made today, he thought, positive progress.

"Yes, the visit was special," he said. "I'm glad you came with me."

Margaret stood in the yard, trying to hold onto the image of Robert as he disappeared. The Robert inside the house and the Robert laughing with her about the farm. The image that she couldn't shake was Robert riding away in the carriage. Was this another Arran, she thought? Would something she wanted be taken away? Could Mrs. Blacknell change his mind?

Mama was waiting with a grin of approval for her daughter, when Margaret stepped inside the house. Margaret was immediately overcome with emotion and fell into her mother's embrace. Liza said it right, Mama thought. She saw it with her own eyes. Magic happened when Robert and Margaret were together.

But Margaret's tears flowed from fear, not happiness. Mama was too excited to sense it.

26

The Frozen Bay

Margaret counted the full moons over Bay Chaleur until she would see Robert again. She wished for a small number, so counting the weeks, days or hours would never do. Too painful she thought, with those large numbers. Four was easier to count.

The last moon to count was the month of the Colborne picnic. It was scheduled for the last Sunday in September and intended to be a celebration of the new hall. She thought of inviting Robert, but Mama abruptly told her about the rules of courtship.

"Nice girls don't do the inviting," she said. "You'll just have to go to the picnic and see him there."

So many unknown rules, she thought, realizing she hadn't paid much attention to her sister's courting. And what if Robert doesn't attend the picnic? The number of moons would increase.

She paused wondering how her whole world was wrapped around Robert. The picnic was her countdown date. Her mind was preoccupied with Robert and it had to stop one way or another. This was far too time consuming and complicated.

Maybe Janet had the right idea, she thought. Go away to school and let the courting fall to second place. If she continued with schooling, there would be more time for reading instead of thinking about Robert all day. She brushed that aside knowing she had created her own distraction with the constant thoughts of Robert.

During Janet's Saturday visit, she eagerly shared stories about her life outside of Colborne. Life in the town, away from the farm. She worked in the hospital in Dalhousie as an aide alongside the nurses and the local doctor. During supper, the words flowed with enthusiasm as she described her new independence and enjoyment of nursing. A brief mention of her courtship with Edward raised Mama's interest.

"Edward's decided to move west to the big woods," Janet announced.

Mama stared into her daughter's eyes for confirmation.

"I won't leave, so he's going alone," Janet continued. "Bay Chaleur is enough wilderness for me."

She looked around the table for agreement. There was nodding about the wilderness of Bay Chaleur and only Mama nodding about Edward.

Everyone heard the stories of the trees in the west. They were twice as big as the New Brunswick pines and beckoned the men who had skill, an axe and the will to take the risk.

Mama didn't hesitate to tell Janet how good everything would be without Edward, and Papa never found the words for his daughter's courting. He kept quiet, adding nothing to Janet's announcement. After a short pause, it was time to change the subject.

"Besides, there are new friends at the hospital," she said.

Janet bubbled as she continued to describe her new life filled with friends and the pleasures of helping people. It was evident Janet had found herself. Margaret listened, not sure how she should react. It was a bold statement for a young woman in Colborne. Her work was more important than her beau.

Mama felt sad for Janet, now alone without a man. But her happiness with Edward out of Janet's life overruled all of her emotions. There was something about Edward she didn't like.

"Oh Mama, you need to be less critical of everyone who isn't like you," Janet said. "He's a good man and wants the challenge of the forests far from here."

And that was it. Janet refused to talk about it further.

"I've decided," she said. "It's over." She wanted to shut down the whispers and her mother's concerns.

"Besides, nurses support each other," she said. "We don't need husbands to feel whole."

It made Margaret question her own feelings all over again, but only for a short time.

The questions and doubts disappeared the next week when Margaret received an invite to the picnic from Robert. On Saturday morning, Mama pointed to a letter Papa collected at the Postmaster's house. Without hesitation, Margaret whipped it off the table and ripped it open, before Mama could finish her sentence. At the same moment, courting shifted back to the number one spot. In an instant the encouragement she found in Janet evaporated along with the idea of attending school. They both plummeted to second place after Robert's invitation arrived.

Mama was soon preoccupied with the picnic preparations. The Colborne church ladies collected their best recipes to share with the community and Mama stood at the forefront. From dairy to baked goods, it was bragging time and a time to share new creations. This year, maple syrup captivated the entire community. It was all things maple. It replaced molasses, a former favorite from Arran, and satisfied everyone's sweet tooth. Papa called it a gift from Bay Chaleur. He always pointed out it was available on their own land.

Papa had his own reasons to look forward to the picnic. The men saw it as a time to relax and share stories about farming, fishing and working in the sawmill. Their camaraderie and conversation differed from their wives and daughters and they continued to share the latest pranks played on the unsuspecting young.

The day of the picnic brought out the best in the Colborne Community with friends and family celebrating more than the completion of the hall. As

Mama walked passed the patchwork of picnic blankets decorating the field, she grew proud of her family's good fortune. Thanks to Papa's dream, they traveled a long distance from a life of tenant farmers on Arran, to a new life she never would have imagined years ago. There was much to be thankful for.

At the same time, a feeling of melancholy overcame Mama as family and friends gathered around the Murchie blanket. Her eyes welled up as she briefly thought about Duncan and those difficult days. A time she would never forget.

The afternoon sun cast its long shadows on the blanket as the final crumbs of apple cake disappeared. The stories and laughter covered the events of the summer and plans to complete the harvest.

Margaret insisted Robert should head home and avoid traveling in complete darkness. She looked at him expecting the typical quick goodbye, but instead he wrapped his arms tightly around her for an endless minute. He released his embrace and slowly walked toward the carriage. He knew several months would pass before they'd be together again.

Robert headed north along the coastal road, reflecting on the changes since his very first trip to the office in Dalhousie. Back then, he didn't know the location of Colborne Settlement and now he was a frequent visitor. The quiet ride along the bay didn't match the loud thoughts inside his head. He knew he had a decision to make.

When Robert walked into the house, he found everyone eager to hear about the picnic. Even Thomas was asking questions and curious about the event.

"We all should've gone," Robert declared. "I'm not sure why I was the only one."

"You wanted to be alone with Margaret," Rebecca teased.

"Well, that maybe so, but I could've shared part of the day with all of you," he offered.

Mother sat knitting, not getting involved in the teasing. The girls were doing a fine job of making Robert blush, she thought. Thomas wanted to know what was so funny, but no one would answer his questions. After Robert described the picnic and shared some maple sugar butter, Mother couldn't hold her tongue any longer.

"Will you be taking Mary to the harvest picnic in Dalhousie in a few weeks?" she asked, putting down her needles to take in his full response.

Robert looked at his mother with a scowl.

"No, Mother," he said. "Mary is not my choice, she's your choice."

Mother was surprised at Robert's quick answer. She picked up her knitting so she wouldn't glare at her son, but didn't want the conversation to drop.

"Mary's a lovely woman but she doesn't have the same interests as me," Robert added.

Mother couldn't believe her ears, he didn't even know Mary. She stood up trying to take the upper hand.

"How do you know?" She asked. "You haven't spent any time with her."

Robert looked down, afraid to give away too much of the information Sarah uncovered. Mother would be angry with Sarah if she knew her own daughter was snooping around and gathering information on her friend's daughter.

"Mary's brother talks about her all the time," he replied, quickly trying to cover up.

It was partially true and Robert didn't think his mother would ask Mary's brother so he kept going.

"She doesn't read much and she needs to be treated with special care," he said. "That just won't work for me, I need a farmer. Someone who wants to get her hands dirty."

He knew Mother couldn't argue with that. She was a farmer and knew the hard work it took to make a farm a home.

The conversation was over and Mother sensed it. She would have to find a way to stop Robert's attraction to Margaret. This was not how she envisioned Robert's future.

But time was on her side with the upcoming harvest. Robert would be busy over the next few months. Enough time to find a nice Irish girl who knows how to farm. She smiled thinking about Robert's future wife. She would be a woman just like her.

And just as Mother predicted, the end of the harvest season kept Robert and Margaret apart. She relaxed expecting a long cold winter between the two, unaware of the extent of their ongoing correspondence. Robert found time to write short notes and letters to Margaret every week and Margaret responded with news about the Colborne farm.

Before long, signs of an early New Brunswick winter appeared along the bay. The shore line was gripped in ice and a steady east wind off the bay built snow drifts typical for late January. The settlers prepared to spend the bitter cold months indoors, huddled by the fire. Only the bravest would spend extra time in the barn, caring for the animals.

Margaret continued her work at the McPherson farm, staying with the family during the week. The weekends were back home where Liza and Margaret compared stories about their domestic work. Each weekend, Margaret helped Papa with the barn chores. It was a special time for James Murchie as he eagerly worked to make a farmer out of his youngest daughter.

Despite the Bay Chaleur wind and the freezing temperatures, Margaret cared for the animals without prompting each Saturday and Sunday. She called it barn farming, and grew fond of caring for the cows in the cold damp barn. She was convinced they were tired of the long winter too.

The bitter winds off the bay did not extend as far as the Eel River Settlement. The five miles inland was a small advantage, a distance Robert appreciated every winter. Nothing could protect Eel River from the snow, however, and it collected in huge drifts around the farmhouse. At one point, Robert shoveled snow drifts just to clear the windows. Overnight, the Blacknell children took turns checking the fires and adding more wood to keep the house warm.

By late February, Robert grew tired of the cold and snow. He wanted a change from the winter monotony and needed to feel the warmth of Margaret's energy. He thought a visit to the Murchie farm would demonstrate his interest beyond the weekly correspondence and give him a chance to validate the magic.

Robert's mind was made up. This spring he would actively court Margaret and secure her hand in marriage. She was one of a kind and Mother must learn to accept her. He realized how protective his mother was and for some reason she was less of a problem over the past few months. Perhaps she had softened her opinion but he could never be sure. Even so, she continued to warn him of Margaret's impulsive behavior.

"I cannot decide these things for you," she said. "But I can advise and I'm not certain on Margaret. At least she's a Protestant, the only wife you can have."

Robert didn't expect more from his mother. She was living in the new world with old world ideas.

Early Saturday morning before the barn work, Papa handed Margaret the letter he retrieved from the Postmaster.

"He's coming to visit," she announced, without taking a breath. "I didn't even ask him and he'll be here in two weeks."

Papa just nodded. This was not the time to argue with his daughter. He knew better. He had learned how to live with so many women in the house.

The next two weeks felt like two months to Margaret. She was unaware of Robert's intentions but hoped there was more. Her eyes had read Robert's words over and over since the letter arrived. She couldn't believe the words were still visible on the paper. What was the meaning behind, he longed to see her? The words didn't sound like Robert. How could she wait until the weekend?

With only two days remaining, no amount of sighing could make the clock move faster. Daydreaming became her escape from the constraints of time. Margaret found herself leaving food on the stove for too long, standing still with a broom in her hand or lost in thought while the McPherson children called her name.

27

Saturday Afternoon Visit

The overnight coating of wet snow was a welcome hint of winter's weakening grip on Bay Chaleur. Robert knew the snow would fight the warming sun well into April. Northern New Brunswick had taught him well.

Robert prepared the sleigh for the trip knowing the roads would be passable, yet slow with the shallow sleigh ruts to navigate. As he turned onto the coastal road, the crisp east wind caught Robert's attention. The warm feelings he had for Margaret were no match for Mother Nature's hold on Bay Chaleur.

Margaret was in the barn when Robert turned up the road. She ran out to help with the horse and sleigh and caught her first glimpse of Robert's smile. At that moment, time stopped. The days apart melted away and the magic instantly returned. Robert stepped out of the sleigh and gave Margaret a hug, lifting her completely off her feet. Once the horse was taken care of, they headed toward the house holding hands as they walked on the snow packed path.

Janet was home for the weekend and stared at the two from inside the kitchen.

"She's too young for Robert," she exclaimed. "Robert should be courting someone my age."

Mama quickly interrupted. There wouldn't be any sister arguments today.

"This isn't the time for creating problems," she said. "It's time to welcome Robert."

Mama knew trouble was only an argument away when the two sisters were home. She hadn't expected Janet to be jealous, especially with her nursing decision.

"If you can't be cordial, you'll need to stay away from Margaret and Robert today," Mama ordered. "This is Margaret's time and I don't want you to create problems."

Janet thought about Robert's Irish heritage and why Mama was so willing to welcome him. Somehow, the Eden and the Bathurst dock made Robert special, different from Edward. She shrugged her shoulders, in an attempt to release the tension of her mother's rules. She would let the issue go, Edward was gone and his heritage didn't matter to anyone.

Janet looked at her mother. For some reason, this visit had Mama on edge. Was Mama afraid her baby Margaret would never leave the house? Nonsense, she thought, so why was she so touchy? As she glanced toward the door, Robert and Margaret entered the house.

"Welcome back," Mama said. "Let me take your coat and boots and get the tea ready.

She looked at Margaret, signaling with her chin to move toward the sitting area.

"The fire will warm you from the journey," Mama said.

Margaret looked at her mother, wondering why she was behaving strangely. What could she be up to, she asked herself? As quickly as the question came into her head, it left. Robert was sitting in front of her. She didn't want to think about her mother at the moment.

Robert welcomed the warm fire and placed his hands above the rising heat before sitting in the chair next to Margaret. The conversation continued from the picnic as though time stood still. The harvest, the farms, and a few touching moments about the McPherson children filled the sitting room air. Robert wasn't much for formal visits and he wanted the Murchies to see him as a friend and not a stranger. At the first opportunity, Janet joined the conversation sharing her recent experience as a nurse's aide. Robert listened intently as Janet glowed about what she was doing and how different herbs and medicines were used to treat the sick patients.

Margaret felt the mood change while Janet occupied the conversation. Instead of sharing winter stories with Robert, she was listening to Janet's accomplishments. She tried to look interested but she only wanted Janet to leave. It was too cold to go for a walk so she needed another option.

"Shall we play cards?" she asked. "There are enough of us to enjoy a good game."

Janet was stopped in her tracks, shaking her head at her juvenile sister.

"Cards?" "Nonsense Margaret!" "I have so much to share about nursing and Robert is clearly interested."

Margaret grew impatient with her sister.

"I'm sure your nursing experience is far more exciting than a game of cards, but it's time for some fun," she said. "Let's share some laughs. There's plenty of time to learn about your work and new friends."

Janet felt the blood rise in her neck expanding quickly to her face.

"Well then, let's play some silly game," she said. "Maggie this is so like you to play instead of learn."

Margaret felt the direct insult but ignored it. This type of back and forth had been going on for years. She knew Janet was trying to make her look young and impulsive, but she would have none of it.

Robert sensed the tension between the two girls and had experienced bickering like this between his sisters. Expecting Robert to be alarmed, Margaret tried to down play Janet's comments.

"Well Janet, having a little fun doesn't hurt now does it?" she said. "We've all worked so hard this winter keeping warm."

Mama and Papa listened in horror from the kitchen as the two girls attempted to keep Robert's attention. Papa was usually silent during the spats, but this time he couldn't hold his tongue.

"Janet, can you come into the kitchen?" he asked.

Mama took a different approach. She walked into the room and tried to intervene.

"Robert, do your sisters argue too?" she asked.

He smiled, looking directly at Mama.

"Of course, they do," he said. "I wouldn't expect anything else."

Mama relaxed. She knew her daughters' behavior wouldn't change his mind about Margaret.

Janet headed toward the kitchen with her head down. She realized she had gone too far, still treating Margaret as her baby sister, instead of the young woman she had become. After taking a few steps, she turned back toward Margaret.

"I'm sorry, that was wrong," she said, shocking everyone with her words.

Those words hung in the air, like an early morning fog, instead of a clear recognition from Janet. No one could see through them until Margaret stood up and hugged her sister, accepting her apology. The two laughed and went back to the conversation with Robert. It would be a turning point in the sister's relationship. Mama never understood what happened that afternoon, but it didn't matter, her daughters weren't arguing.

When the low sun signaled Robert's departure time was approaching, he stood up and headed into the kitchen. Margaret quickly followed, but Robert politely asked her to wait. He needed to speak with Papa, he told her.

Margaret sat back in the chair, wishing she could keep the sun from dropping below the horizon. The setting sun always takes Robert away from me, she thought, wanting a few more hours of daylight.

As Robert stepped into the kitchen, Papa stood up, sensing something urgent in Robert.

"May I have a word with you?" Robert politely asked.

"Of course," Papa said, the words cracking with concern. "Is something the matter?"

He overheard the arguments between Janet and Margaret but didn't think it bothered Robert. It was the typical conversation when the two sisters were in the house.

"It's about Margaret," Robert said, not wasting any time to ask his question. "I'd like your permission to marry her."

Papa stood completely surprised with Robert's question unaware that his mouth was wide open.

"Margaret?" he asked, closing his mouth to form the word. "You're asking me if you can marry Margaret?"

He knew Robert was fond of his youngest daughter, but didn't expect a marriage request so quickly.

"Yes." Robert said, not adding more to his answer. He didn't think he needed to say anything more.

"Most certainly," Papa replied. "Yes, you may marry my daughter Margaret. The Murchie family would be honored to have you as a son."

Margaret listened from the sitting room, barely able to breathe when she heard Robert's question. She wasn't sure how to react, or what to say. Marriage? It was what she dreamed of but didn't expect it to happen so fast. Robert turned from Papa and headed back to the chairs by the fire. Margaret was beaming.

"I'm sure you expected me to ask you first." Robert said, realizing Margaret could still say no to his proposal. "I needed to make sure your father wouldn't object before I asked you."

As Margaret was taking it all in, Robert got down on one knee.

"Margaret will you be my wife?" he asked, staring deep into her blue eyes.

Margaret stood still for nearly sixty seconds, a lifetime of quiet for her. "Yes, yes, Robert, I will!" she replied, grinning from ear to ear.

Robert enveloped Margaret with his two arms, pulling her close to him, and touching her lips for the first time. It was Margaret's first kiss. Robert's lips were soft and salty and she instantly wanted more of them. When she felt Robert's arms relax she kissed him again and they remained in a locked embrace.

The excitement lasted well into the evening in the Murchie house, after Robert's departure. It was difficult for Margaret to let Robert leave and head back to Eel River that afternoon. She didn't want the feeling or the day to end.

"I'll be back soon," Robert said. "I love you Margaret Murchie." And with those words, he headed down the road on the sleigh.

Margaret's head was spinning, there was so much to think about. Another new beginning. Life kept changing and this change was as big as the move from Arran to New Brunswick for her. She would leave her home in Colborne for another in Eel River.

And then it dawned on her. What about Mrs. Blacknell? Was she supportive? The uncertainty of Robert's mother would weigh on the happy day. Things are never simple, Margaret thought.

Robert was in a daze as he headed north along the coastal road, oblivious to the cold east wind. He hadn't intended to propose to Margaret, but it just happened. It was the magic. The magic took over.

28

Dalhousie

Early Monday morning Robert met with the Reverend at the Anglican Church in Dalhousie to arrange the marriage date. The Reverend was available the following week, but Mother intervened and requested Robert to wait until the next month.

"Why do you need more time?" Robert asked, suspecting she was trying to stall the marriage.

She shrugged, trying to appear small, while giving Robert a sense of guilt. It wasn't the first time Mother tugged at her son's emotions and it wouldn't be the last. Robert succumbed and agreed to delay the marriage one month. It was a fine line between giving in to his mother and moving forward with his life, but if it helped the acceptance of Margaret, he agreed. A one month delay would be a very small sacrifice.

Mother was still in shock from the announcement and needed the time to adjust. Robert arrived home after his trip to the Murchie farm and surprised everyone with the news. He was barely inside the house before the words reached every corner of the Blacknell farmhouse. And then his early Monday visit to the Reverend. It was all happening too fast and Mother felt stranded, left behind by her son's decisions.

Truthfully, she wanted to delay the marriage for a year but knew Robert would never agree. A month wasn't long enough to find an Irish farm girl, so the delay wouldn't stop the marriage. It was the amount of time she needed to come to terms with Margaret Murchie moving into her house. She shuddered at Robert's impulsiveness. Was Margaret's behavior changing her son?

As the couple waited for their special day, the April thaw softened winter's lock on the Restigouche River's ice. Large ice sheets flowed to the east disappearing into the warming waters of Bay Chaleur. Margaret imagined she was one of those large ice floes, heading into places unknown. She pictured a future with more surprises than the voyage across the Atlantic from Arran. But circumstance and chance had brought Margaret and Robert together and she wasn't worried where her new journey would go.

Margaret entered the rectory with Mama and Papa by her side. Mama was filled with excitement as her youngest daughter prepared to marry the man who saved her family. She held Margaret's hand tightly to let her feel a mother's love.

"Margaret, you'll always be our little girl," she said as they walked through the door.

Papa rarely showed his emotion toward his daughters but today was different. He hugged her and put his lips next to her ear.

"I love you dear Margaret," he said. "Robert's a great farmer."

Margaret smiled as she listened to her father words. Of course, he admired his skill on the farm. The farm was Robert's treasure. Margaret left her parents and moved toward Robert. It was the Reverend's turn to speak.

Annie Hamilton and Matthew Blacknell were also standing beside the young couple. They were about to witness a marriage, neither of them had ever expected. Individually, they marveled at the events leading up to today in Dalhousie.

The woman standing in front of Annie was not the young Margaret she had gone to school with back on Arran. This Margaret had become a beautiful bride standing next to the handsome, Robert Blacknell. Many of the young women along Bay Chaleur wanted to be Robert's wife, but that honor would go to Margaret.

Matthew remembered the first time he met the younger Margaret. She had arrived on the Eden with her brother John, in search of their family. Tender moments, he thought. The two tired, yet excited children on the dock in Bathurst. Alone. During those days in Stonehaven, no one could have predicted this future.

Matthew was honored to be part of this special day and proud of his cousin Robert. He glanced over at Mary Blacknell. He saw a mother holding her thoughts together, barely smiling, and afraid of what was next. It was clear to Matthew she was still dealing with the sudden news. It was sudden for everyone, but that might have been Robert's plan, he thought. There wouldn't be time to react.

The ceremony was brief and after a few short minutes Robert and Margaret were declared Mr. and Mrs. Blacknell. After a kiss that made the couple blush, they were off to a new life together. Almost everyone celebrated with them.

The obligatory paperwork was followed by a cup of tea and a piece of cake. After a few stories and more laughter, Matthew headed toward his carriage for the long ride back to Stonehaven. Robert watched his cousin walk away, realizing today would never have happened without Matthew's insistence to emigrate. Robert rushed toward him, filled with an appreciation only Matthew could understand.

The newlyweds were ready to head to Eel River and start a new life together. The ride to the Blacknell farm was filled with optimism. Margaret had many questions about living with Robert's mother but knew better than to ask with Mother sitting in the carriage with them. This was her new challenge. The challenge of gaining the approval of Mrs. Blacknell.

Mother concealed her concerns during the marriage ccremony, knowing it was Robert's day. Deep down she knew his choice of a bride was his decision, she wished for a louder voice. It would take time to learn how to share Robert with another woman. Especially with a woman she barely knew anything about.

As the carriage made its way south along the coastal road, the two women were preparing for life in the same house. The household chores of cooking and cleaning would need to be shared but the house belonged to Mary Blacknell. Margaret wondered if her role would be more like a domestic than Robert's wife. She would soon find out as they turned west along the cove road.

Rebecca and Sarah were intrigued with the thought of Margaret as their new sister-in-law.

"Margaret, you'll need to take your share of chores," Rebecca teased, almost reading Margaret's mind.

"Can you chop wood?" Thomas asked.

Robert let the conversation go for a few miles before he jumped in.

"What do you suggest Margaret should do?" he asked.

Thomas listed all the chores he currently owned. It was the perfect tension relief for Margaret and her new mother-in-law. Laughter followed Thomas' long list.

"There's no getting out of your responsibilities," Mother answered.

"If Margaret takes your chores, what will you do?" Robert asked.

"Advance my schooling," he answered, while catching his mother's nodding approval.

Soon Thomas would leave Eel River and attend college in Fredericton. Mother wondered if sending her son away to school would prevent this type of marriage or create more problems.

Robert expected his marriage would bring many changes to his life. His family would never be the same, yet it was exactly what he wanted. Margaret was his new wife and he would spend the rest of his life with her. He smiled as the carriage reached the farm. His future was decided. The Blacknell farm had increased by one.

29

Margaret in Eel River

Robert insisted on putting the horse and carriage away, letting his family disappear into the house. He wanted to enjoy the couple's first quiet moment together alone, without his family. Nervous laughter filled the barn as the conversation drifted back to Thomas' list of chores for Margaret. It was silly, but encouraging. Margaret could be a part of the Blacknell household.

They were alone at last. The barn was the starting point of the Blacknell farm and today it became a place of solitude for the two newlyweds. Margaret wrapped her arms around Robert feeling the magic of the day. It was a kind of excitement, calmness and gratitude, all at the same time. A floating feeling that carried her well into the evening.

Robert sensed the special connection he had with Margaret. Only three years had passed since their first dance in Colborne and yet so much had changed. He responded to Margaret's embrace with his own squeeze.

Reluctantly they headed into the house, with a bond and feeling of togetherness neither had ever known. It was Margaret's first time at the Blacknell farm, the farm she would share with her new husband. There was so much to take in and learn as she looked around and marveled at the house. It was much larger than the Murchie home in Colborne. It might be larger than any home in Colborne, she thought.

Mother prepared tea and a small meal for the family. It was awkward at first, Margaret wasn't a guest and hadn't established her place. The reaction she had to the outside of the house continued as she made her way to the sitting area. She remained quiet not knowing how to take in everything around her.

"This will take time," Mother admitted, looking directly at her new daughter-in-law. "But we'll figure each other out."

Robert kept his head down, trying not to look at Margaret and make her smile. He recognized his mother's words as a small step toward acceptance. Margaret would be on her best behavior for a while, he thought and Mother might be extra difficult since she didn't get her way. Margaret was not her choice.

When it was time for bed, Mother left the sitting area first, encouraging her children to follow.

"It's time for bed," she declared.

When no one moved from their books and needlework, she became more direct.

"Let's leave Robert and Margaret alone to enjoy their first night together," she said.

Suddenly, Sarah realized her Mother's intentions, blushing while she pushed Thomas out of his seat.

"Let's go Thomas," she said. "Take your book up to bed with you."

Rebecca followed behind after giving Robert and Margaret a hug. As she left the room she turned to look directly at her new sister-in-law.

"It's nice to have you with us, Margaret," she said.

Robert moved closer to Margaret and put his arm around her as the flames of the fire sparked in front of them. It was time to reflect on their special day.

"How'll we ever match this excitement?" Robert asked his new bride.

Margaret smiled and caressed Robert's face in her hands.

"Oh, we will," she said. "This is the beginning of our adventure. What started on the Eden has led us to here. Who knows what's next?"

Robert smiled, acknowledging the unpredictable path that brought them together. Their future was full of possibilities.

"There's so much ahead," he said, his desire to plan, taking over him for the moment. "We'll face many challenges, many unknowns together."

He stopped, realizing a discussion about plans would break the spell and ruin the mood of the evening.

It was a marriage filled with optimism and defined by a sense of togetherness. They both knew the future in the wilderness of Bay Chaleur would place demands on the strength of their relationship. Tonight, however, they could enjoy each other. There wasn't any need to rush. They had a lifetime ahead.

When they were ready to fall asleep, there was a completeness to the day. Margaret closed her eyes, barely believing her good fortune. In the early hours of the next day, she awakened to the sun rising into the bedroom window. How perfect, she thought.

She glanced over toward Robert but he wasn't there. Jumping quickly out of bed and gathering a cover for her nightdress, Margaret made her way toward the stairs. As she turned, Robert was heading toward her with two cups and a teapot in his hands.

"Good morning Mrs. Blacknell," he said.

Margaret blushed and reached over to hug Robert, almost knocking the cups out of his hand. Never giving up a chance to be equal in any conversation, she stared into Robert's eyes.

"Good morning Mr. Blacknell," Margaret replied.

"Will you join me in a cup of tea in our bed?" he asked.

This was a side of Robert she hadn't seen before.

"Of course," she replied. "What a special treat. I didn't know where you were when I woke up."

Robert was filled with emotion as Margaret stood in front of him in her nightgown and messy hair.

"This was not what I expected," Margaret said, staring at the tea pot.

Robert knew he had the advantage. He laughed, feeling a sense of completeness.

"Oh, and what were you expecting?" he asked. "Chores? Chopping wood on the first day of our marriage?"

He knew the chores were waiting, but wanted to cherish the first morning with his wife.

"I love you Maggie," he said.

Margaret felt the warmth of love flow all over her body. It was the first time Robert called her Maggie. It sounded sweet. She jumped back into bed and Robert joined her. The tea was the starting point of a many long conversations between the two. The farm, the kitchen, Mother, cleaning. So many topics. They discussed having children, knowing that it was expected of them.

"How many?" Margaret asked.

"Five," Robert answered.

"Let's see how we do with one, then we can decide," Margaret replied, her excitement rising. There was so much to look forward to.

Settling into the Eel River farm was better than Margaret expected. To her surprise, Mother was less opinionated than Mama. She allowed Margaret to establish herself as Robert's wife and share the kitchen responsibilities and cleaning chores. Misplacing plates or burning a meal wasn't followed by a lecture.

Mother remembered how difficult it was to join a family. She had done it many years ago in Ireland when she joined the Blacknells. She wanted to make Margaret feel the Blacknell house was her home too. Her willingness to make Margaret comfortable, didn't stop her from having concerns about Robert's choice. She had seen the impulsiveness of Margaret at a young age and hoped she had calmed down. Mother would watch closely. She now had a bird's eye view

30

Children

It wasn't long before Margaret was expecting her first child. After several days of nausea, she grew concerned. Not knowing why she felt so horrible, she asked Robert how he was feeling.

"Do you feel like throwing up?" she asked early one morning.

Robert assured her that his belly and general health were good.

"How long have you felt this way?" he asked.

"Close to a week," she replied.

Robert had no experience with pregnant women so it didn't occur to him, she was carrying their first child.

"Well let's keep an eye on it," he said "And let me know if it gets worse."

When the nausea continued, Margaret shared her concerns with Mother the next morning while preparing breakfast.

"How're you feeling?" she asked. "I've been having an upset belly for several days now."

Mother stopped, resting the spoon on the table and shifting her focus to find Robert. When she didn't see him within eyesight, she called his name. Robert arrived in the kitchen almost on demand, but he continued to head toward the door. Mother realized he hadn't heard his name called, so she tried to get his attention before he left the house.

"Where're you going?" Mother asked. "Didn't you hear me call you?"

Robert was oblivious to the conversation taking place in the kitchen. He had chores to attend to and was heading outside to get started. He stopped, apologized and looked directly at his mother. It was exactly what she needed.

"You could be expecting a child," she asserted. "Margaret's upset belly is typical when you're carrying a child."

Robert immediately looked at Margaret who had just heard the same words. They locked eyes and Robert reached for his wife. They would later laugh at having Mother tell them they were expecting a child, but now it was time to understand more.

"How can you be sure?" Robert asked.

"I'm glad someone knows what's wrong with me," Margaret said, acknowledging her mother-in-law's experience.

"You've had four children so I'll need your guidance and help if I'm carrying a baby," she said.

Robert was thrilled but continued to ask questions. For once, he didn't have all the answers.

"Are you sure?" he asked his mother. "Can it be true?" "Our first child? What should we do? Should we check with the doctor?"

So many questions, and so much to think about. Robert immediately started to plan.

Mother intervened, trying to calm everyone down.

"Let's see when the doctor is available," she said. "We can have him check on Margaret the next time he's in Eel River. There's nothing to worry about."

The words fell over the kitchen like a warm blanket as Robert and Margaret continued their embrace. They wanted to hold each other all day, but the chores were calling.

Those chores took on a whole new meaning when Robert walked into the barn. He was no longer taking care of his father's family. He smiled as he thought about taking care of his own child. His own family. There was a new purpose in his life. A child. A child he had created with his wife, Margaret. There was a skip in his step and a happy tune in his whistle.

Margaret didn't know what to say. She had never seen a doctor and didn't know why she needed to see a doctor now. The only woman she had seen pregnant was Catherine. But she hadn't seen Catherine during most of her pregnancy. Only at the announcement and then once the baby was born.

A wave of concern enveloped her. Concern wrapped with excitement. It was good to know why she was nauseous, but she wasn't sure what the next several months would bring. How did Mother know, she wondered? Other than her nausea, what else told her? What happens next? Margaret needed to know more.

She suddenly realized she needed to talk to her own mother. She couldn't recall a single conversation with Mama about having babies and now that was all she wanted to talk about. Robert wouldn't be able to leave the farm, there was too much work to do. The only choice was to write a letter and invite Mama to the Blacknell farm. She wanted her mother's wisdom.

Two weeks later Doctor Ellis was in the settlement and checked on Margaret, at the request of Mother. He declared the baby would arrive early in the new year. Margaret listened to every word the doctor spoke, but didn't know what to say. For the first time in her life, she was sitting across from a doctor, and on this important day, she didn't have one question to ask. Nothing to ask about childbirth. The words simply didn't form. She was tongue tied.

Robert wasn't any better as the doctor described his wife's health. Robert stared at the doctor with a blank look. He didn't have any questions either. Childbirth is a complete mystery, she thought. No one talks about it.

"I should see you in a few months during a visit to the settlement," he said. "Eat well, rest and get plenty of sleep."

And with those final words, Dr. Ellis left the farm.

"It'll be important for me to keep my regular activity," Margaret said without hesitation.

Robert smiled recognizing nothing would keep his wife still.

"Only if you promise to be careful," he said, trying to look strict.

Margaret and Robert went back and forth a few times about the level of activity, until Mother jumped in and made a suggestion.

"The energy Margaret brings to the family is an easy thing to watch," she said. "Margaret, you'll need to stop when we see your energy shift."

Margaret agreed and laughter filled the room. The tension of the doctor and the unknown left. Mother was the calming force. The voice of reason.

Margaret waited for a response to her letter from Mama. She knew it could take weeks but checked with the local Postmaster every other day. In the meantime, she worked in the fields with Robert and tended the animals. The farm was productive and kept the family well fed and cared for. With a child on the way, Robert wondered if he should work beyond the farm. Many farmers had found extra money working, but Robert quickly ruled it out. He wanted to be around his family.

Mama arrived on a Saturday to see her youngest daughter. Papa came along to see the farm. He wasn't ready for a conversation about having babies, but Mama insisted he join her for the trip, so he decided he wanted to see Robert's farm.

Mama shared as best she knew with Margaret, trying to remember all the important details. For Margaret, the mystery wasn't completely solved, especially when she overheard Mother and Mama whispering in the kitchen. Whisper voices again, she thought. What is so secretive about having babies?

She decided not to confront the whispers, asking more questions of both women. They answered politely, leaving out many details, fearful of scaring Margaret. By the end of the visit, Margaret knew more about giving birth, but was convinced there was something the older women weren't sharing. Mama insisted she would learn more when the baby was born. None of this made sense. No one wanted to talk about childbirth, yet everyone had children.

Mama struggled to say goodbye as she stood in the kitchen, ready to leave. There were risks ahead for her daughter and she knew many women didn't survive childbirth. Mama reached for Margaret, enveloping her with both arms. She would be back before the birth, she promised.

The next six months went quickly. The cycle of the farm kept everyone busy with little time to worry about Margaret's pregnancy. The number of cows at the Blacknell farm had increased over the years and now milking demanded more of Robert's time. Thankfully, Margaret liked the routine of the cows.

"Would you take on the milking chore?" he asked Margaret as they were walking into the field. "The cows seem to respond to you."

"I like that idea," Margaret replied. "It will bring me out to the barn twice a day, and I can check up on you."

They both laughed and Margaret headed toward the cows. Farming was something they could do together, outside the house, but she knew a baby would change all that.

Robert increased the size of the farm operation and started to sell milk and crops to nearby farmers. He was harvesting more than enough hay to keep the cows and horses healthy over the winter, so exchanging with the other farmers made sense. Soon, the general store in Eel River was asking about the Blacknell butter and eggs.

Things on the Blacknell farm were about to change. Margaret awoke the morning of the birth with contractions across her entire abdomen. She nudged Robert.

"I think this is it," she declared. "The contractions Doctor Ellis told me about have started. I've been awake for hours and they are getting stronger. Shall we get prepared?"

Robert was in the middle of a deep sleep and didn't respond when Margaret described her contractions.

"Robert, Robert, wake up," she said.

It took Robert a few minutes to figure out where he was.

"The contractions?" he asked.

"Yes, the painful ones that tell when the baby is ready to be born," Margaret replied.

He suddenly realized this wasn't a dream and sat straight up in the bed.

"Shall I get Mother?" he asked.

"I think so," Margaret replied, her voice getting softer. "I'm in so much pain, she'll know what to do."

Robert jumped out of bed. He was wide awake now and rushed down the hall to Mother's room.

"Mother, can you join us in the bedroom?" He asked while knocking on the door. "Margaret is having painful contractions and we need your help."

It was all Mother needed to hear. She was needed and a grandchild was on the way.

"Let me get dressed and I'll be right there," she replied.

Robert returned to Margaret and knew immediately that her pain level had increased. Margaret couldn't get comfortable.

Within a few minutes, Mother was standing over the bed reassuring Margaret that everything would be okay.

"Nice deep breaths dear," she said. "This baby needs nice deep breaths."

Margaret hadn't experienced pain like this before and had no problem accepting the advice of her mother-in-law. Margaret could barely speak. She tried to remain quiet, taking deep breaths to reduce the pain that had overwhelmed her body. A midwife didn't live in the settlement so Mother and Robert would deliver the baby.

It was four hours before sunrise, yet the entire Blacknell house was awake.

"How can we help?" Sarah asked.

"What can we do," Rebecca added.

"I'll add more wood to the fire," Thomas said.

Mother had no trouble assigning tasks and getting everyone busy.

"Get the water boiling Sarah," she shouted.

Sarah and Rebecca hurried to the kitchen. It was a whirlwind of activity. No one wanted to miss the moment.

As Margaret's contractions got closer and closer, Mother sent Rebecca for more towels and blankets.

"Get the softest ones you can find," she asked. "The baby will need a soft wrapping."

Rebecca was thrilled to help so off she went. Robert wasn't leaving Margaret's side. He stroked her forehead and hair as he winced with every contraction.

"Robert, take a deep breath," Mother ordered. "You'll pass out if you keep breathing like that."

At 10:45 A.M. a baby boy became the youngest member of the Blacknell family. Margaret's color returned to her pale skin and baby Blacknell found comfort in his grandmother's delivery and parent's embrace.

William Wadsworth Blacknell had arrived, bringing happiness to the magical couple and creating a lasting bond between Margaret and her mother-in-law. When the doctor showed up at the house later that week, he declared William and Margaret healthy. The new baby, William, became the center of the Blacknell farm.

Mama couldn't wait to see William. There was something special about meeting her daughter's first baby. It was different than John's children. They were special too, but this was Margaret's child.

Papa insisted on traveling to see his new grandson, despite the coming thaw and potential work at the sawmill. The mill was a large part of Papa's life. His hours had increased and gave the Murchies more money than the farm. It was another freedom he enjoyed about Bay Chaleur. He knew this would never have happened on Arran. But this time, the sawmill would have to wait, their new grandson was more important.

They would travel in a few weeks. Papa thought it was enough time for Margaret to rest and adjust to motherhood.

Liza was busy with the Cook family, and Janet was completely absorbed with nursing. Both sisters unable to join them. Mama didn't mind going without them, they would meet William in due time, she thought.

When they arrived in Eel River, William was over two weeks old and the Blacknell farm was beginning to settle into a routine.

"He's beautiful," Mama declared. "Do you think he will keep his red hair?"

Robert laughed, looking directly at Margaret.

"I hope so," he said. "It's a reminder of his mother."

Margaret wasn't so sure, she knew the challenges of living with red hair. She shook her head, attempting to make William's hair change color.

William was a beautiful child. He had the coloring of his mother and the features of his father. Everyone in his family saw themselves in this tiny baby.

"He has my chin," Mama said proudly, pointing to the tiny face looking up at everyone. And so, they began, one by one, declaring their similarities to William.

"When you put it all together, we all make a William," Robert said laughing.

Papa chuckled at the silliness of these women, as he watched his wife search for her features in her new grandson. Stories about babies and childbirth filled the afternoon connecting the two families together with this little boy.

Mother was in her element describing the morning of the birth and how strong Margaret was during William's delivery. Robert remained quiet, taking it all in. Baby William was now the bond, the connection between his mother and his wife.

The mothers in the room shared stories of their children's birth and what they knew after delivery. Margaret was surprised how little the mothers were willing to share. She took her queues from Mama and Mother, not revealing all the details. She vowed she would ask her mother sometime in the future about the secrecy of childbirth. The whisper voices among the women. For now, she was content with sharing her new baby with his grandparents. This mystery would wait until later.

31

The Sawmill

William's first year filled the family with new milestones. First steps, first words. All the cherished events. For the Blacknell family, William was the first child to ever accomplish any of these milestones. He had captivated his young mother with his personality and his father with his tenacity. William was a good baby. He slept well and never seemed cranky.

"He's Robert," Mother remarked. "Robert was the best baby."

It wasn't long before Margaret was expecting their second child. Only this time the baby would arrive around November, at the end of harvest season. A busy time at the Blacknell farm for a newborn and baby William, approaching his second birthday.

Margaret was better prepared for this pregnancy than her first one. She recognized the nausea and the loss of her waistline before too long. The symptoms were more familiar now, giving her confidence.

But knowing a child was on the way, was one thing. Questions remain about pregnancy and childbirth. There were too many unanswered questions. No matter how Margaret approached the topic, Mother or Mama remained aloof with vague answers.

The excitement of having a second child wasn't a worry for Margaret. Mother was never too far away and Sarah or Rebecca were always ready to share in caring for William.

Away from the Blacknell farm, things were changing. Papa had increased his hours at the sawmill, shifting the farm workload and allowing Mama to purchase new quilting fabric at the store in town. There was something special about quilting with fabric that had never been worn. Mama felt rich.

Papa decided to work the early shifts at the mill, allowing time to complete any farm chores after he arrived home. It was a good compromise. He never felt too far from the farm and the mill gave him skills he was proud of. The mill men were a second family to Papa.

The Colborne settlers quickly saw another advantage of the nearby sawmill. The mill's lumber and shingles were the perfect upgrade to replace the barns and homes built with only logs. Soon the mills were operating several shifts, just to keep pace with the newfound demand.

For many of the Colborne men, the time spent at the sawmill was the best part of their day. The work was difficult but less monotonous than farming and warmer than fishing several miles out in the bay. At the sawmill, there wasn't a need to fight the weather all day.

On a day like any other, Papa arrived at the mill and immediately started moving the large logs to the saw's entrance. As he pushed a log onto the carriage feeding the central blade, he noticed the newly cut boards starting to jam. Without calling for assistance, he rushed toward the saw, losing his footing on the wet and bark filled floor. As he struggled to regain his balance, he fell directly under the powerful saw. John observed his father lose his balance and ran over to help, but he was too late. John could only watch in horror as the saw cut his father's body into pieces directly in front of him.

Papa died instantly and John stood absolutely frozen, unable to move. He stared at his father's lifeless body, almost willing Papa to say something. He didn't notice the eerie silence engulfing the mill as the machinery stopped and voices stood quiet.

Without talking, the mill men split into two groups. One group surrounded the center saw to cover the horror from John's eyes, while the other group walked John out of the building. Once outside, they struggled to find the right words, anything to console him.

Inside the mill, the first group retrieved the body after John was out of view. They all knew he had seen the worst. He didn't need to see them pull his father out from under the saw.

John sat in shock, completely dumbfounded, holding his head with his hands.

"Can we take you home?" one of the men asked.

He could see all the men standing around him but couldn't hear the words coming from their mouths. The men kept talking, offering to stay with John or take him home. Nothing worked. After a few minutes John stood up. It was time to do something.

"I need to go to my mother," John said, barely speaking loud enough for others to hear. "She needs to know what happened. What happened to Papa."

Catherine's brother Daniel, one of the youngest mill workers, agreed to take John to the Murchie farm.

"I'll go with you," Daniel offered. "It'll be best if I go. The others will find the undertaker to take care of the body."

"I can't leave, I won't leave," John said. "I must stay until the undertaker comes to take Papa."

John was barely functioning. He was in a state of shock, a state of complete disbelief. He pushed aside Daniel's arm, wanting to head back inside the mill to find his father. There's a chance Papa's okay, he wished, trying to restart the day in his mind. As he headed toward the steps, Daniel tried to keep him outside, but John wouldn't listen. He had to see his father.

Once inside the building he walked toward the main saw, wishing for a different outcome. As he moved closer, he noticed a body lying lifeless on the floor, covered in a blanket. There was blood everywhere. His legs started to buckle and the men rushed toward him. They agreed he could stay and wait, but he must wait in a different area. Away from the tragedy he would replay over and over.

As the morning turned into the afternoon, the hours felt like days had passed. The guilt of bringing Papa to the mill started to eat away at John and the guilt for not preventing his father's fall took hold.

When John and Daniel eventually left and arrived at the farm, Mama was immediately concerned.

"Where's Papa?" she asked. "Why aren't you at the mill?"

John tried to be gentle but his words were blunt.

"Papa's dead," he cried.

Mama reached for the table in an attempt to steady her legs from collapsing. She didn't believe John.

"Dead?" she asked. "When he left this morning, everything was fine"

John nodded, trying to remain strong for his mother. After he described the accident, he reached for her, but she pushed his arms away.

"I told him not to work in that sawmill," she screamed, her voice angry at the world. "It's your fault John. You made him do it. You killed your father."

John knew this wasn't the time to argue with his mother. She had to blame someone and he understood the reason for her anger. And he couldn't argue, he was already blaming himself.

There was no describing the grief John felt. His mother's anger was directed his way. He had yet to face his sisters and feel their despair. All the decisions he made were coming to the surface. It was true Papa followed him to the sawmill. They both enjoyed the work and the friendship at the mill. Now what? Could he stay at the sawmill after the accident? What about the farm? There were many more decisions to make.

John was awash with emotions yet he knew there would be challenges with keeping the Murchie farm. He tried to push those thoughts aside, but they kept coming back. Everything the Murchie family wanted in their new homeland was now in question. Was this emotion or logic? John couldn't decide.

He didn't know if Mama could keep the farm running without Papa. John was managing the Stewart farm and Robert had his family's responsibilities in Eel River. What would they do if Mama decided to stay? What if she couldn't manage it? Could they sell it and have Mama move in with John or Robert? What about Liza and Donald? Janet? His head was filled with questions and there were few answers. It all happened so quickly and he needed to talk to his sisters.

The news arrived in Eel River later that evening with Liza and Donald. They had traveled to Eel River with the intent of collecting Margaret and bringing her to Colborne. Mama needed her children with her at the Murchie farm.

"There's no need to take a small child with you," Mother said. "Robert, you go with Margaret. We can care for William and manage the farm for the next few days."

Robert accepted his mother's offer without argument. His mother-in-law needed comfort now. This would be a difficult time.

The wake and funeral were surreal. Papa was a young man, not yet fifty years old. Too young to be buried, everyone said. Isabella and Neil sat with the family, afraid of speaking. There were no words to lessen the sadness surrounding Colborne.

The community and Papa's closest friends offered to help Mama but she was barely functioning and unable to accept. The impact of Papa's death had not moved past her first reactions of anger and grief. She had yet to deal with her livelihood or that of the farm. John decided the difficult conversations could wait for now.

Papa was buried in the Colborne Cemetery overlooking the bay that had become his new home. There were several other Arran names on the tombstones in the graveyard, forcing John to think Papa was among old friends. This is not how Papa had planned it, John thought. His desire to leave Arran brought the family to Colborne, but this was not his expected ending.

Once all the visitors had gone and daily life started to creep back in without Papa, Mama refused to get out of bed. Liza and Janet decided not to push it and let her sleep for a few days. Janet took a leave from her work in Dalhousie and Liza came home every night from the Cook family.

"Mama, it's time to feed the chickens," Janet started on the third day.

"There's nothing for me to get up for," Mama replied.

"You need to get out of bed," Janet pushed. "You need to get up for us. We know you miss Papa and we miss him too, but we'll lose the farm if we don't take care of it."

It took another few days of nagging, pushing and visits from Isabella. Eventually Mama got out of bed. She had barely eaten over the past five days and her clothes hung on her like they were made for a much larger person. Janet held her as they walked to the kitchen.

"Let's have some bread and tea," she said.

Slowly Mama came back to the family.

At first, John's only choice was to manage the farm. He couldn't bring himself to go back to the sawmill so he spent his mill time back at the Murchie farm. It was another way to numb away the pain and guilt of losing his father. After a month of little sleep and running two farms, John decided it was time to bring his sisters together to discuss the family options. He needed their input and more importantly, their help.

"If we come together, we can help Mama," John told Liza.

Liza was the daughter Mama listened to. They had a special relationship and Mama thought Liza always listened to her. There weren't any arguments, like the other two daughters. Janet would push and Margaret would distract. John knew Liza's voice would be heard.

Many of the Colborne families grieved along with the Murchies, but not long after the burial, John sensed a sharp change in attitude. One afternoon at the General Store, several Arran friends started a conversation about the farm. When John heard their type of questions, he grew angry.

"What do you mean take the farm off our hands?" John asked. "We aren't giving it away. The Murchie farm isn't for sale."

He left the store in a huff, almost forgetting the flour he had purchased. The questions and conversation had to be shared with his sisters. They needed to know which families to trust. He thought he heard Uncle

Neil's voice at the store, but wasn't sure. None of it made sense to him.

Margaret traveled to Colborne with Robert for the family meeting. It was the first one since the funeral so emotions were still on edge. When Margaret and Robert entered the house, John pulled them aside to share what he had learned at the store. Margaret stood with her mouth open, not believing what she heard and trying to understand their motive.

"These are Mama's friends," she said. "And family, if it was Neil."

When Janet came into the room, Margaret pulled her aside without giving her the information John had shared.

"What are your immediate plans?" Margaret asked.

Janet was taken aback by Margaret driving the conversation.

"What do you mean my immediate plans?" Janet countered. "Are they of your concern?"

Margaret saw Janet's posture change and realized there was a misunderstanding.

"Look I don't mean to be difficult and now isn't the time for us to argue," she said. "We need to discuss the farm and Mama. Some people are trying to take the farm away from Mama."

Janet couldn't believe that someone would try to take the farm.

"That's nonsense Margaret," she said. "Your vivid imagination is at it again."

The conversation quickly turned into a frank but blunt conversation.

"If you don't believe me, go ask John," Margaret said.

Janet walked over to John and with her hands on her hips looking for answers. John saw her coming with daggers looking straight at him.

"What?" he said.

"Why don't I hear about these farm stealing stories?" she asked. "Why must I hear it from Margaret?"

John just stood still, shaking his head. So much to discuss and now there was an argument.

"Where's Liza?" he asked. "Let's discuss it all together, all of us."

Once the story was repeated for all to hear, Janet went quiet. Liza had the same reaction that Margaret had. It made no sense. These were family, friends.

"Maybe not," John said. "The farm is a nice piece of property overlooking the bay. The harvests are good and the amount of cleared land is very attractive for building a larger farm. Papa proudly did more than the grant required."

John was looking for the goodness in everyone, Janet thought. She had seen difficult conversations with sick patients and many friends and families aren't always nice to each other.

Once the Murchie children stopped talking, Robert suggested the family review Papa's will. It could take a few weeks, but the family needed a legal opinion to ensure Mama and the farm were safe. Robert was confident the will would state Papa's wishes for the farm and everyone agreed.

"Mama's not capable of making difficult decisions right now," John said. "She just lost her husband and the anchor in her life. I'll check with the solicitor in Dalhousie about the will."

Janet had another idea. Maybe the farm should be sold. Only Mama needed a place to live. She could move in with John or Margaret. Liza would eventually marry and leave the farm. No one would be left. This was an opportunity not a problem.

"Why don't we sell the farm now?" she said.

Janet thought the idea was worth saying. It was a choice the family could make. After the words left her mouth, the entire room went silent.

"Thankfully Mama isn't here to hear you say that," John said.

Margaret couldn't believe her ears and a shocked Liza had to be reminded to close her mouth. Liza eventually weighed in.

"What's wrong with you?" she asked.

Janet tried to explain her logic but no one would listen.

"We need to consider all choices," she said. "It might be quiet for now but it will come up again."

"It is time to focus on Mama," John declared.

The conversation was over.

32

Healing

The Colborne farm wasn't the same without Papa. The entire farm was in mourning and even the animals sensed something was different. Reminders of Papa were visible everywhere. The cleared land, farmhouse, and barn, the entire Murchie farm displayed Papa's hard work.

Mama tried to look beyond the constant reminders without success. She saw him in every room or walking in from the barn. She waited for him to join her at the supper table, setting a place for him every night. The daylight hours were painfully long for Mama, but the evenings were even longer.

Janet spent most evenings talking with Mama about the past. They shared stories about Arran, the family or anything Mama wanted to talk about. Mama needed to touch every moment she had shared with Papa. The conversations could go well into the early hours of the next day.

Eventually, Liza chose to leave her domestic role with the Cook family. She would live at home and care for her mother. Janet could return to Dalhousie and nursing, with the promise of coming home when she wasn't working. It was their best option.

The farm started to suffer. Managing two farms proved too difficult for John and signs of neglect started to show. There was only time for the basics, forcing John to wonder if Janet's thoughts about selling the farm were correct.

"Do you think we should sell the farm?" he asked Liza, late one afternoon after the animals were safely in the barn.

The timing of the question could not have been worse for Liza. She was dealing with her own issues while trying to pull her mother back from despair.

"Sell the farm," she repeated, hearing the words come out of her own mouth. "Is that what you said? You've been talking to Janet, haven't you?"

John was surprised by Liza's reaction. He sensed there was more to the response but couldn't hold back. He was tired and wanted to be heard.

"I can't do it alone," John declared. "The farm's too much. I have my own farm and family to care for."

The burden of the Murchie legacy had fallen to the oldest daughter and the only son. There were clear signs the two were buckling under all the responsibility.

"I know, I want to help but Mama's too fragile," she said. "There's no time to sleep, with housework and Mama to care for."

They agreed a family discussion was necessary. The farm was the family's prize and neither wanted to give it up.

Eventually, with the constant coaxing from Liza and Janet, Mama started to crawl out of the dark place she occupied. After six months a few flickers of light appeared. It started with baking a birthday cake for John and spending time with John's children. Eventually, she was quilting and talking about visiting a few friends. A tiny space in the hole left behind by Papa began to fill in.

Not long after Mama returned to quilting, Bessie McNeish, another Arran widow, came to visit. Bessie gradually showed Mama how to live without a husband and within a short time, the two women became inseparable. Malcolm McNeish had died a year earlier and left Bessie with a farm and grown children. The two widows from Arran grew stronger together as they accepted their future lives without their husbands.

During the depths of Mama's darkness, John received word from the solicitor regarding Papa's will. The farm was bequeathed to Mama provided she did not remarry. Once she took another husband, the farm would go to the four children. Divided evenly. John, as executor of Papa's estate took his responsibility seriously, but had concerns about telling his mother not to remarry.

John knew a decision had to be made, but wanted to discuss it with his sisters first. He approached the subject with Liza and Janet knowing it would be weeks before he saw Margaret. The discussion didn't resolve the problem.

"We don't know what will happen in the future," Janet declared. "Mama needs to know the truth."

John tried to reason with her. He wasn't avoiding the truth, he didn't know how to tell her. What if she remarried, what then?

Liza remained quiet. The farm, the house and Mama were a large part of her life. A life she wanted to change, but couldn't. Janet tried to make eye contact with John, but he kept his head down, too unsure of what to do.

"We've an obligation to tell her the truth," Janet enforced, ignoring her sister's silence.

John had heard enough. He had responsibility as the executor and didn't want to upset his mother. Not now, not while she was still grieving.

"We'll tell her next year," he said. "There's no need to upset her anymore."

Janet immediately backed down. John was right, Mama was still grieving, and no one knew how she would react to the will.

"Promise me, we'll tell her in one year," Janet requested, looking at her brother and sister. "Promise me."

It was a heartfelt request and they all knew it. The truth would come out at some point and the children were responsible to deliver the message.

33

Winter in Eel River

James Patterson Blacknell arrived as expected in November. His birth brought a change of focus for the family, still struggling to recover from the loss of Papa. Named after his maternal grandfather, James became the focus of Mama's attention. When she was with him, Papa wasn't on her mind. It made Margaret wonder if a change of location might help her mother recover.

"Why don't you stay in Eel River over the winter?" Margaret asked, unsure of her mother's response.

She hadn't asked Robert, but knew he'd agree. Anything to get Mama back to her old self, he would say.

"What about Liza?" Mama asked. "She needs me."

Both women looked in Liza's direction.

"It'll be difficult, but I'll manage," Liza said laughing. Mama started to smile realizing how important Liza had become. Unknowingly, Liza had filled a space Papa left behind. Mama found a purpose caring for Liza. Margaret seized the moment.

"You can help care for James and William," Margaret said. "They could use your expertise and so could their mother."

The words barely passed Margaret's lips before Mama beamed with the excitement of staying close to the new baby. Without hesitation, she agreed, caring for her grandsons was more important than Liza.

Liza agreed to bring extra clothes on her next visit, so in the meantime, Mama wore a few of Margaret's dresses. She was close enough in size with her daughter so Margaret's clothes could hold her over. Nonetheless, Mama's weight loss was still evident. A strong woman turned thin and frail by the loss of her husband.

Robert shook his head wondering how three mothers under one roof would work. He supported Margaret's request, but saw the perils of three different personalities together all the time.

"How do you plan to manage this?" he asked Margaret.

"I don't know," she said honestly. "Take each day as it comes."

Mary Blacknell became the centerpiece for the next phase in the healing process. She gently pushed Elizabeth Murchie a little every day to rebuild her emotional strength. Slowly Mama grew stronger and Margaret's dresses began to fit better.

The two grandmothers found a lasting connection through their grandchildren, William and James. Mother was widowed with small children back in Ireland and understood Elizabeth Murchie's emotional pain. Before long, they were sharing stories and laughing about bringing up their own children. Quilting and embroidering became a time to share family stories. Occasionally, Margaret noticed a different type of laughter when Mama brought up the challenges of raising her youngest daughter. It was a laughter that filled every room in the Blacknell house.

"Goodness, what an impulsive child," she told Mother. "I never thought she would turn out to be so calm. It's all Robert."

Mother glowed as she heard the nice words about Robert. She had something in common with Elizabeth Murchie. They both credited Robert with improving Margaret's demeanor.

Never giving Margaret credit for positive actions was Mama's way. Mama must be getting better, Margaret thought. But inside the Blacknell house, it was difficult to notice the subtle changes in Mama. It would take a visit from Liza to point it out.

Liza had written suggesting a visit to the farm in a few weeks. Margaret was excited to see her sister and hear how she was managing the Murchie farm with John. Margaret never imagined Liza had a different reason for visiting Eel River.

"Liza's coming to visit," Margaret announced to Robert after collecting the mail.

"Your mother will be glad to see her," Robert said. "Do you think she'll take her home?" He asked.

"I don't think so, but I don't know," Margaret replied, surprised by Robert's question.

She began to think about Liza and her sudden need to visit. Did she have news to share? Margaret would have to wait for the answers. Liza would arrive in Eel River before the post could travel back and forth between the two settlements.

A sense of longing filled Mama when Liza entered the Blacknell farmhouse.

"You look well rested," Mama said the moment she saw her. "How I've missed our talks."

Liza returned the compliments, recognizing her mother's improved health and weight gain. The past few months were the longest the two had ever been apart and Mama needed to catch up. For the rest of the afternoon, Mama sat with Liza and talked about her new grandsons, the farm, and caught up on the Colborne gossip, or nonsense, as Mama liked to call it. There was a special bond between mother and daughter. A bond Margaret or Janet didn't have.

As Liza prepared to leave, she motioned for Margaret to follow her to the carriage. It was clear she had more to share.

"She's almost back," Liza said, pleased with her younger sister "She's almost back to her old self. She's interested in the future again. The stay in Eel River has been good for her."

"Should we plan on bringing her back to Colborne in May?" Margaret asked.

Margaret knew Robert had the farm work scheduled to start and knowing when to bring Mama home would certainly help.

"I suppose, but with Mama getting better, can we talk about the future?" Liza asked.

"Your future or Mama's future?" Margaret asked, trying to find the true reason for Liza's question.

Liza blushed and looked at her feet.

"Mine," she said.

Margaret pulled Liza toward the barn, attempting to get her inside, and out of the cold wind.

"What is it?" she asked. "Are you and Donald getting married?"

Liza smiled, revealing there was more to share.

"It's not that simple," Liza said. "There are a couple of decisions we need to make. Donald stopped working at the Colborne ship builder and plans to go west."

"Just like Edward," Margaret interjected.

"Yes, Donald heard about Edward and all the others working in Wisconsin," she said. "The money and work is good they say."

This is horrible, Margaret thought. What will Mama do? So much change since Papa died. How will she react?

"Please don't share with Mama," Liza asked. "She's doing well and I don't want to change her progress."

"What about the farm?" Margaret asked. "Why don't you and Donald take the farm?"

Liza couldn't believe Margaret's suggestion, then realized Margaret didn't know about the will.

"Are you serious?" Liza quizzed back. "The farm is Mama's and by law, I am only entitled to one fourth of it."

Margaret didn't know how to react.

"What?" she said. It was the only thing that came out of her mouth.

Liza shared what she knew about the will, hoping Margaret wouldn't get angry. A silence fell over the two women as Margaret attempted to understand.

"We have to decide when to get married," Liza said, refusing to keep quiet. "Donald's out of work, so that's another challenge. At least Papa isn't here to disapprove."

Margaret continued to keep quiet. So much information and Liza had her own big decision to make. And the will, what should they do?

"I'll talk to John about my plans," Liza said. "The farm will fall on his shoulders when I leave."

"We need to meet again in a few weeks," Margaret insisted, unable to keep quiet. "Is Janet aware of your plans?"

As much as Margaret didn't want to ask, she had to. Janet would be upset if she heard it for the first time at the meeting.

Liza shook her head.

"I've only told you," she said. "Please keep it private for now."

The discussion left Margaret concerned for her mother and the farm. Mama couldn't stay in Eel River forever and the farm needed constant care. John would know what to do, Margaret thought. Robert would have an opinion but there was little doubt, the burden of the Murchie farm would fall upon John's shoulders.

34

Return to Murchie Farm

Mama returned to the Murchie farm when the weather warmed and the roads were good for travel. She was a changed woman, ready for life on her own and filled with a confidence to live without Papa. She had been away from the farm long enough for everything to feel inviting and new when she opened the door. The kitchen, the sitting room belonged to her. She wasn't a guest or a visitor. She was home.

Liza and Donald had kept the farm running and Mama insisted they should stay. Donald had relieved John's burden of caring for two farms giving Mama the impression he would continue to manage the farm. She tried to convince Liza to take it over.

"But Mama, it's not mine," Liza told her, not knowing how to reveal the details of the will.

"I can give it to you," Mama pushed. "Your father left it to me so I can do as I see fit and I want you to have it."

Now Liza was in a bind. It was time for Mama to know Papa's wishes, she thought. She is healthy and strong again.

"Let's talk about it with John when he's here next," Liza offered without looking at her mother.

Besides the will, the Murchie family avoided talking about the sawmill. There was a fear any conversation would turn towards John and how his work at the mill caused Papa's death.

John and his mother had barely spoken before she left for Eel River so he wasn't sure how she would react to seeing him. As he pulled off the main road onto the Murchie road, he felt the tension build in his entire body.

Time is a great healer, he thought, hoping Mama had softened from blaming him for Papa's death. Time hadn't healed his wounds, however and John continued to have nightmares about that horrible day. He saw Papa falling over and over in his dreams. It continued to fuel the guilt he lived with every day.

He worried how the conversation would flow, knowing he couldn't avoid visiting Mama since her return to the farm. Today, he would keep everything light and share his three children with their grandmother. It was a page out of Margaret's book. John's children were the perfect distraction.

"Mama, you look well rested, John said walking into the kitchen. "Eel River must've been good for you."

Mama reached over to hug John.

"I know terrible things were said after Papa's death," she admitted, starting to cry while holding John. "I've thought about it over the past few months and want you to know it was my first reaction to the bad news."

Mama wanted John to know she understood it was an accident. "I'm sorry," she said.

John took in his mother's words. "I'm sorry too," he responded, barely able to speak. "It was a horrible day. A day I will live with for the rest of my life."

And with a few soft words, a mother and son tried to connect their grief and love for Papa. They needed to make sense of the past few months and find comfort together. John knew the accident was something between them. A wedge that would need more time.

The three children watched as their father and grandmother unwrapped from each other and tried to move on from the past. They quickly stole Mama's interest as they tugged on her dress demanding attention. James, Isabella and Elizabeth ran behind their grandmother as she headed into the sitting area.

"Let's read a book" she said.

The children surrounded her feet waiting for the words. Mama smiled as the three gazed up at her. It was good to be back in Colborne.

With Mama occupied at the moment, Liza pulled John to the corner of the kitchen away from Mama's view.

"We need to talk," she said. "Mama wants me to take the farm and that's not possible."

Liza was confident her brother would understand.

"I don't want to run it while I can only own a quarter of it," she declared.

John stopped smiling and looked concerned.

"Did you tell her about the will?" he asked.

"No, I couldn't," she said. "Not today, not now. She just got home."

John wasn't sure what to do. If they sold the farm, there wasn't a place for Mama to live.

"Can't we leave it the way it is right now?" he asked. "It's working."

Liza folded her arms across her body, unhappy with her brother's question.

"It's not working," she said. "It can't continue much longer and we promised Janet we would tell Mama about the will. She'll understand Papa's wishes."

John hadn't seen an angry Liza for many years but there no mistaking it. Her two eyebrows became one and her nostrils flared.

"Before you say anything Liza," he said trying to prevent an argument. "How can we make it work?"

Liza turned her head away from John and tried to remain calm as she responded.

"It can't work because Donald and I are planning to move west," she said. "Donald doesn't want to farm. He wants to work in the big woods timber."

Now John understood the gravity of the problem. The whole situation was bad. The only sister available to take the farm, didn't want it. He couldn't count on Janet. She was busy nursing and had little interest in farming or Colborne. Besides she wouldn't last a month farming, he thought. Was it possible to run the two farms, he wondered? It was the family's only choice.

"Liza, I need your help to transition," he asked. "Can you give me at least a month?"

"Yes, but not more" she replied. "Donald is planning to leave and find a job in Wisconsin," she added. "The Rogers young men from Colborne are heading out west in a few weeks. Donald has plans to go with them."

"What about marriage?" John asked expecting a thoughtful answer.

"We were married last week," she blurted.

John had to sit down. He couldn't believe his ears. Liza was married! And no one knew.

"Donald will send for me once he's settled," she continued.

"Does Mama know?" he asked, wanting to know if he was the last to find out.

"No, she has been wrapped up in her own grief, I couldn't tell her," Liza said. "We'd planned this for months before Papa died and didn't want to wait any longer."

John thought about the timing of everything. It would take Donald more than one month to settle and call for Liza. He was convinced he had a little more time. More than a month to solve this problem.

"We now have two secrets from Mama," John told Liza.

He wondered how life got so complicated.

"Let's start by telling your family about your marriage to Donald," John said.

"I'll do it when the time is right," she answered. "For the past few months, no one was interested in happy events. I'm not sure the family is ready."

Liza was right. Everyone was still in mourning.

Donald took center stage when he entered the kitchen from the barn later in the afternoon. Liza waited until he sat down at the table next to her before she whispered the details of the day into his ear. John had left with the children for the Stewart farm, so only Mama was in the house, sitting across from them.

Liza looked at her mother and tried to imagine the upcoming reaction to her news. There's no time like the present, she thought.

"Mama, I have some good news," she started.

"Oh, I need some good news dear," Mama replied. "What is it?"

"Well, I didn't know when to tell you or how," Liza started.

"What is it?" Mother interrupted.

"Donald and I were married last week," she answered looking directly at her mother.

A large smile came over Mama's face.

"That's very good news," she said. "I'm happy for the two of you."

Liza didn't sense any concern in her mother's voice. She watched her mother finish supper, expecting a few words about Papa, but nothing was said. As Mama rose to leave the table, she embraced both Donald and Liza.

"This is good news," she repeated.

The day ended with one less secret. It was now up to John to manage the first one. Liza partially relaxed knowing there was more, more to tell about their future plans. For now, it would wait. She could be Donald's wife.

35

Partridge Island

The nursing life in Dalhousie consumed Janet's time, forcing her to stay in town most weeks. It was challenging as the population of Bay Chaleur grew, bringing new families and their children to the many settlements along its shoreline. Janet shared a love of helping people with her new friends, the nurses in Dalhousie. They were a tight knit group of women who chose nursing over marriage. They were different for their time. Janet took great pleasure watching her sick patients get better, but she wanted more. A greater challenge.

Soon she would get the opportunity. Rumors were spreading about sick immigrants arriving across the many ports in the province. With each passing month, the horrors of the rumors grew. Every port was impacted, from St. John to Miramichi. Small numbers of these sick arrivals turned into stories of spreading death. It wasn't long before requests for doctors and nurses went out across the province.

When Janet first heard about the need, she was immediately interested. This is my calling, she thought, excited at the chance to leave Dalhousie and head south. She didn't think it was possible to travel alone so she decided to ask a few of her friends to join her.

"We can work in St. John," she excitedly told them. "Most of the ships are arriving there and it's the largest city in the province."

Reluctant at first, because of the distance, Gertrude and Bridget eventually agreed to go. Janet was too convincing for both women to say no.

Janet decided St. John was everything Bay Chaleur wasn't. A large port city without surrounding farms, she told them. She actually didn't know anything about the city, but her enthusiasm filled in the details she needed.

Janet traveled to Colborne to share the news of her upcoming plans and date of departure. Unexpected, Janet arrived at the farm in the middle of the day, just in time for dinner. Liza and John were in the barn when she arrived and they dropped everything when she rode up the road.

"Is everything alright?" John wanted to know.

He wondered what she was up to. Janet loved the element of surprise.

"Of course," Janet replied. "I'm leaving Bay Chaleur in a few days and wanted to say goodbye."

She didn't wait for more questions. Her excitement couldn't keep her quiet.

"I'm heading to St. John to help with the sick immigrants," she said proudly.

"St. John!" John exclaimed. "Why so far away?"

"They have the biggest need," Janet replied, convinced her family wouldn't understand.

They knew about the difficulties crossing the Atlantic, but they wouldn't understand why she wanted to help. She went into the house to find her mother. Mama was as surprised as John to see her.

"Well, what brings you home?" Mama asked. "It's nice to see you."

Mama's voice changed when she learned of Janet's plans. She listened as Janet explained the need in St. John, worrying as the numbers and types of illnesses were described.

"Is it safe?" Mama wanted to know.

"As safe as any place with sick people," Janet replied.

Truthfully, Janet hadn't given it any thought. It was an adventure and one with a purpose.

Mama attempted to change Janet's plans, fearing her daughter would become sick from the immigrants. She had seen the illnesses on the ship and knew the suffering. What could Janet do to help them, she asked?

Janet would have none of it. No one was going to change her mind, not even her own mother. She respectfully told Mama nothing would stop her, forcing the two women to change the discussion.

After Janet said her goodbye to Mama she headed toward the kitchen where Liza was patiently waiting. Liza motioned her to sit, then promptly shared her news about Donald. Janet couldn't believe the words coming from Liza's mouth. Liza married?

"Where's Donald?" she asked. "Is he working the farm with you too?"

Liza shook her head, trying not to show any emotion. Donald had left a few days ago and she missed him already.

"He's heading to Wisconsin," Liza said, folding her arms across her chest.

Janet was confused, trying to makes sense of what she just heard.

"Wisconsin, but didn't you say you were married?" she asked.

"Yes, and I plan to join him once he's settled," she said. "Mama thinks he's coming back. Please don't tell her my plan."

Janet promised to keep it quiet, not sure what was going on with her family. So much had changed since Papa died. And Wisconsin didn't make sense. But then, St. John was just as confusing. The Murchie children were expanding their footprints in this new country, she thought.

As Janet said goodbye to Liza, John walked toward his two sisters.

"We need a family meeting to discuss the farm," he said. "Do you know how long you'll be away?"

Janet shook her head. Her plan didn't include a return to Bay Chaleur. At least for now.

"Let's meet in the new year," she said. "We'll have more time to think about it."

John agreed and the three Murchie children said their goodbyes, letting the secret live a little longer. Liza and John were scared for their sister, but Janet showed little concern.

As Janet headed back into town, she thought about her family and their questions. Why was everyone so concerned? Should she be? Her family's questions were obvious and she should have known the answers. She shrugged it off. This was her adventure, not theirs. Besides, they were set in their Bay Chaleur ways, unable to understand her point of view. What difference did it make? They didn't know anything about St. John or caring for sick patients.

As Janet justified her lack of answers, she decided to inquire about the hospital and St. John. It was too late to explain everything to her family, but not too late to prepare for life in the city. So far, the only information she had, was a collection of stories shared with the other nurses or the visiting doctors.

As she dug deeper, the information caused her to pause and wonder about leaving Bay Chaleur. The hospital wasn't in the city of St. John, after all. It was on an island in the Bay of Fundy, known as Partridge Island. Doctors and nurses were stationed there. This wasn't exactly what she had in mind.

Janet's world dimmed as she realized it was time to make a decision. She could continue to nurse and live in Dalhousie or leave for an island in the Bay of Fundy. Nursing on Partridge Island would be different because she would be helping large numbers of sick people. But living on the island was far from what she wanted.

After a day of hand wringing, Janet decided her commitment to help the sick on Partridge Island was the only choice. The visiting doctors described the island as a quarantine, a way to protect the city and the province from any illness arriving on the immigrant ships. To the nurse in Janet, it made sense. To her adventurous spirit, it felt more like a punishment.

Each immigrant ship was required to stop at the island, the doctors told her, and clear their passengers. Only the sick stayed on the island until their health improved.

The three girls, excited at their upcoming adventure, prepared for their travel to St. John. It was a two day journey from Dalhousie, covering more than a few hundred miles to the city of St. John. They would travel on the mail coach, with one overnight stop in Northumberland County.

On the day before their departure, Bridget changed her mind and decided to stay in Dalhousie. It would be left to Janet and Gertrude to make the journey.

"Bridget allowed her family to talk her out of it," Janet said.

Gertrude agreed, confirming their pioneer attitude.

"She's too scared to leave Bay Chaleur," Gertrude said.

They felt smug in their willingness to take risks and leave their home. It would be the continuation of a great friendship. Two young women ready to stick together in their great adventure.

"I can't lie, I'm nervous about this" Janet said, putting her emotions out for Gertrude to hear.

Janet wanted to care for people but she knew this would be a big challenge. Perhaps her biggest.

"I don't think this will be like the work in Dalhousie," she said.

Gertrude remained quiet not knowing how to answer. She had the same fear as Janet so she nodded as Janet spoke, trying not to burst with nervous excitement.

The overnight stay was at the mail stop on the south side of the Miramichi River, a community booming from shipbuilding and the timber trade. They had traveled south for a hundred miles yet despite the distance from Dalhousie, everything looked the same.

The locals at the mail stop tried to convince the two women to stay and forego their trip to St. John.

"The Miramichi's the greatest river in the province," they said. "And we've the best young men, if you're looking for a groom."

Janet and Gertrude avoided looking at each other. They knew the moment their eyes met, the giggles would erupt. Janet nodded trying to remain polite. It was enough of a hint to keep the conversation going.

"If it's nursing you're after, the immigrants are arriving here with illnesses too," one of the men said. "We know you're traveling to St. John but we've plenty of sick patients here in Chatham. We could use your help."

The man sounded a bit desperate, but Janet was determined and kept her head down. How could they move from one small town to another?

Finally, Janet and Gertrude looked at each other, not knowing how to say no. Janet spoke first.

"We'll come back here when we're finished in St. John," she said.

It was the only thing she thought would end the conversation. Gertrude stiffened with Janet's response, deciding to voice her opinion later. Now was not the time. Not in front of these strangers.

After a meal at the stop, they went into their small room for the night. Finally, Gertrude let her feelings be known.

"How could you say that?" Gertrude asked. "This is no different than Bay Chaleur."

Janet knew Gertrude was speaking the truth.

"I felt bad," Janet said. "They need our help too."

"Well I left Dalhousie for St. John," Gertrude said. "Not for Chatham."

"I'm sorry," Janet replied.

There was nothing more to say. Gertrude wanted the city and not country living. Janet would never make that mistake again.

The next leg of the trip took the better part of a full day, traveling for over a hundred and fifty miles both inland and along the coastal road. When the mail coach finally arrived in St. John, the two women couldn't help but stare at the city's damaged buildings.

"Why are so many buildings burned?" Janet asked as she gathered her belongings from the coach.

The driver was familiar with the city of St. John, traveling this route between the north and south of the province weekly, so he knew its history.

"Several fires have destroyed whole sections of the city over the past several years," he said. "You are witnessing a city in recovery from three fires since

1837. This business district was hit the hardest in that '37 fire."

Janet and Gertrude nodded as they heard their driver's answer, their eyes lost in the deep scars of the fire damage. With all the vacant lots and disfigured buildings, they felt small in the port city.

The driver saw their hesitation and directed the two towards a small building down the street. Janet started walking toward the office, with Gertrude not far behind. It was easy to feel unimportant, surrounded by people moving up and down the city streets. This wasn't the farm or even the open spaces in the town of Dalhousie.

The two women kept moving until Gertrude stopped mid step.

"Where are we?" she asked. "This is confusing to me."

They laughed and grabbed each other's hands and headed to the registration office. After a few more steps, the mail coach driver called out to the two women.

"Did either of you leave this satchel on the coach?" he asked, waving it high enough for both to see.

Janet looked at Gertrude and started to laugh. The bag belonged to Gertrude.

"It's mine," Gertrude yelled as she ran back to the coach to collect it.

With all their possessions in their arms, they continued toward the registration office. Once inside they saw an orderly routine, very different than their first impression of the city. After waiting a short time, they heard their names called.

"Miss Murchie, Miss McLean," the voice behind the desk said. "We need a few things, before you head over to Partridge Island."

After a mailing address and a signature, the women were given hospital clothes and directions to the boat for the island.

"Take these and make sure you keep them washed," the voice said.

They stepped out into the street and started to laugh.

"This is it," Janet said. "Last day on the mainland."

Gertrude was too busy giggling to understand the truth behind that statement.

As they made their way toward the boat, they seemed to be the only people walking away from the city. The wharf was filled with arriving immigrants heading in the opposite direction. So many ships, so many passengers. And there were more ships waiting in the harbor.

"Have you ever seen such a busy place?" Janet asked Gertrude.

"I thought Dalhousie was a busy port with a few ships in the harbor," she replied. "How can anyone keep track of this?"

They found the boat for the island and climbed in with their satchels and the new hospital clothes. The damp air of the Bay of Fundy forced Janet and Gertrude to huddle together as they left the dock. The powerful rip tides tossed the small boat in all directions, making Janet think about her decision, once again. When the boat finally approached the dock, one of the oarsmen attempted to prepare the women for the stark appearance of island.

"It's desolate but don't worry, the boats travel back and forth a few times a day," he said. "You can always visit St. John."

They had climbed off the dock steps when Janet realized what he meant. It was desolate. There were only a few trees and a small number of buildings scattered about.

"This is our home for the next several months," Janet announced, unsure of what to expect inside those stark buildings.

36

Blacknell Daughters

The Blacknell house was empty without Mama. She had blended into the daily routine, active in the childcare of her two grandsons while showering them with attention and love. It would take a few weeks to adjust to the void she left behind and find a new pattern without Elizabeth Murchie.

Margaret was surprised how she missed her mother's voice in the morning and ongoing advice. The daily tidbits of child rearing and housekeeping instruction strengthened their relationship in ways Margaret never thought possible. She witnessed a fragile widow and not the domineering mother she experienced as a young girl.

The spring fields and increased daylight hours demanded Robert's time outdoors. Each day, Margaret joined him in the barn chores and tended to her two young boys. The young couple continued to rely on their bedtime conversations to discuss the lives swirling around them.

After Robert pulled the bed covers over his body, Margaret announced she was expecting another child. Robert embraced his wife, holding her long past the point when fatigue numbed his arms. It was a welcome surprise, Robert wanted to share his love with more children.

"We'll need to travel to Colborne soon," Margaret said, immediately changing the focus to her mother.

She thought the news about another grandchild would be good news, but there was more for Robert to hear.

"Liza wrote about Janet leaving for St. John," she said.

Robert sat up in disbelief.

"What's in St. John for Janet?" he asked, realizing this news changed everything in Colborne. "Now we truly have a problem with the Murchie farm."

They spent the next hour discussing Mama and the Murchie farm. Managing two farms was too difficult for John, and Liza would soon follow Donald to the Wisconsin woods. The options were shrinking with Janet in St. John. Everything seemed temporary, barely held together. The family needed a long term solution, something more substantial than their casual agreements.

"What about Sarah?" Margaret asked, without thinking.

At the moment Robert heard the innocent question, he realized how little time he had spent with his two sisters. He knew very little about their future dreams. A sense of guilt fell over him as he listened to the words settle.

"Sarah's courting Samuel Dixon despite Mother's complaints," Robert answered. "Perhaps, but truthfully I don't know."

The question kept Robert awake most of the night, revealing few answers. Would Sarah marry Samuel despite Mother's argument? Would she live in Stonehaven or could they settle in Colborne? His thoughts swirled as he imagined the conversation between Sarah and Mother. As quickly as the questions about Sarah came and went, thoughts about Rebecca took over.

The more Robert thought about it, the more he realized he hadn't fulfilled his father's role with his youngest sister. He didn't know if Rebecca wanted to farm.

After only a few hours of sleep, Robert decided to talk to Rebecca first. It would be the start of many conversations, he thought as he walked toward the barn. He would find time for his sisters, time to listen and understand their dreams. He found Rebecca tending to the chickens, unaware of her brother's approach.

"There you are," Robert said, watching his sister jump at the sound of his voice. "Oh, didn't mean to alarm you."

Rebecca laughed at her reaction, then quickly got down to business.

"I need to talk to you," she said. "You've been so busy, but I need your help."

Robert stood taller, feeling the importance of his sister's request and confident in his decision to find her this morning.

"Michael Connors --," Rebecca said, before Robert interrupted.

"I've heard talk about you and Michael at the McGarvie store but I pushed it aside, disbelieving that gossip," Robert said. "Please tell me it isn't true."

"It's true," Rebecca answered, holding her head high.

Robert shook his head, unsure of how to give his youngest sister advice while realizing the family challenges just got worse. He knew the Connors family from up the north road. They were hard working Irish, with a recent grant and many months of land clearing ahead. It wasn't the work that bothered him, the problem was, the Connors family were Catholic.

He released a sigh, loud enough for Rebecca to hear. Their mother would never allow this relationship. She barely approved of Samuel Dixon, a Protestant from Bandon. Michael Connors would completely unravel the family.

"I know what you're thinking," Rebecca said. "But if I love him, what difference does it make if he's from a different religion. You married Margaret and Mother didn't like her."

Robert was caught. He knew better than to argue about Margaret with his youngest sister. Rebecca had found someone she loved and Robert's words would do little to change her mind. He reminded her of the family's reasons for leaving the Timoleague farm. She pretended to listen before shrugging her shoulders and leaving the barn.

Robert felt defeated. He expected the conversation with Rebecca to be easier, but now another issue had surfaced. Solving the Murchie farm would have to wait, he had more important responsibilities to tend to.

Within a few weeks, Mother heard the gossip about Michael Connors. Rebecca didn't try to hide her feelings when Mother pointedly challenged her daughter with the gossip. Mother settled it immediately. Rebecca was forbidden from spending time with Michael. A deep fracture now shattered the Blacknell family. Rebecca would never know how the news about Michael reached her mother, but she immediately blamed Robert.

Sarah wasn't much help. She was engrossed in her own world with Samuel Dixon while Mother continued to push another young man.

"The relationship won't work with Samuel," Mother declared. "There are other young men closer to Eel River."

Sarah trusted her mother had good intentions, but her feelings for Samuel started back in Ireland. How could she ignore them?

Mother pushed Sarah to meet other eligible bachelors with an eye on one prominent businessman, David McGarvie. David's family were the owners of the dry goods store in Dalhousie. Early one morning, Mother decided it was time to pick up a few yards of cloth in town. Sarah loved to quilt, and her eyes lit up at the suggestion.

When they arrived, the McGarvie store was busy with a few local patrons including several of Mother's friends. Sarah left her mother and approached the counter to select her cloth. David McGarvie moved over to assist Sarah as her mother kept talking, while closely watching her daughter from the distance.

"He's the perfect groom for your daughter," one of the church ladies remarked.

In no time, the ladies were hatching a grand scheme to bring David to Eel River for tea with Sarah. Mother brushed it off, suggesting Sarah would select her own beau. A slight chuckle followed Mother's remarks. The church ladies knew better.

"Did you take notice of David McGarvie?" Mother asked on the ride home. "David's a prominent businessman in town, he's been making a name for himself at the family's store."

"Oh Mother, I don't need to take notice," she said. "Samuel is waiting in Stonehaven. One day, he'll ask Robert for my hand."

The conversation continued at home as Mother tried to encourage her daughter to move beyond Samuel. After supper, Robert noticed how Mother captivated Sarah's attention at the quilting frame. As he approached the two, Mother stopped talking. She didn't want to revisit the scars of courting around Robert. There wasn't anything more to say, she would find another way to convince Sarah.

Sarah was relieved when Mother left the room.

"Do you have time to talk about courting," Sarah asked. "It's a big decision and Mother is sticking her nose into it.

"Let's do it later tonight," Robert said. "The house will be quiet."

After their mother and the children went to bed, Sarah didn't waste any time.

"I'm not sure about Samuel or David," Sarah said. "I just don't know."

There was an innocence in her voice.

"You don't have to decide as quickly as I did," Robert told her. "Take your time and don't let Mother tell you what to do."

"Easier for you," she said.

Robert knew Mother would smother her oldest daughter.

"If you want to get to know David, we can invite him over for tea the next time you see him," Robert suggested. "That'll keep Mother happy too."

Mother was surprised when she learned about David's upcoming visit.

"He's coming for tea, and to meet you," Sarah said, feeling her skin turn bright red.

Always practical, despite the tension building inside, Sarah tried to remain calm and put everything in perspective. When David arrived on time, Mother pointed out how dependable he was.

Sarah couldn't hide her feelings after he left.

"He's so handsome," Sarah said, blushing for everyone to see. Rebecca and Thomas had been sitting in the kitchen listening to the afternoon unfold. They looked at each other after the outburst and laughed. Sarah immediately covered her face. She had shared too much.

"If it makes you feel better, I like him too," Thomas said, loud enough for his sister to hear.

Thomas was preparing to leave for Fredericton and continue his schooling. An education was his dream and their prosperous farm would make it a reality. For a moment, Robert wondered if he should worry about his younger brother.

"What about Samuel?" Rebecca asked.

The room went silent while Sarah shook her head at her sister. There were too many decisions for Sarah Blacknell to make and now wasn't the time for Rebecca to ask.

Margaret invited Mother to join them for the Murchie farm visit. She knew the two mothers had built a strong bond and thought they would enjoy a grandmother's conversation again. As the carriage made its way south along the coastal road, Robert reminisced about the first visit Mother made to the Murchie farm. Mother laughed as Robert shared how nervous he was on that ride. Things were different now. Margaret and Mother had found common ground. It seemed like a long time ago.

They talked about Papa and how the Murchie family had changed since his death. The children were no longer drawn to Colborne. Only John remained steadfast in his place. Janet was far away and Liza continued to wait for Donald. Again.

When they turned up the road, Margaret noticed John's carriage was next to the barn. This will be a good visit, she thought, we can have a discussion about the farm. She turned around to catch the view of the bay. The mountain steps across Bay Chaleur were still calling her to visit. She smiled thinking of that first day with Liza and Janet on the beach. So much time had passed with so many changes.

The five cousins found playing outdoors more exciting than staying inside with all the adults. The two grandmothers followed them into the yard, trying to keep them out of the hay fields.

The conversation inside the house was predictable. Liza was waiting to join Donald. He had arrived in Wisconsin but lived in a logging camp deep in the woods. Not a place for a young woman, he described in his letters. Their choices were few until Donald found work near a small town or settlement. Liza would wait until then.

A long term plan would also wait. Not much had changed at the Murchie farm. John hired a few farm hands to help during the harvest and Mama still thought the farm was hers.

"We could move to Colborne," Robert said after they arrived home. "It's a beautiful piece of land and we could make it our home."

Margaret wasn't sure. She had grown to love her life away from Colborne. It was a level of independence that made the bonds and the visits stronger, she thought. They were only a short ride away.

"Do we need to make a decision now?" she asked.

"Not now, we just need to think about it," Robert said. "We need to be prepared."

That was Robert. Always prepared, Margaret thought.

"Do you ever let things happen?" she asked.

"They happen as planned," Robert said.

Margaret leaned over and hugged her husband. He was so predictable.

37

Immigrant Ships

Janet and Gertrude headed toward the hospital building following the directions from the oarsman. As they made their way along the narrow road, the wind cut through their clothes, forcing the two women to crouch down with each step. What would the island feel like in the winter, Janet wondered. They picked up their pace, moving easily over the gravel, while holding their belongings close.

Partridge Island felt strange. It seemed lost in the middle of the bay. In the middle of rough waters and missing something. Once they opened the doors to the hospital, Janet discovered the missing piece. It was life. The sense of sickness was everywhere.

Inside the door, the room was in a constant state of chaos. People everywhere lying in cots, while others moved from place to place. It didn't demonstrate the structure and order Janet expected. She searched for someone to talk to. Someone who wasn't walking briskly away from them. Eventually they made their way through another door and found a room that appeared to be the office.

"We're here to register," Janet said, hoping the man behind the desk would listen.

The man looked up and struggled to answer. He had the appearance of someone who hadn't slept in quite some time.

"We have seventy beds and many are filled with the sick," he said.

Janet knew immediately he hadn't heard her.

"We're here to help," she said, trying to get his attention.

"Clean up and come back if you can tonight. We could certainly use your help."

He waved his arms toward the door, suggesting they leave. After the two women left the office, he ran after them, shouting.

"Your housing is off to the right," he said, pointing. "It's those barracks."

As quickly as he ran out of his office, he ran back in. Janet looked at Gertrude, trying not to laugh. So far, Partridge Island wasn't what she expected. It had to get better.

They made their way to the barracks and unpacked after locating their room. It had been a long day since they left the Miramichi coach stop and Janet was tired.

"Let's get some sleep," she suggested.

Gertrude wasn't interested in sleep.

"We must go back to the hospital," she said. "That's the reason we came here."

And so their days and nights began. There was little time to relax and no time to visit the city of St. John. They spent each day shuffling between the hospital and their small room. The doctors called it the shipping season with new ships arriving daily in the harbor. Sleep was never a priority.

Janet discovered there was much more to the chaos on Partridge Island. As the ships approached, they raised a yellow flag to announce they were carrying sick passengers on board. That signal sent a team of nurses into action, separating the sick from the rest of the passengers, as soon as everyone debarked.

But even the ships without the yellow flag were thoroughly inspected for illness. There were fierce rumors about ship captains not following the rules and arriving with sick and dead passengers. The New Brunswick government stood firm against these practices but the short shipping season across the Atlantic forced many ruthless ship owners to push every limit.

They were desperate for a quick turnaround in the port of St. John. If their ship was held in quarantine, the owner's business would suffer. The competitive timber business would find another captain.

Sick patients for quarantine were constantly arriving. It took the two women several days to adjust to a sense of complete helplessness. It took them much longer to understand why this was happening.

Whole families would enter the hospital and only a few would leave alive. In other cases everyone would die. Families were frequently separated, not knowing if they would see each other again. It was a chaos driven by sickness and fear of death.

"Some of the deaths are ship fever or typhus," the doctor said. "It doesn't matter what age the patient is, young or old, all are vulnerable. Others have consumption, and will need to rest."

It took time, but soon Janet started to tell the difference. There was little hope for the ship fever patients. Their temperatures spiked and rarely came down. She recognized consumption patients by their cough. A cough with blood in it.

Partridge Island would leave a lasting mark on Janet and Gertrude. They would witness only a few of their patients walk out of the hospital.

"We weren't nursing in Dalhousie," Janet told Gertrude. "But now we are."

The ships didn't stop. The sick grew in numbers and the death toll continued to rise. The two women worked at the hospital all day and night. Janet's body grew tired with each new arrival but she knew she couldn't stop.

"I'm needed here," she would tell Gertrude. "For the first time in my life I feel I'm making a difference."

With her head held high, Janet moved from patient to patient, giving fresh water and washing their faces with cold cloths.

Toward the end of the fall, Gertrude was the first to slow down. They had been working long days without a break and the fatigue was beginning to show.

"I'm staying in the room today," she said. "I had cold sweats all night and didn't sleep well."

Janet left her and headed to the hospital. What if she's sick and not just tired, Janet thought. What can I do to help her? She had been too busy with all the patients to give Gertrude her attention. After a long and tiring day at the hospital, Janet returned to the room with food and water, hoping to see her friend sitting up. Instead, when she opened the door, she found Gertrude still in bed and barely moving.

"Wake up, wake up," Janet yelled, while pulling on her arm.

Gertrude just moaned and wouldn't move. Janet held her up and forced her to drink water. That's when she noticed the blood stained cloth.

"I'm here, please drink," she begged. "Drink this water."

Janet ran to the hospital after forcing Gertrude to swallow a full mouthful. She had to find a bed for her. Once in the hospital, she would get better, Janet thought. Food and water and constant supervision. Inside the hospital she searched for the first doctor she could find.

"Gertrude's sick, she's coughing up blood," Janet told him. "Is there a bed for her?"

The nurses nearby stopped to listen. A sense of gloom filled the room. Each nurse was instantly evaluating their own health.

"Let me look at her," the doctor said. "I can go over within the hour."

After looking at Gertrude, the doctor couldn't hide his diagnosis.

"She needs to rest," he said. "I'll come back tomorrow and check on her."

Janet couldn't believe the doctor. How could this be happening?

"Consumption," the doctor told Janet. "Gertrude has consumption."

Janet sat down trying to take it all in.

"Try to keep the windows open a little during the day," he said. "Gertrude needs plenty of fresh air. Even this cold air will do."

Barely able to speak and weak from the illness, Gertrude made a few murmurs indicating she heard the doctor.

"I'm here," Janet said. "I'll be your nurse."

The hospital wasn't the same without Gertrude at her side. It was difficult to focus. They had shared every story, every horror witnessed and now there wasn't anyone to cry or laugh with. Janet wanted Gertrude back but she watched her friend get weaker every day. The improvement the doctor expected didn't come. Janet realized it was time to go home. Home to Bay Chaleur. Gertrude needed her own bed and her family around her.

Janet informed the hospital of her plan to leave. Once the schedules were confirmed, Janet wrote letters to both families. She didn't want to stay overnight at the mail stop at the Miramichi. She asked for someone to meet the coach and take them home.

The letter set off a flurry of activity. John was unable to leave the two farms during the harvest. Mama couldn't travel the hundred miles. It was simply too far. They needed a man to make the trip. Reluctantly, Mama and Liza took the carriage to Eel River. Mama would ask Robert to make the trip.

The Blacknell farm had several farm hands to call upon and Mama hoped Robert could go. After sharing the terrible news about Gertrude, there wasn't any hesitation from Margaret and Robert. Janet was asking for help. Margaret saw the trip to the Miramichi as a stronger bridge for their relationship. It was time to help Janet and that was that. Robert would go and Margaret would stay in Eel River with the children.

38

Return to Bay Chaleur

Robert left Eel River early Friday morning to meet the mail coach. It was difficult to plan the exact meeting time, but based on the letters from Janet, the late coach would be pulling into Miramichi around supper time. He wanted to be ready when the two women showed up. They shouldn't wait for me, he thought.

The weather was fluctuating between a cold drizzle and a steady downpour. He needed shelter, it was too cold to wait outside in the rain. The Miramichi stop had a small pub and inn, so he headed over and stepped inside. The room was filled with passengers waiting to head north with the carriage. It was nice to witness New Brunswick's growth.

When the mail coach finally arrived, Janet jumped out to find Robert. When their eyes met, she started to cry. Her stoic demeanor fell apart directly in front of him. Gertrude's illness and the love she felt from her family overwhelmed her.

"Thank you, thank you," she said, leading Robert to the coach. "Gertrude needs her home bed, she can't stop coughing and sneezing. The ride here has been so difficult."

"Your family wants both of you home," Robert said as he collected Gertrude and carried her over to his carriage. He shook his head as he noticed the blood on the blankets. This is worse than he originally thought.

They spent a few minutes trying to make Gertrude comfortable. Janet wrapped her with Robert's extra blankets and despite the rain, attempted to keep her dry.

"Have you eaten?" Robert asked. "We can ask the pub for some bread if you'd like."

Janet nodded. She hadn't thought about eating since they left the island. After Robert returned with a few pieces of bread from inside the pub, they headed up the portage towards Bathurst. Janet let out a large sigh. Gertrude was almost home. After one night in Colborne, she would be in her own bed.

It took ten hours to make the hundred mile journey. The rain added to the delay, forcing Robert to move slowly along the coastal roads in the darkness and against the blinding rain. It appeared to relent as they headed up the Murchie road.

The house was aglow with lamps in every room and fires in the stove and fireplace. It was the exact greeting the wet and weary travelers needed. Robert pulled the carriage next to the house and John appeared to help carry Gertrude inside. She was soaked and barely moving.

John and Robert carried Gertrude to a spot Mama had set up next to the fireplace.

"We'll remove her wet clothes and blankets here," she told them. "John, give Robert some of Papa's clothes to change into."

Liza helped Mama with Gertrude. Once she was ready in dry nightclothes, Robert carried her to the bedroom Mama had prepared. Already weak from illness, Gertrude didn't speak as Robert laid her head on the pillow and covered her with several quilts.

Janet changed into dry clothes, grateful for her family and home on Bay Chaleur. The family gathered in the kitchen, ready to talk and learn about Janet's work on Partridge Island. Janet wasn't ready to share any stories. The emotion of Gertrude's illness overshadowed what she had seen during the past several months. It wasn't time to share.

The conversation changed toward the farm. Another touchy subject, Liza thought. At least Janet is home now and we can discuss the future. After warmth was restored to both Janet and Robert, everyone decided it was time for bed. The next morning would have its own challenges.

Gertrude's family arrived the next afternoon from Dalhousie to collect their daughter. After a few greetings and nice words, they rushed to leave. They weren't at the Murchie farm to socialize. Gertrude's mother tried to remain strong as she watched her husband carry their daughter to their carriage, but it was too much. She had said goodbye to a vibrant young woman heading to St. John and now she was watching her motionless daughter placed into the back of the carriage.

"Gertrude needs to be home," her mother said with tears rolling down her face. "She needs my care."

It was an emotional goodbye for Janet holding Gertrude's hand as her father slapped the reins to move the carriage.

"I'll visit next week," Janet said. "Once you're settled at home, I'll stop in."

Janet watched as the carriage made its way down the road with Chaleur Bay in the background. She had seen so much in a short time in St. John. Now she was watching her best friend leave her. Possibly forever.

Janet knew her life would never be the same. The farm was different than St. John and Partridge Island. It was a safe place. Not a place of chaos. And nursing would never be the same without Gertrude. She would need to find something else for her life. It wasn't Edward. He was probably married by now, she thought. And there's Liza, foolishly waiting on Donald.

She made her way to her old bedroom, feeling a sense of comfort in a place she knew. She would think about the farm. Maybe it was time to forego adventures and become a farmer.

Robert left the Murchie farm before Gertrude's family arrived. There were chores to finish before the cold weather made its appearance.

"The house was visible from miles away, the night we arrived from Miramichi," Robert later told Margaret. "You would've been proud of your family last night."

Margaret knew exactly what Robert meant. The Murchie family took care of each other.

39

Spring Thaw

It took several months before Janet adjusted to life back on the Murchie farm. No one was surprised when the word came about Gertrude's death in December. Janet knew her friend was too ill and too tired from helping others to survive. She had seen the immigrants on Partridge Island as sick as Gertrude and feared the worst for her friend. Despite the cold and the snow, Janet found her way to the Bay Chaleur beach. She needed time alone and time to remember Gertrude.

The funeral was held in town with a burial schedule in the spring, after the thaw. Janet shared the best stories with Gertrude's mother. She wanted her to know how many sick patients Gertrude had helped.

Farming became Janet's outlet. Taking care of the barn animals was rewarding. She could disappear for hours in the barn after John had left for home. Liza always headed back into the house to care for Mama while Janet enjoyed the time by herself.

As the Restigouche River released its annual grip on the large ice sheets, Janet decided her future plans. She would spend the spring and summer months working the fields with John. The Murchie farm would be hers. John couldn't hide his enthusiasm, when she shared her plan with him.

"I'll do anything to help you," he said.

They now had a plan, he thought. If Liza left, Janet could take over.

Liza agreed, privately wanting to leave tomorrow. She had grown tired of waiting for Donald, but would never share her concerns.

"Donald will be calling for me shortly, so I can do it for now," she said, smiling to deflect her thoughts.

John and Janet rolled their eyes imagining when that letter would come.

"You know best," John said, not revealing any skepticism.

The Murchie family could keep their last secret a little longer and Mama would feel protected with Janet at home. If things worked out, the farm would stay in the family, John thought. They hadn't solved the problem. Once again, it was pushed into a future discussion.

Over the next two months, Janet and Liza would spend their days in the fields. Planting season was demanding during the long days and shorter nights for sleep. It was hard work for the two young women, yet they managed to hide their exhaustion. By the end of June, Mama noticed Janet was slowing down. She watched her for a few days expecting to hear about the fatigue of farming, but Janet remained quiet.

The following week, Janet awoke one morning with a blistering headache. She didn't want to alarm anyone so she rushed to the barn to avoid the family. John saw the pained look in her face immediately when he arrived.

"What's wrong?" he asked. "Your eyes are barely open."

"A bit of a headache," she replied. "It'll go away soon."

John didn't agree. "Let's get you back into the house," he said. "I can do this today."

As Janet walked past her mother in the kitchen, Mama saw the ashen look on her face.

"Looks like you need a rest, dear girl," Mama said.

"I think the past few weeks of farming were too much for me Mama," Janet replied. "I need to take a rest now."

John waited until Janet was behind closed doors.

"I think she's more than tired," he said. "I've never seen Janet look that way."

Mama checked on Janet throughout the night placing a cold cloth on her forehead. The cold sweats started after midnight and turned into a fever the next morning. As the second night wore on, Mama realized she needed Liza by her side. She needed someone who could think clearly.

"What about getting John?" Liza asked. "He'd know what to do."

Liza followed Mama into Janet's room.

"This is worse than I thought," Liza said after seeing Janet. "She's burning up. I'll get John."

Liza raced out of the house and was gone before Mama could stop her. It would take her an hour to make the return trip to and from the Stewart farm, but it didn't matter, this was an emergency.

Alone, Mama tried to think. She was filled with fear, a fear of not knowing what to do. She hadn't seen many high temperatures in her lifetime so she tried to remember how the elders handled fevers on Arran. She immediately thought of Duncan, but his fever didn't look like this.

As she stared at Janet's pale skin, her mind raced to the family's journey across the Atlantic. There were several high fevers on that ship, but those were different, she thought. Without answers, she continued to wash Janet's face with the cold cloth.

The loud footsteps and voices of John and Liza could be heard before they entered Janet's room.

"Let me get the doctor," John suggested, after seeing Janet. "Is there one nearby or do we need to go into town?"

"We can't ride anywhere tonight," she said. "It would be too cold this time of the night, too cold for Janet. I know she can't take it."

Liza was surprised the conversation was going nowhere.

"What about Bridget, Janet's friend?" she asked. "I'll go get her."

And with Liza's quick thinking and action, she was back in the carriage and off to Dalhousie. On the way up the coastal road, she thought about Janet. She was so sick, so vulnerable. Why have you done this to yourself, she questioned. First Gertrude, now you.

It would be mid morning before Liza arrived at the farm with Bridget. Janet barely responded as Bridget looked at her, trying to understand her sickness. Before long, she stepped out of the room and sat next to Mama in the kitchen.

"Janet's very sick, Mrs. Murchie," she said. "I haven't seen many patients like this but she's having trouble breathing and needs fresh air. I've been told clean clothes are a necessity, wash everything and do not touch anything she touched."

Mama froze at the Bridget's words. In her mind, she went over the day Gertrude arrived at the farm. What had she touched? Mama had touched everything. Everyone had touched Gertrude's blankets. What did Liza touch? As her mind was racing through the list of people, Bridget broke her trance.

"She'll also need constant care," she said. "Can someone watch her over the next few critical days?"

"Yes," Mama answered overwhelmed by the circumstances.

"We don't know how people get this sickness, so you will need to be careful," she finished.

An eerie silence fell over the house after the Bridget left with Liza.

"What is it Mama?" John asked. "What did Bridget tell you?"

Her eyes welled up as she looked at John.

"We could all get Janet's sickness," Mama blurted. "Bridget told me not to touch Janet's clothing."

John didn't know what to do or say. He thought about the past few months, they had all touched Janet's clothing. It didn't make sense, what was wrong with her clothing? He had also touched Gertrude and the blankets.

"What about Gertrude?" John asked.

The questions kept rolling off his tongue.

"Who touched Gertrude's clothes," he asked.

"Is there anything left in the house from Gertrude? She stayed here overnight."

Overwhelmed, Mama started to cry as the entire house fell into a panic.

"I want to be strong, but I can't," Mama said. "I don't know what to do."

Janet never walked out of her bedroom again. The fever lasted for two weeks and Mama sat beside her for the duration. While Janet was sleeping, Mama would tell her stories of her childhood in Arran. Stories about the house, the school and the island. Mama never tired of repeating the stories.

"You were brave to care for sick people," she told Janet. "Always helping others. We love you Janet. Don't leave us. We need you too."

The words felt hollow after Janet's death, but Mama found solace in them. Mama watched Janet take her last breath. She thought about Janet's first breath and the years of risk taking. The years of being her own person. That was Janet. She didn't want to be Liza or her younger sister, Margaret. She had to be Janet.

Sadness gripped the Murchie family once more. Margaret and Robert traveled to Colborne, leaving the children behind with Robert's sisters. Mother was still active but three little ones made it a challenge. John and Catherine were the last to arrive. The house felt empty. No children and only adults feeling the emptiness of Janet's death.

"Janet wouldn't want us this way," Mama said. "Let's get the house ready for her wake. Many of her town friends will be paying us a visit, so let's get cleaning."

And with Mama's words, the Murchie family cleaned each room, reminded by the Bridget's words. While the others were cleaning, Mama pulled Robert aside. She was still haunted by Bridget's caution.

"I know you were in contact with Gertrude and Janet the night they came back to Colborne," she said. "Are you feeling alright?"

Robert thought about that fateful night. The rain, the blankets, Gertrude's coughing and sneezing. What had he touched? Everything.

"Feeling fine," he said, silently questioning his recent fatigue.

He brushed it off. This wasn't the time to think about himself. It was time to help Margaret's family.

As Mama predicted, the wake brought Janet's friends to the farm. Mama didn't know many of them or their families. It was Janet's life away from the country. Her life in town. They shared many stories of Janet making Mama proud as she heard them.

"We all loved her," they said, walking out the door.

"We only get together for funerals these days," Margaret lamented.

"I guess we are getting old," John replied.

"I hope not," Margaret sighed. "Our lives get in the way"

"Let's try to do better," John agreed and thought about how his sister had changed.

From a self-centered compulsive child to a sister trying to bring everyone together. He was right. They were getting old.

40

Moments

The ride back to Eel River seemed longer than usual, Janet's death weighted heavily on both Margaret and Robert. They had time to discuss the family and the two farms. Once again, the Murchie family had more changes and uncertainty.

"The farm must stay with John and Liza," Margaret said. "They can take care of Mama too."

They couldn't ignore Liza's future.

"Who knows when Donald's going to return," Margaret said. "I don't think he's coming back for Liza."

Robert didn't agree.

"He doesn't seem like the kind of man who would stay out west without her," he said. "They've been together a long time."

"We'll have to wait, just like Liza," Margaret said, almost smiling at the irony of the situation.

They knew there would be a problem if Liza left. Mama had grown accustomed to her presence.

"We've talked about moving to Colborne," Robert said. "Would John object?"

Margaret shook her head. The farm had been Papa's dream. The reason for leaving Arran. Land ownership was the draw that put the Murchie family on the ship. The family needed to protect it and keep it for the Murchie grandchildren.

"John has his own now," Margaret said. "He doesn't need the Murchie farm. But I'm sure he wants it protected as much as we do."

"Sarah could take over the Blacknell farm," Robert said.

Sarah hadn't decided on Samuel or David, so Margaret wasn't convinced.

"What about Rebecca?" Margaret asked, knowing the rumors and Mother's rule about Michael.

"She's been quiet lately, planning something," Robert said. "I'm almost afraid to ask."

They turned onto the cove road and headed toward the farm. It had been a long few days in Colborne. Margaret looked at the Eel River and suddenly thought about Aunt Isabella.

"What about the MacNairs?" she asked Robert.

"Who?" he asked.

"Isabella and Neil, Papa's sister's family," Margaret said.

"Oh, didn't John tell you about Neil, asking to buy the farm?" Robert asked.

Margaret suddenly remembered the conversation with John at the general store in Colborne. She shook her head, giving Isabella the farm wouldn't do, she thought.

Mother was awake when they rode up to the house. She was anxious to hear how Elizabeth Murchie was doing.

"You must be tired," she said.

"Yes, it's been an emotional time," Robert replied.

Margaret nodded not realizing how focused Mother was on Robert.

"It's time for a good night's sleep," he said.

They were asleep within minutes of getting into bed. The difficult decisions about family, farms and emotion had taken their toll. It would be many weeks before a routine would return to the Blacknell household.

The children made their way into the bedroom early the next morning, excited to see their mother.

"Get up, get out of bed," William cried, as he shook her arm.

Margaret looked over at Robert still asleep next to her. She found it odd. He must be extra tired, she thought.

In the kitchen, Margaret and the children enjoyed breakfast. Each child wanting to share the events of the past few days. Mother joined them at the table to add to the conversation, pointing out their activities.

"William was the big brother this week," Mother said. "He made certain everyone completed their chores."

Margaret glowed when she met William's eyes.

"I'm so proud of you, my little man," she said.

Margaret thought about the conversation with Robert the night before. Two farms to deal with and only two Murchie children as options. What about the grandchildren? She looked at her young son, convinced he could have the Murchie farm when he was older.

After breakfast Margaret returned to check on Robert. On a normal day he would be in the barn by now. When Margaret opened the door, Robert was still asleep. She leaned over to kiss him and felt his hot skin with her lips. Immediately she ran to the top of the stairs for Mother.

"Come see Robert," Margaret pleaded. "His body's on fire. He must be sick."

Mother rushed up the stairs to the bedroom. She found Robert asleep with sweat beads along his forehead. Mother reached for Margaret to steady herself.

"Is Robert sick with consumption too?" Margaret asked.

The two women stared at the man they both adored. Mother was slow to reply, not wanting to confirm Margaret's question.

"I don't know," she said.

It was all she could say. Mother sent Thomas to get the doctor.

"He's usually in town, but ask at the general store," she said. "They always know where he is."

When the doctor arrived, he thanked the two women for collecting him.

"It's nothing but a fever," he said. "Plenty of sleep and tea and he'll be back in the barn in no time."

Neither Mother nor Margaret heard all the doctor's words. Once they heard fever, the panic took over.

"Rest is needed for Robert," he said in a louder voice, forcing Margaret to listen.

Thankfully Robert heard the doctor's words and spoke first.

"I'll stay in bed today," he said.

"A few days, perhaps a week and you'll be ready for the barn," the Doctor said, as he left the room.

Mother walked the doctor to the door, questioning the diagnosis, and looking for confirmation. He remained firm, Robert would recover from his fever.

Margaret trusted the doctor's words but pleaded with Rebecca to travel into town and find Bridget. She knew Janet's trusted friend could help the family, once again.

Bridget arrived and immediately took charge, ordering all the women to boil water and wash everything. No one argued. They all wanted Robert healthy. The children tiptoed around the house over the next days, as their father gained back his strength.

After a few weeks, the Blacknell family settled into their regular routine. Robert returned to the fields and Margaret to the cows. The doctor had been right all along, it was only a fever, but Mother refused to let Robert out of her sight.

Robert's illness softened his mother. She eventually agreed Sarah could marry whomever she wanted telling her daughter both Samuel and David would make good husbands. Mother's change of heart only complicated matters as Sarah struggled to decide.

Michael Connors was another story however, and she remained steadfast on her objection. Rebecca remained quiet, taking in all the changes in Mother's attitude.

For Margaret, every day since the fever was an extra day with Robert. In her mind, she had come close to losing him, a feeling she never got over. As she prepared the morning tea for breakfast, Margaret thought about the special moments in her life with Robert, certain there would be many more.

But first it was time to celebrate the morning. She carried the tray with the tea pot and two cups, step by step up the stairs, taking extra care not to stumble. It was a short distance to share a few moments with her husband and pause the clock, before the day took over.

About the Author

Ann Webster grew up listening to family stories shared by her grandmother. Eventually those stories turned into a passion for genealogy and the discovery of where and how her ancestors lived. While the characters and the story in *The Distant Steps* are pure fiction, many genealogy discoveries are its foundation.

Made in the USA
Columbia, SC
01 July 2019